THE PRINCESS AND THE PROPHET

H . BEDFORD-JONES

THE PRINCESS
AND THE PROPHET

H. BEDFORD-JONES

ILLUSTRATED BY
JOHN RICHARD FLANAGAN

ALTUS PRESS • 2018

© 2018 Altus Press • First Edition—2018

PUBLISHING HISTORY

The Princess and the Prophet originally appeared in the December 1941–March 1942 issues of *Blue Book* magazine.

THANKS TO

Everard P. Digges LaTouche and Gerd Pircher

TABLE OF CONTENTS

THE PRINCESS AND THE PROPHET

Prophet or not, Nostradamus was a good physician;
and in this fine novel of a fascinating period he
shares with Mary of Scotland and other people
the light of an able writer's brilliant portrayal.

IN THE courtyard of the post tavern at Chouzy, the first crossroads outside Blois, a dreadful thing was taking place, and going from bad to worse: A dog was held by two lengths of rope about his neck. One ran to the pump, the other to a hook in the stable wall. Both were taut. Thus, the dog could move scarcely at all to either side, and only slightly forward or back.

He was a great gaunt dog, with long lean head and long curled tail. He was plastered with filth; his coat was matted with briars and brush and blood. Red streaks of bloody flesh showed through his dark fur, and blood dribbled down his legs to the cobblestones. He stood at the point of fury, eyes rolling savagely and lips curled back to show white fangs—but he was quite helpless.

The innkeeper spoke uneasily, as he looked on.

"Better send for a pike or a boar-spear, Jacques! You'll never kill him with that whip."

The burly, bearded Jacques held a long-thonged whip of braided leather. He glared at the dog; the beast growled murderously, with such terrific pent ferocity that Jacques fell back a step. Furious drunken speech poured from him in a torrent.

"I'll kill him, never fear. He's mine to do with, by the saints! I found him in my fowl-yard with half a dozen hens dead and eaten; and his life pays for it. Some kind of wolf, no doubt. A devil's in him!"

"More truth than poetry to that," said the innkeeper, crossing himself. "A devil is in his eye, surely! Why not let him be judged and killed by the provost?"

"Because I want that pleasure myself," snarled Jacques, a peasant by his garb. He coiled the whip and lashed out.

The dog could not evade. Plunging on his rope, he took the blow, gave no sign of pain, but fastened his lambent eyes on the man and voiced a low growl so deadly that the watching grooms cried anew that Satan was indeed in him. He eyed Jacques as a man would do, tensely, with a personal hatred.

"Well, well, *mes amis!*" exclaimed a hearty voice. "Honest Frenchmen at your pleasure, eh? No welcome for travelers? No itching palm for minted coin? The world must be coming to an end, indeed!"

Everyone turned. Even Jacques swung around, all astare. Into the courtyard had come a stoutly built, powerful man with grizzled beard and big nose and bold eyes, leading a horse. On the horse sat another, younger man, drooping in the saddle. Little of his face was visible, thanks to a bloodstained bandage about his eyes and head. Tied to the saddle was a sword, and beside it a quiver of long shafts and a long bow in its case.

The grooms sprang to assist; the innkeeper hurried forward. The big man helped his companion from the saddle, led him to the pump, and put his hand on it. Obviously, the younger man was blind. Now he spoke, but not in French.

"What is going on here, Angus Dhu? Was it a dog I heard growling?"

"Aye; these French peasants are as bad as English—always killing something. Now wait here, Malcolm, till I get us settled and learn if they can get a surgeon from Blois." Black Angus beckoned the innkeeper and slapped the fat purse at his girdle, and spoke in fluent but badly accented French.

"Now, good host, show me your rooms! One of the best, mind. Have a drawer bring wine to my friend, while we're gone. We met robbers in the woods—killed three of them; but a broken sword has left my comrade hurt and blinded. Come along…. Your best rooms, mind!"

They departed inside the inn. A drawer came out with a pewter cup of wine and gave it to the hurt man, who thanked him in excellent French. Slightly bearded, this blind Malcolm, wearing a leather surcoat stained by armor and weather. He stood at the pump and drank the wine, then faced around at queer sounds.

Jacques, coiling his whip anew, began to lash out at the dog, cursing him the while. The animal crouched, belly to stones, growling but not whimpering as the thong slashed into him cruelly. Suddenly, unexpectedly, he flew into life.

Too rapidly for eye to follow, he caught the lash between his jaws as it landed. He caught it, jerked it, pulled it from the hand of Jacques. He gathered the whip beneath him. Astounded, Jacques bellowed oaths while the grooms fell to laughing. One of them got a pole and began to scrape at the whip, raking it away from the dog's paws.

Blind Malcolm left the pump and moved toward sounds.

"Here, here, what are you doing?" he demanded. "Whipping a dog? Torturing him? That's not man's work, my friends!"

Sharp cries of warning arose. For with hands outstretched, he was moving directly at the animal. His foot struck against the rope; grasping it, he moved on toward the dog. No one dared to intervene.

"The beast will tear out his throat!" cried a tap-boy, horrified. "Stop him, stop him! You, monsieur! For God's love, turn again!"

The dog crouched, with savage tense growl. Malcolm, almost beside him, paused, reached down, and laughed.

"What's this, beastie?" His words came not in French, but in English. "Are these French rascals tormenting you also? Then we're both fallen among evil hands. And we both need help, God knows!"

The dog rose upright, abandoning the whip, so that the groom raked it clear of him. The great beast stood waist-high to Malcolm; instead of flying at the outstreched hand of the Scot, a low sound like a groan escaped him, and he thrust his nose into the reaching palm.

"Devil take me if you don't understand English speech, eh?" exclaimed Malcolm, and stroked the long head and neck. "What's this? Blood?"

Jacques, however, whip in hand once more, turned to those around.

"You hear? You hear?" he demanded. "A damned foreigner? Aye, an outlander by his speech! Satan is in him as well; look how the dog knows him!"

Amazed cries broke from the others, seeing man and dog at peace and understanding. Jacques, however, bared his teeth in a burst of rage.

"You, foreigner!" he bellowed angrily. "Away from the devil's beast, away from him! Stand aside, while I rip the life out of him!"

"Peace, whoever you are," responded Malcolm. "Yours is the devil's work, it would seem; the dog's a friendly soul. Leave him alone. When my comrade returns—"

"The beast is mine, not yours!" burst forth Jacques. "Away from him! He's mine to kill—ha! Take your hand away from those ropes!" he added in sharp alarm, as Malcolm's fingers found the knots about the dog's neck. "Fool, leave them be! Don't dare to turn him loose! Hands off—hands off, or I'll teach you a lesson!"

What with hatred of foreigners, fear, anger and cruel resolve,

"I am a physician—by name Michel de Notredame."

the bearded Jacques flew into a tempestuous passion. He lashed out with insensate frenzy. The whip curled about dog and man. Malcolm shouted at him, turned and staggered toward him, cursing him in helpless rage. Jacques backed away, but struck again, desperately trying to check this bandaged figure. He struck again and again, while Malcolm drove at him.

IN THE midst of this scene, Black Angus came bursting out of the tavern with a roar of dismay and fury. Too late! Blinded though he was, Malcolm reached the burly peasant and grappled him, tearing the whip from him. A knife slid into the peasant's hand, and he launched a deadly thrust—only to have knife and arm knocked aside as Black Angus hurtled into him.

"Here's what you seek, madman!" cried the Scot, whipping out his dagger. "And what you want, you shall have to the hilt!"

Whether drunk or sober, the bearded Jacques was by this time a madman indeed. He hurled himself upon Angus, screaming imprecations. The two figures came together. After a moment the knife tinkled on the stones, and the burly peasant staggered backward, clutching at his chest; Black Angus, with poniard reddened, flung a harsh word at him.

"Fool! Steel is my business, not yours. Give my compliments to your master the devil!"

Jacques coughed something; his knees loosened, and he fell on his face and was quiet. A groom ran to him, half turned him over, then let him slip down again, and furtively crossed himself. Silence fell on the courtyard and upon the staring men.

ANGUS WENT to Malcolm, slipped an arm around him, and walked him to the bench beside the tavern door. He aided him to sit, and straightened up as the innkeeper came out.

"Small beginnings, grave endings," said Angus. "From the beating of a dog comes the death of a man. Who's this bearded fury, good host?"

"He belongs to the Vicomte d'Oger, monsieur," said the innkeeper, "and has a farm just outside the village. A violent and terrible man; none the less—"

"None the less," said Angus sardonically, "he is dead. Eh, Malcolm? What is it?"

The younger man had reached up, pulling at his sleeve.

"The dog, Angus. Free him."

Black Angus cocked an eye at the great hound. "Be damned if I do!" said he. "That beast is dangerous."

"Not so. He understands English. Go try him yourself! I'll not stir from here till he comes with us."

Angus rolled his eyes resignedly. "I'll humor you," he growled; "but I'd not lay hand on that brute for all the wealth of St. Andréws!"

Gingerly enough, he approached the dog, stopped, and began to speak—not in English but in broad Scots. Almost instantly the ears of the beast pricked up; he stood looking at Angus, his tail lifted and wagged, and from the astonished man broke a sharp exclamation of surprise.

"He's not English, Malcolm! Scots he is—and a friend, by his eye."

"Set him free, set him free," said Malcolm impatiently. "Loose the ropes; I'll call him and he'll come to me. You'll see."

Angus was none too sure. Poniard ready, he advanced warily. The dog looked up at him, and as he later swore, smiled into his eyes. Angus put down a hand to the ropes, worked at the knots with the point of his dagger, and they came apart. Cries of fear escaped the grooms, who scattered hastily, but Malcolm called the dog and extended his hand, and the animal went to him and crouched at his feet.

The staring landlord pointed to something beside the pump.

"There is a collar that broke from him," said he to Angus. "It has a brass plate with something writ in a foreign tongue."

Angus strode over to the spot, picked up the broken piece of leather, and came back to Malcolm and the dog. He looked at the metal plate, and knit his brow.

"I can read big letters, but not script," said he. "Here are big letters first, and script afterward. Five letters, Malcolm; damn it, man, why haven't you your eyes?"

"Bad luck, Angus Dhu," said Malcolm. His lips were tightly set, as he fondled the dog's head. "Hellfire's in my head and eyes; but spell the letters. What are they?"

"*T* is first," replied Angus. "Then *H*. I know it by the crossbar. Then an *O*. That's simple. Then *P*.... No, wait! It's the one like *P,* only different. *R,* that's what it is! And last comes the two strokes with the leaning bar—*N,* that's it. Does it make sense?"

"Thorn," said Malcolm. "Thorn! Eh? Why, the dog's head jumped up at the word!"

"He's looking up at us. By the saints, that's his name, of course! Thorn!" cried Angus, and the dog's head and gaze swung to him. "That's his name, Malcolm, Thorn! That's why it was on the collar. But the plate isn't brass. These fools took it for brass; if it's not ruddy gold, then I'm an Englishman!"

"Take care of it," said Malcolm, and sighed. "I'm done up, Angus. The pain's more than I can bear. Did ye ask about a surgeon?"

"Must send to Blois. It's not far; the court's there, and—" Angus broke off suddenly. A low oath escaped him as he swung around. "Oh, the devil! Here's trouble."

Hoofs clattered and muttered warnings flew among the grooms. Into the courtyard rode an officer, gayly resplendent, and six archers. A low word escaped the landlord.

"God save us all! The provost's lieutenant!"

The officer had seen the body of Jacques. He drew rein with a sharp cry.

"De par le Roi! In the King's name! What have we here, you damned rascals? Murder?" He dismounted and strode arrogantly to the landlord and Black Angus. "Speak, speak! You, landlord, you dare to kill without authority?"

"Not I, your worship, not I!" The landlord fell on his knees, stones or no stones. "The dead man is Jacques, the villein of M. d'Oger. This foreign gentleman was attacked by him, and killed him."

"Eh?" said the officer, and bent his brows upon Black Angus. "You?"

"I, monsieur," said Angus, composedly.

"Then you shall be bound and taken before the provost—"

"Not so fast, monsieur," said Angus. "Haste is a fast horse, but precaution's a better one. You've no authority to lay hand upon me, and you'd best not try."

"Indeed!" The officer regarded him with a sneer. "Indeed! You are, no doubt, the good St. Michael himself, to be independent of the authority of France, and to kill peasants who are the property of gentlemen!"

"Not St. Michael," rejoined Black Angus. "If you'd said Saint Andréw, you'd have been closer to the mark, monsieur. I'm Angus Douglas of Kilspindie, sergeant of the Scots Archer Guards, at present returning from furlough in Scotland to my duty. And I'm subject only to the authority of the Captain of the Guards, the Earl of Arran, or of His Majesty in person, or of the Dauphin or his good lady, Mary Queen of Scotland. Outside of which, you or any other authority in France will get your fingers damned well burned if you lay them on me."

An officer of the Scots Guards! That was something, indeed. It was so distinctly something, that the provost's lieutenant swallowed hard.

"Have you any proof of this claim?" he demanded.

"Certainly, under the hand of the Earl of Arran and of His Majesty as well," said Angus. He produced a folded pad of vellum. "There's my passport, and you'll note that it requires all officers of the realm to give me aid and support on demand."

THE LIEUTENANT unfolded the vellum, glanced at the writing, and nodded. Then he looked at Angus with sudden interest.

"Can it be that you're the two gentlemen who were attacked by thieves on the road hither from Veuve, earlier in the day?"

"We are," said Angus, pocketing his passport again. "And except we were taken off our guard, there'd have been little trouble. My comrade here, Malcolm Campbell, who's on his way to take service in the Guards, was grievously hurt when his sword splintered and bits of the steel blinded him; but we killed three of the rogues."

"And wounded four others," added the lieutenant. "Word

was brought of the matter, and I was sent to investigate. Well done, monsieur! You have my permission to kill a dozen peasants if you desire; you've rid us of a most troublesome gang of robbers who have plagued our roads for the past year!"

"Soft words salve no wounds," said Angus dourly. "My comrade is sore hurt. I ask your aid in sending to Blois for a surgeon. The court is at Blois, so there must be no end of doctors and surgeons about—" He broke off sharply at a word from the innkeeper. The head of Malcolm had fallen back, and he had slumped in a faint. "The devil! Here, someone lend a hand— help carry him to our room! The dog will hurt no one. Down, Thorn! Down!"

So presently, Malcolm was carried away, with the huge dog quietly following; but Angus did not go along, for the lieutenant detained him.

"Wait, monsieur! The chateau of M. d'Oger, whose man you have just slain, is not a league from here. A physician from the court is there now as the guest of the Vicomte. I heard of it only this morning; he must be still there."

"Who is he? Maître Ambroise Paré of Paris?"

"I do not know. But, if it please you, I'll send him at once. I'm riding there now, as I must make report of this other incident. I'll undertake to have him here well inside the hour."

Angus seized his hand. "Good! Thanks, with all my heart, monsieur! Do this, and if ever you have need of a friend, come to me and I'll serve you to the utmost!"

Angus departed to the side of his comrade, well pleased; he needed help imperatively, and any of the court surgeons or physicians would be excellent. The lieutenant mounted and clattered off with his men, equally delighted; an officer of the Scots Guards could be a bad enemy but a most valuable friend.

The dead man lying on the cobblestones was forgotten. He was of no importance to anyone, except perhaps to the Vicomte d'Oger, who could replace him very easily. Yet in his death, the bearded and violent Jacques had served as an essential cog in the grinding mechanism of destiny.

In these days when blood and war and ruin swept the world, destiny often depended upon such trifles. It was the spring of the year 1559. A woman of twenty-six had just recently become Queen of England. A girl of seventeen, already Queen of Scotland, was soon to become Queen of France as well, and had a better claim to the English throne than its incumbent. Assassination, treachery, bloodshed, were everywhere; law was prostrate, justice a mockery; religious strife was rising to fury. Only the strong could survive, or so men said.

Yet this whole savage warring scene was actually being managed by the slender fingers of women. It was they who pulled the strings, to which danced puppet statesmen and warriors and kings. Behind the scenes, they ruled the social world, and upon the stage it was they whose abilities were dominant, with three of them predominant above all the others—Elizabeth in England, Diane de Poitiers in France, and Catherine de Medici in her own place.

Black Angus thought of these things as he sat watching at the bedside of his comrade. He thought of Scotland, which he had just now seen given over to fire and sword, to murder and plunder and factions. He washed the wounds of the great dog and thought of men broken on the wheel for opinions, or burned alive for their beliefs.

"The world's a damned sorry place," he told himself, and wagged his grizzled beard, and looked at the flushed face of the unconscious man on the pillow. "The greater rascal a man is, the greater lord he becomes; a prince is another name for a scoundrel. What in hell's name is the use of being honest and true and brave, when the only good woman in France is the King's mistress, and the only future open to a soldier is to betray his master or break his oaths? What's the use of decency, anyway?"

HE GRUNTED. Then, leaning forward, he felt under the leather jacket of the unconscious Malcolm and touched something there, sewn to the leather.

"There's wealth," he said. "And a title of nobility, the captaincy of an army, anything the heart of a man could desire. Merely for a broken oath and honor laid aside. Why not? There's no honor left in the world, and damned little decency. Why not chuck it all and take what could be had for the asking?"

The answer to his temptation and to his questioning was at this moment approaching. He heard a coach roll into the courtyard, and knew that the physician had arrived; and he came to his feet expectantly.

But Thorn, the Irish wolfhound, rose stiffly and stretched his great length and height to full size, and his shining intelligent eyes were fastened upon the door as it opened, as though he had risen in homage to some presence more than mortal.

It was, however, only a man in a black gown and the square biretta of a doctor, who stood there.

In this moment Black Angus of Kilspindie had a queer impulse to salute this man with deference; he fought back the impulse. The physician's impressive air was hard to define; he was not a tall man. Gray-bearded, very ruddy and hearty of cheek, bright and piercing of black eye, long of nose, the visitor met the gaze of Black Angus and nodded pleasantly.

"So this is the place," he said in French, with a distinct accent. "A man hurt?"

"My comrade," Angus replied, indicating the bed. "His sword broke as he warded a blow; the splinters blinded him. I have done what I could."

The visitor halted and looked at Thorn, who pricked up ears and wagged tail.

"So!" said the deep, pleasant voice. "There are two who have need of me; perhaps all three! Who is this young man?"

"A recruit, coming to join the Scots Guards," said Angus. "And who are you?"

*"What is it?" she went on. "Your air is strange; you
speak strange words. Yet Thorn says you are a friend."*

The visitor looked at him for a moment, a quiet, contempla-
tive moment.

"Friend," he answered at length, "I am a physician, by name
Michel de Notredame. And I will thank you to observe one
thing: the truth."

ANGUS SWALLOWED hard, then stood rebuked and
silent. A servant entered, bringing warm water and cloths.
Maître Notredame drew a stool to the bedside, sat down, and
began very carefully to remove Malcolm Campbell's bandage.

"How was he hurt?" he questioned, and Angus told him,
repeating his words. Notredame shook his head slightly, cleansed
the wound, made a lengthy examination, and looked up. "My
pupil and assistant, Brion, is outside. Kindly tell him to enter."

"Madame, I put my life in your hands," he said.
"I'm Malcolm Campbell.... Unless you can help me,
I'm a lost man—and Scotland is lost with me!"

Angus went to the door. Another man stood waiting in the corridor; a younger man, with pointed beard and sparkling eyes, who came in and handed his master a case of instruments and tiny vials. He, too, leaned over and examined the wound with care.

"Luckily, he is unconscious," he remarked. "The eyes are not injured, master, but it is a delicate matter. Do you wish me to get out the splinters?"

"No, my dear Actæus," said the physician. "No. This young man is of the greatest importance to the world. Prepare everything; the work is mine."

He rolled back his sleeves and fell to work upon the wound. The skin and flesh above the eyes was torn and ragged and badly messed about by the ministrations of Angus. With deft fingers, Notredame worked upon the hurt. His instruments glittered like needles. He drew out tiny slivers of steel, he explored the flesh, he cleansed it again; then went to work replacing the skin. All the while, Malcolm lay senseless and Black Angus stared hard. At length, Notredame nodded and straightened up.

"Now the bandage, Actæus," he said. "And first, the salve of Avicenna. Sit here. I'll take the dog in charge—"

"No, no, master!" exclaimed Brion, whom the physician called by the intimate name of Actæus. "A dog? Such work is not for you. Let the beast wait for me."

"This is no beast," said Notredame, leaving the stool and stooping to examine the hurts of Thorn, who nuzzled his hand. "This is one of those rare animals that approach the human strength of spirit and intelligence. What sort of dog is he, good soldier?"

"An Irish wolfhound, I'd say," rejoined Angus dourly. "My friend and I are Scots."

"So I understood." The physician smiled at the dog and began his work. "Foreigners in this pleasant land of France, all of us. I myself am from Provence, this hound from Ireland, you from Scotland."

"And the Queen, from Italy," said Angus, under his breath. Notredame glanced up.

"The Queen? Oh, Catherine de Medici, yes. A great woman, in her way; she will rule France; yet France will never belong to her. Are you going back to Scotland soon?"

"I've just been there, on furlough," Angus said shortly.

"Indeed!" Notredame, while he spoke, was anointing the wounds of Thorn with salve and cleansing them. "And you do not know where the dog came from?"

"No. Who told you that?"

Notredame smiled, and stooped to lift the broken collar that lay on the floor.

" 'Thorn is my name,' " he said, reading the inscription.

Angus started. "So you speak English? You read it? Does it give the name of any owner?"

"That is all it says." Notredame, having finished his task, watched Brion for a moment. The bandage was adjusted. Malcolm still lay unconscious. From among his vials the healer selected several and mixed a potion in a silver cup he took from a case. "Give your friend six drops of this in water, not in wine, every hour. Here is a quill to measure the drops. Pour it between his lips. With morning, his fever will be gone. In two days, he will leave his bed and go on to Blois with you. In a week, only the scar will remain; and it will vanish soon. But he must come to me when you reach Blois, that I may treat the wound again."

"His eyes?" questioned Angus.

"They're not hurt." Notredame put the cup aside and nodded to his assistant. "Wait for me in the coach, Actæus; we'll go back to Blois from here."

Sunset was approaching. The room was filled with ruddy light. Brion departed; the physician leaned back in his chair, his long, slim hands quiet in his lap, his gaze fixed on Black Angus. It was a calm, meditative gaze, searching yet serene. The very essence of the man was composure, an absolute composure eloquent of inward power.

Thorn came to him, put his head on his knee, and licked his hand. Notredame paid no heed, but continued to study Black Angus reflectively.

"Well?" broke out the Scot. "There's nothing wrong with me, at least."

"Much," said Notredame gravely. "But first, there is so much to say! These are strange times, when such a man as you, the very soul of honor and loyalty, could be tempted to betray his trust."

The rugged features of Angus set hard; had it been possible, he would have turned pale, but he was not that type.

"What do you mean?" he demanded gruffly.

The calm voice spoke on: "Henri II is the king; his queen is

Catherine de Medici; his son François is the Dauphin, married to Mary Stuart, Queen of Scotland. These two, a boy and a girl, are heirs of destiny, my friend, children of ill fortune. Henri is a good man, a strong king. His mistress, Diane de Poitiers, is one of the wisest and noblest women in the world, and by her counsel France is ruled. In spite of her, all about us is corruption and treachery and intrigue. You may well ask what is the use of honor and loyalty!"

"I did not!" Angus started slightly. "I asked you nothing, physician."

"Then ask yourself, soldier. What's the use of loyalty to a doomed cause? What's the use of honor, when leaders are dishonored? What's the use of fighting, when the enemy outnumber you?"

Tiny beads of sweat broke out on the brow of Angus.

"That's enough!" he said hoarsely. "Are you man or devil?"

"A physician; you yourself named me." Notredame nodded. "And a friend. Now look, soldier! Harken while I resolve the mystery, though I fear you'll not comprehend my words. You hear my words, not my thoughts. Yet thoughts are actual things like words. Thoughts are a force, an exertion of energy. Sometimes, though very rarely, a man can feel and understand them, as other men hear words. I am one of those rare persons."

"Devil's work!" muttered Angus, eyes wide.

"No. All that is noble is God's work, comprehended in two words *courage* and *faith*. Bear this in mind, soldier." The physician rose and extended his hand. "Farewell. Bring your friend to me at Blois in three days. Either I or Brion will see to the wound there. And keep a stout heart!"

Black Angus gripped the long, firm hand. He sought for words and found none, and in silence saw the visitor depart. Then he wiped the sweat from his brow, felt a touch, and looked down to see Thorn nuzzling him, looking up at him.

"Stout heart!" he muttered. "You, Thorn, are great of heart yourself; you shame me. How the devil did he know what I'd been thinking about? Well, best get busy with that medicine, I suppose."

He prepared the dose and trickled it between Malcolm's lips. The younger man opened his mouth; his fingers gripped on those of Angus, and he spoke.

"You, Angus? I'm burning up; a touch of fever. But the pain's all gone."

"Then sleep and gain strength. Your eyes are not injured; the physician says you'll be all right in a couple of days."

Malcolm sighed and smiled, and slept. But Angus looked out at the gathering darkness and stroked his grizzled beard, and frowned.

"Who is he? How does he know so much?" he muttered. "Flesh and blood, by his grip, yet more than mortal man by his words. When I told him Malcolm was a recruit, he gave me the lie! He knew; but how did he know? Who'll tell me that, now?"

At all events, his temptation was clean gone; the very thought of it made him snort with scorn. Black Angus of Kilspindie was himself again.

CHAPTER II

B LOIS WAS intolerably crowded. Gone were the days of King François, who dragged from one royal residence to another an attendant court of twelve thousand souls. Under the businesslike rule of Diane de Poitiers, inefficiency and graft were cut to a minimum; none the less, Henri II loved magnificence, and the size of his court left few empty beds in the royal chateau or the town.

Black Angus had good reason not to seek the guards' barracks at present. Therefore he got a temporary room in the town, and after a long night's sleep, accompanied Malcolm Campbell in search of the physician Notredame. The latter's lodgings were soon found, for he was a man of great note, the most famed physician in all France.

Notredame they found not, but Brion was there, and he saw to Campbell's wound. A merry fellow, this Brion, who jested right and left, removed the bandages and replaced them with a heavy strip of plaster, and gravely asked after the health of the dog Thorn.

"He's doing well; we left him in our room," said Campbell. "What's that on the wall, a mirror? The first I've seen in France! Now for a squint at myself, Angus."

He looked, and did not know himself. The plaster disfigured him. In place of the shaven, high-boned features he knew so well, with the gray eyes glittering under straight black brows, he beheld a face blurred by dark beard in ragged lengths. He had not shaven since leaving Scotland. He gave Angus a wry grimace.

"Safe enough, eh? At least, until I've done what I came to do."

"Careful, messieurs," intervened Brion with a gay chuckle. "I warn you that I speak English, so tell no secrets! Also, my master left a message for you," he said, turning to Campbell. "For three days you're not to leave your room, except after dark. On the fourth day, remove the plaster from the wound and then seek her whose mother sent you."

At these words, Campbell felt his heart contract for an instant. He shot a glance at Black Angus.

"You talked? You told him, then?"

"Upon my honor, I told him nothing!" exclaimed Angus, equally startled. "Did I not say he knew everything? This is like the things he said to me at the tavern."

"Master Brion, what did your master mean by those words?" Campbell demanded.

Brion shrugged. "A wise man never asks Maître whence came his knowledge! From the stars, perhaps, since he's a famed astrologer. I only deliver the message, monsieur."

"Monsieur, what is your desire?" asked Diane.

"Very well. As I may not be in France very long, let me pay your master's fee now."

"He said that you could pay it at your next meeting, monsieur. He said you would meet him again where you least expect it."

"Thank you. Good day." With a brusque gesture to Angus, Campbell strode out of the room, out of the house, and paused not until they stood in the street. Then he turned to his companion, making no secret of his alarm.

"Angus, something has slipped; perhaps word has got here ahead of us. We know English spies are everywhere, their agents are everywhere. This doctor probably is a friend and has taken this way of warning us."

"Like enough." Black Angus looked troubled. "Well, with that patch, that leathern coat, and that beard, you look like any rascally countryman. As you see, beards are in fashion here. You're safe from recognition, so go back to our room and wait. I'll gather news and be along presently. Good advice, to venture out only at night!"

"But how the devil am I to reach the Queen, in secret?"

"Wait and see. I can manage that for you, once I return to duty."

They separated, Campbell retracing his steps to their lodging where he kicked off his shoes, loosened his doublet, and disposed himself comfortably. Thorn stretched out at his side, and Campbell's hand strayed over the long lean head affectionately.

Thorn was still very stiff from his hurts, but his famished look was gone, and his neatly brushed coat lent him an entirely new appearance—an air of dignity, of breeding, of alert nobility.

"You're a prince among dogs, old fellow," murmured Campbell. "And devil take it, I'm a dog among princes! One suspicion of my errand, and my life's not worth a groat. And here this doctor's assistant blurts it out to my face! This place is filled with Scots and with English, with lords and princes of France, and none of them to be trusted. Devil a one! Yet I must reach the Queen, for Scotland's at stake!"

He was a different person now from the drooping wounded man of the highway. Strength was back in him, the gray eyes were alight with youth and energy and shrewdness; when he moved, his step had the balance and precision of trained muscles and alert fighting ability.

When the door burst open, Campbell glanced up quietly. Angus came in, breathing hard.

"Now the devil's to pay! However, I've got the mystery solved."

"Sit down and catch your breath," said Campbell. "There's wine; I'll drink with you. Bad news can wait."

"This can't," growled Angus. None the less, he crossed to the table, poured wine into two mugs, and brought one of them to Campbell. He emptied the other at one quaff. "My fault, comrade," he said. "At the crossroads tavern, I told that provost's officer our names: A sad mistake—not for my sake, but for yours. I met a couple of comrades from the Guards; they tipped me off the captain's watching the roads for you. We must have slipped into town by sheer good luck. No one's looking for me, it seems; just for you."

Campbell frowned, puzzled. "What captain?"

"Why, the Captain of the Scots Guards, man! The Earl of Arran. Hamilton, head of the house of Hamilton, next in line to the throne of Scotland, after Mary Stuart!"

Campbell caught his breath. "Good Lord! Then the worst has happened; we've been betrayed at the other end; a messenger has come through ahead of us!"

"Obviously."

"Get back to your duty, then. You're safe. Wash your hands of me—"

"Go to the devil," snapped Black Angus, and dropped into a chair. "My leave has three days to run; I stick with you. But that's not the worst. The Dauphin hasn't yet arrived; he is on the way from Fontainebleau to join the court. Mary Stuart is with him, naturally."

Campbell's heart sank. "Bad luck. My errand is to her, or to Madame Diane."

"Oh, *she's* here right enough! And the King," said Angus. "Look, d'ye see why that physician knew so much? He had picked up word. These surgeons and barbers and doctors hear all secrets. His warning was good; stay indoors. Queen Mary will be here in three days, and that's what he meant. He's a friend, right enough."

"I dare not wait three days," said Campbell slowly. "But you can't help me reach Diane de Poitiers."

"No," said Angus gloomily. "Only a Frenchman of the court could help you there, and you can't trust any damned Frenchman. Or can you?"

Campbell shook his head. So Hamilton, the Earl of Arran, Captain of the Scots Guards, knew of his errand! This was frightful news.

His thoughts went back to Leith in Scotland, and to the indomitable, stern woman he had left there struggling to hold the Stuart inheritance together: Mary of Guise, Regent of Scotland for her daughter Mary Stuart, a woman of the lion's breed, a true Guise. No one could be trusted, she had warned him solemnly. No Frenchman; not her own brothers, not the Duke nor the Cardinal of Lorraine. He remembered her very words.

"Only one of two persons, Monsieur Campbell! Only my daughter Mary Stuart, Queen of France; if you cannot reach her, get the message to the Duchess de Valentinois, Diane de Poitiers, beloved of Henri II—the wisest woman in France, the most able, the most powerful. She has been as a mother to my own daughter, Mary. Trust her. No one else, not the Dauphin, not the King himself! And God preserve you."

Black Angus jerked up his head. "We've had no supper. I'll order it at once."

"I've ordered it. Compose yourself," said Campbell. "You don't know the details of my errand, Angus."

"No. I don't want to know 'em. Must be something big, if Arran, or Hamilton as the English call him, wants to wring your neck."

"Right. If he fails, he loses his own neck. I must reach Diane de Poitiers tonight or tomorrow. I must!"

"As well hope to reach the moon, as the King's mistress," Angus said gloomily.

"Well, think! There must be some way. Here's supper, and

high time too. I'll take Thorn out for a walk when it's dark; does me good to be on my feet. I may think of something," said Campbell, and said no more. Two of the servants from the tavern at the corner were at the door with the dinner he had ordered. It would not be wise to let them hear foreign tongues in speech. Everyone was a spy in Blois, these days....

The dinner was served; the wine was poured; the two servants departed.

"I'll want some decent clothes and a sword," said Campbell.

"You can't reach Diane tonight," Angus objected, his mouth full. "She retires early. She's up at three or four in the morning, to start her horseback rides and cold baths, her beauty treatments. Think of it! A woman of fifty-nine, holding the King's affection against all comers, supremely beautiful, without a mark of age—"

"Court clothes," said Campbell. "Now, at once, before I take Thorn out. They may be looking for a ragged Scot, not for a courtier with a dog."

"Give me five minutes to eat! It won't be dark for an hour."

"Dark enough. And a hat, mind, like these courtiers wear."

"What about your leathern coat?"

"Under my doublet. Get me a fat man's size. Anything at all! And a sword."

Black Angus swore, and sighed, gulped down his wine, and shoved back his chair.

"You're daft! Sheer daft!"

Campbell smiled, but made no response. Angus donned his hat and strode out.

Daft? Perhaps; urgency drove at him, and Campbell felt himself yielding to it. A queer sense of urgency it was. Not for himself. He was a mere pawn in this game. But upon his success or failure hung many lives, the destiny of kingdoms, the triumph of good or evil in this world—more than he could envisage in his mind's eye. And, if this man knew of him and his errand, failure lay close and bitter; this man known to the French as the Captain of the Scots Guard, to the English as Hamilton, to the Scots as the Earl of Arran and next in succession to Scotland's throne! Now it was the game that mattered, not the man, and the game must somehow, somewhere, be won this night or forever lost, and Scotland with it.

SUNSET PASSED. Shadows crept down upon the valley and town, the lordly chateau stood darkling against the sky with lights glowing from its windows. Black Angus came tramping heavily up the stairs and into the room, a candlestick in one hand, clothes flung over his other arm.

"Malcolm! I've been thinking. About this dog, Thorn. It was a gold plate on his collar, d'ye mind? He must have broken away from someone here, at court, either Scot or English."

"Precisely my own line of thought," broke in Campbell, seizing on the garments. "Well, well, it's a slim hope, Angus. Good garments, and a fair sword. Thanks, greatly."

He was stripping as he spoke, to dress again. Wide hard shoulders, the arm of a swordsman, no great muscles, but rippling silk, steely tough. Into his leathern coat, and jerkin and doublet and long hose, all in a rush of haste.

"What's driving you?" demanded Angus. "You're not going alone?"

"I am that," said Campbell, buckling tight the sword-belt. "If I'm not back in two hours, give me up and get back to your comrades with morning. I'll not incriminate you, should they take me. If I have any luck, I'll send you word of it."

"You daft fool!" growled Angus, staring at him. "You can get nowhere; you can reach no one, of an evening!"

"There's always a first time." Campbell put out his hand and wrung that of Angus. "Stout heart! You're a grand comrade. Come, Thorn! To heel—that's right. Well trained, beastie. Farewell, Angus! Until later."

He was out and gone, descending the stairs with Thorn at his heels, a long, hugely graceful shape. And so to the streets, hat cocked over ear, sword pricking up the folds of his cloak, and that drifting silent beast padding at his side. Whither? He knew only vaguely, but turned aright. One could not miss those buildings along the height. All the world pointed thither, even of a dark night; soldiers, guards, courtiers, pages, messengers, friars, horses, carriages. Where the court lay, there was France.

Above the town on a little plateau was the former citadel that had now become a palace. Campbell knew that on the opposite side of the chateau lay the gardens and pleasure walks, and with this objective he followed the circling road, unhurried now.

On this north side of the buildings, however, also lay gardens and terraces, by which Campbell's road passed. Here was the famed Perchoir aux Bretons, the Perch of the Bretons, a terrace where in olden days the Breton nobles were wont to await the pleasure of Queen Anne de Bretagne. These terraces were laid out in paths and hedges and flower-beds, perfumed and blooming under the touch of approaching summer.

Aware of a number of scattered figures on these terraces, Campbell turned into one of the graveled walks. His steps were aimless. He was led by desperation, not by design. To reach his goal by any accustomed channel was impossible unless he revealed his name and errand; this was out of the question. In a day of plot, intrigue, and assassination, high personages were guarded with utmost care by their retinues and servants.

"Oh, it's fantastic; I'm sheer daft, as Angus said," he reflected as he followed the path under the brightening stars. "Thorn, your new master is a fool, an utter fool!" At the low words, Thorn's long muzzle found his hand with a touch of reassurance, and he fondled the sleek head. "Why, beastie, you're close to human! I do believe you understand my words. Be off, then! Look for your old master and bring him to my aid, for any man owning such a dog as you must have a spark of honor and chivalry."

As though he did indeed understand the words, Thorn stiffened suddenly. A low, tense whine escaped him, and he was gone into the darkness.

Campbell walked on, oppressed with a sense of his own folly. In his heart, he knew all this was sheer madness; it was no more than the flickering fancy of a lately fevered brain, urged by desperation.

Best return to town and let Angus seek some way of reaching Diane de Poitiers, he thought gloomily. These masses of royal buildings, glowing with lights, were sinister; here was peril, everywhere was peril. His name was known, men were seeking him—

In upon his thoughts broke the whine of Thorn, a joyous, impetuous, eager whine, followed by a burst of voices in surprise and astonishment. Campbell whistled curtly. Women's voices! The dog came with a rush, bounding over the flower-beds, to leap upon him shoulder-high and whine again with gladness. Then Campbell was aware of three figures in the starlight, coming toward him.

Thorn went leaping back to them. He circled around them and returned to Campbell, who looked at the three women and swore under his breath.

"Now you've done it, Thorn," he muttered. "What's this, eh?"

His words were in English. To his startled surprise, they were echoed by the foremost of the three.

"Just what I was about to ask, monsieur! Who are you and how did you find my dog?"

"Oh! The devil!" ejaculated Campbell. "Your pardon. You speak English, madame?"

He could see little of her except the vague shape of flowing garments.

"Naturally." Her voice was impatient. "Who are you, I say? Of the court, by your attire, but I don't recognize your voice."

CAMPBELL HESITATED; his brain raced. Danger, danger! Yet Thorn was pressing against the woman, licking her hand; now the dog came back to him with new eagerness, so that despite the crisis, a laugh escaped him.

"Your dog, say you? Yes, only a woman would let such a dog fall into the hands of barbarous peasants who tried to kill him by torture—"

"By the Rood, this passes endurance!" came the woman's angry voice. "Your name, and at once! Or I'll call the guards if you prefer."

"Wait! For God's sake, madame, wait!" exclaimed Campbell. "Do these women understand English?"

"No; they're two of the Queen's ladies. I'm Anne Haworth, lady of honor to Mary Stuart."

"Haworth!" he exclaimed. "Not Sir John Haworth's daughter? Why, madame, I talked with your father in Perth—why, this is blessed news! I can trust you, I can trust you—"

"That's more than I can say for you," she rejoined tartly. She had come closer, and stood peering at him in the starlight.

Campbell hugged Thorn's head against his thigh. This woman—could he trust her, indeed?

"What is it?" she went on, more gently. "You speak strange words; your air is strange; yet Thorn says you're a friend. That means much."

Campbell came to a decision.

"Madame, I put my life in your hands," he said, almost under his breath. "I'm Malcolm Campbell; I've just arrived from Scotland with an urgent message from the Regent to either Mary Stuart or Madame de Valentinois. I've no means of reaching either one. By ill luck, my mission has become known. I'm being hunted now by the Earl of Arran and his friends. Unless you can help me, I'm a lost man—and Scotland is lost with me, more's the pity!"

"What? Why, this can't be possible!" she exclaimed softly. "Have you anything to vouch for such a story?"

"Thorn will vouch for me," he said; "and I've a letter sewn

under my shirt. And if you turn me over to the guards, they'll kill me fast enough."

"Strange!" she replied. "I'm serving the Dame de Valentinois at the moment, since my mistress has not yet arrived; I can take you to her, can pass you through the guards…. But—shall I? How can I trust you? It means to stake my own honor and reputation and future upon your word. If you're an assassin and I bring you to her, then I'm lost."

Campbell's heart sank. "Do as you will, madame," he said hopelessly. "I've shot my last shaft, and can do no more."

The two Frenchwomen were whispering and laughing together. From the road near by, where groups were talking or walking, lifted a man's voice that carried clearly to them—evidently one of the Scots Guards.

"Aye, there's gowd i' the purse if ye lay hand on him, and slit his wame before he can talk, says the Captain! They say he's son to old Murdoch Campbell o' Glenlyon, and a master swordsman, so take no chances."

"Why, it's of you he's speaking!" said Anne Haworth.

"True," said Campbell. "You have but to utter my name, madame, to win Hamilton's favor."

"The devil take Hamilton, and his cousin to boot!" she snapped. "You speak French? Good. Remain with these ladies while I make arrangements." To the women, she said in rapid French: "Mesdames, allow me to present a Scots gentleman, an old friend of mine, the Sieur Malcolm Glenlyon, newly come to court. Tell him of the stars, and advise him of the ways of courtiers, until I return."

Campbell bowed to the two women, who immediately exclaimed upon hearing his excellent French. Anne Haworth moved away, then paused and called Thorn. But Thorn, under Campbell's hand, merely whined slightly.

"Go to her, Thorn!" said Campbell, laughing a little. "And come when I call again."

"He shall not!" floated back her indignant voice; but Campbell paid no heed. The sudden crisis was past; the dice had fallen for him, and in the sharp reaction he found it difficult to concentrate his attention upon the gay speeches of the two French ladies. He was conscious, too, of physical weakness, for the strength had gone out of him.

Yet he forced himself to talk and laugh with the two, to meet their jests with brisk repartee, until one of them asked after a friend, a young noble, serving with the French contingent in Scotland. Campbell, as it chanced, knew the man. This at once made things smoother, and all three were talking amiably when Thorn came leaping out of the darkness to paw at Campbell's chest and lick his cheek. And after him came Anne Haworth and a short, cloaked figure, whom Anne presented in few words.

"Monsieur Glenlyon, I have spoken with my lady, and she has sent her secretary, M. Guillaumont, who will conduct you to her presence at once. She is most anxious to hear your messages from Fontainebleau and our friends in Paris."

This was, of course, for the ears of the others, to whom Campbell bowed and made his excuses. He and Guillaumont started away together; they were at the road, when Thorn came bounding after them, and in spite of calls from his mistress, remained with them as they approached the buildings.

"The animal seems to like you, monsieur," said the secretary dryly. "A good presage, for this is a very curious business. I am taking you by way of the royal apartments, where we shall encounter only the French Guards."

"Madame Haworth must have talked fast," said Campbell, and the other laughed.

"Evidently. But I must ask you for your sword and poniard when we gain the apartment of my mistress."

"As you like."

Campbell cared now for nothing. Let them watch him, let them be suspicious, just so that he reached the woman who ruled France! He was suddenly uplifted, carried out of himself, filled with new strength and joy. The impossible was accom-

plished! But he must send word, he remembered, to Black Angus and set his comrade at rest.

And now, suddenly, they were within the flare of blazing cressets. Guards saluted the well-known Guillaumont. Swaggering courtiers and nobles appeared on the stairs and in the corridors, staring with insolent hauteur at Campbell; then on, amid magnificence of carving, of surroundings, sufficient to stagger one fresh from the less ostentatious palaces of Scotland.

From somewhere drifted music of viols and singers. Shrill French tongues chattered volubly on every hand. Campbell was aware of a handsome, arrogant man aglitter with jewels, talking intimately with a younger but more powerful figure. A few words reached him; they were talking English. He bent to the ear of his guide.

"Who are those two gentlemen we just passed?"

"One, monsieur, is the Captain of the Scots Guards. The younger man is his cousin, Monsieur Hamilton, a gentleman of the Dauphin's entourage."

Campbell chuckled to himself. Under the very eye of Arran, who was seeking high and low for him! Angus would appreciate this. And that other man, that Hamilton—eh? The one Anne Haworth had mentioned.

He began to be very curious about Lady Anne Haworth, as he fondled the ears of the great dark hound stalking along proudly beside him.

Then they were mounting a stairs, passing into a narrow corridor, passing a guard at a farther door and entering a large antechamber. Guillaumont touched him on the arm and asked for his weapons; and Campbell knew he had reached his destination. He was about to be received by the mistress of the King of France.

CHAPTER III

DIANE DE POITIERS, now Duchesse de Valentinois, sat over her embroidery, as was her custom of an evening. As she worked, she discussed details of construction with Delorme, the architect of the glorious chateaux she was building. The Bishop of Meaux, her nephew, was chatting with several of her ladies, and in one corner, softly plucking a lute which he held to his ear, being afflicted with deafness, was the poet Ronsard, her fervent admirer.

By birth a great lady, she was yet greater by character and ability. Her private apartment reflected the calm poise, the serenity, that marked her out; it was simple, quietly luxurious, but not ostentatious. Depraved and vicious as was the court, her portion of it remained, like everything she touched, calm and well-ordered.

The circle of Diane de Poitiers held none of those dazzling, licentious personalities given over to depravity. She, who could

discuss Plato and Boethius with a philosopher, business admin-
istration with a banker and the art of poesy with poets, did not
attract decadent minds. Yet she was the mistress of the King
and the mother of his child, Diane de France.

To Campbell, waiting inside the door as Guillaumont went
forward, it was impossible to believe that this woman was nearly
sixty. Her daily regime of horseback rides, cold baths, relaxation
and careful diet, a regime so rigorous that few women would
have endured its necessity of rising at three in the morning, left
her endowed with a youthful freshness that time could not
affect. Her complexion was famed for its purity; Campbell
would have given her thirty-five years, at most. Above all was
her absolute poise, her quiet serenity which nothing interrupted. She was a woman at peace with earth and heaven.

She heard Guillaumont, looked up at Campbell, and beckoned him. Delorme rose, bowed, and withdrew beyond earshot.
Guillaumont, at a gesture, remained. Campbell came forward
and bowed, conscious of her blue-gray eyes and masses of chest-
nut hair, of a quiet voice, of a face that was not beautiful yet
was alight with beauty from within.

"Monsieur, you are hurt!" she said, glancing at his bandaged
forehead.

"A slight wound, madame; it is nothing," he rejoined. She
gestured to the secretary, gave a swift order, extended her hand.
Campbell bowed over it.

"Here is a chair. Be seated, monsieur. First, this curious business of your name; I beg you to explain it. You need fear nothing
from any ears in this room."

He complied, understanding that she was striving to set him
at ease. She smiled wryly over the Scotch names.

"Campbell? Of Glenlyon, is that it? Why, that is almost a
French name, Monsieur de Glenlyon! Excellent! And from
whom is this message you bring?"

"From Madame Marie de Guise, Regent of Scotland," he
rejoined. "It is most urgent, a verbal message— Oh, the devil!

Pardon me, madame, pardon me," he said in confusion, for the head of Thorn had shoved forward against him. "I forgot the dog was here."

Diane broke into quick laughter. She reached out and Thorn went to her, and she touched his head. Then she saw his scars and her eyes widened.

"But he has been hurt! Like you, monsieur!"

"Yes, madame. But my message is more important."

"Perhaps, perhaps not," she said coolly. "A verbal message, you say?"

"Yes, madame. I have a letter from Madame Marie, sewn within my doublet, which will guarantee all that I say." Campbell was confused again. "I can't get it out here. I'll have to take off the doublet to reach it." He broke off, coloring.

"It can wait." Diane smiled a little as she eyed him. "That my good cousin Marie should send you, is guarantee enough for the moment. First, the message."

Campbell met her quiet smile, and felt her composure stealing out upon him. His heart ceased to hammer. Words came to him, words that shocked the listening secretary into pallid incredulity, yet had no effect upon the woman before him.

"Madame, this is the message: Argyll, Stewart and other great lords of Scotland have formed a convention to seize the kingdom and depose Mary Stuart, using religious troubles as a pretext. Much of the kingdom is already in their hands. They are backed by English money and help."

"But then who would be their king?" broke in Diane swiftly.

"The Earl of Arran, head of the Hamilton clan, who is next in line to the succession."

"He? But he is Captain of our Scots Guard here!"

"Precisely, madame. He is to leave France at once and go to England. It has been arranged that he is to marry the new queen there, Elizabeth; the realms of Scotland and England will be united under their rule."

Into the cheeks of Diane, which had the fresh and lovely

smoothness of a girl, mounted a slight color, her only sign of agitation. She laid aside her embroidery, her gaze on that of Campbell.

"Monsieur, this plan could not have been so definitely arranged without French aid and support. We have an army in Scotland now, upholding the Regent."

"Yes, madame. The French commanders take their orders from M. de Montmorency, the High Constable of France. At his orders they will abandon the cause of the Regent and of Mary Stuart. Her Highness the Regent has proof that he has given such orders and is allied in this affair with the Earl of Arran and with English agents."

Guillaumont made a slight noise with his tongue, an involuntary cluck of sheer horror. Diane relaxed and nodded thoughtfully. For a moment there was silence....

From the time the child Mary Stuart had come to France, Diane de Poitiers had acted to her in the place of a mother, arranging every detail of her education and life. She had done the same to the girl Catherine de Medici, the child-wife of Henri II, watching over them with a wise and careful prudence, as she watched over the affairs of the kingdom and of her lover who ruled it.

"THIS," SHE broke the silence gently, "would not be the first time Montmorency has betrayed his trust and his king, nor will it be the last. Well, monsieur? Does this conclude the message?"

"Not quite, madame." Campbell paused. "Her Highness uttered these words: If you give this news to my daughter, tell her to consult Madame de Valentinois regarding it. If you cannot reach her, give the message to Madame de Valentinois and say that she has my complete trust and confidence, and must take what action seems best to her."

"What action seems best!" murmured. Diane. "What action, indeed, will prevent the union of England and Scotland against France? This Elizabeth of England plans well. She is very shrewd. She knows that we face civil war, that we must not antagonize Montmorency, the Constable, that we have just signed a treaty of peace with Spain and must preserve this peace if we are to restore order in France."

"If the King knew of this matter, madame—" suggested the secretary.

Her delicate brows lifted slightly. "If he knew? He would immediately burn with a sense of justice and become the champion of our little Marie Stuart. But France needs peace." She looked at Campbell, with that enchanting smile which melted men's hearts. "M. de Glenlyon, this noble dog possesses a dignity and calm strength which I find in few men. While I speak with him, will you have the kindness to retire with M. Guillaumont and obtain for me the letter which you have mentioned?"

She extended her hand to Thorn, who came to her, crouched submissively, and swept the room with eyes of proud disdain as she caressed him. Campbell rose, bowed, and left the room with Guillaumont, who led him into a small antechamber.

"One would swear, monsieur," said the secretary, "that this dog possesses the soul of a man! Here is your poniard. Permit me to assist you."

Once out of his hot leather jerkin, which he discarded altogether, Campbell cut the stitches that held the folded vellum. Reclad, the letter in hand, he accompanied Guillaumont back to the private room; a guard at the door gestured significantly to the secretary.

"Le Balafré's in there. I think he was summoned."

With a nod, Guillaumont led Campbell in.

Short as was the elapsed time, changes had taken place in the room. The Bishop was gone, Ronsard was gone; but the number of ladies had increased. Diane sat with one hand on the head of Thorn, and before her was standing a commanding figure glinting with jewels and orders, a tall, soldierly man whose beard could not conceal the scar that gave him his nickname of Balafré.

This was François, Duc de Guise, head of that great house which disputed with Valois its right to the throne of France, friend and relative and devoted adherent of Diane de Poitiers.

Diane beckoned to the two, and held out her hand for the letter, which Campbell presented on one knee.

"M. de Guise," she said, "allow me to present M. de Glenlyon, a noble gentleman of Scotland who has just brought me this letter from your sister Marie." As she spoke, as Guise turned to Campbell and bowed slightly, as Campbell bowed in return, she was scanning the lines of writing on the vellum. She continued swiftly:

"Monsieur, your sister is in danger. We must have instant action, without recourse to the Constable or others; this is a matter of family peril, which we both hold close to heart. I wish you to take secret measures to collect ships at the northern ports and to gather a large force of men; it must be done swiftly and quietly."

Guise looked astonished, fingered the great scar on his cheek, and nodded.

"Very well; but what authority pays?"

"Mine," said Diane promptly. "I will guarantee all sums needed. Further, appoint at once only men you can trust, new commanders in Scotland."

"Oh!" said Guise. "By whom, madame? By the Constable?"

"By your brother the Duc d'Aumale, second in command of French forces."

"Oh!" said Guise again, a twinkle in his eye. Diane's daughter was married to Aumale. "Upon my word, madame, my sister must have sent you disturbing intelligence! M. de Montmorency will be most vexed to hear it."

"He will hear it too late," Diane replied calmly, "for his own purposes."

"Excellent!" said Guise, who had small love for the Constable. "And what further?"

"Secrecy, and speed."

Comprehending there was no more to be said, Guise bowed again over her hand, inclined his head slightly to Campbell, and departed. Diane fastened her calm regard on Guillaumont.

"Monsieur, the English ambassador, M. Throckmorton, is involved in this affair, as is the Constable. Now arises the question of the Earl of Arran, Captain of the Scots Guards, whom Queen Elizabeth seems to fancy as a husband."

The secretary shrugged. "Madame, he is in France, in the service of France; and France has prisons."

Diane turned to Campbell.

"Monsieur, will you be in any further danger, now that your message has been given?"

"I think not, madame; it was desired to stop the message, not the man."

"Hm! Guillaumont, you know that man Chaudiere, of His Majesty's suite—the same whom we were warned was a spy and agent of the English ambassador?"

"Yes, madame."

"Go find him now, on the instant. Drink with him. Confide to him that a messenger has arrived from Scotland, with word of a plot. Drop a strong hint that tomorrow the Captain of the Scots Guards is to be arrested."

Alarm seized the secretary. "But, madame! You know what will happen. This man Arran will be warned, will take to flight!"

"Precisely. The English will aid him to leave the country. Prepare a letter, which I will sign tonight, to the lieutenant-general of the kingdom, asking him to make certain that Arran is permitted to leave France; but it must be arranged that his flight takes place via Switzerland. He must be a fugitive, you understand? He must believe himself in danger of his life. You can manage this."

"Certainly, madame," said the secretary, looking more and more astonished.

A laugh escaped Diane.

"Let him ruin himself. Let him escape by devious ways. Let

it be understood that the whole plot is known. This Elizabeth is a proud woman; she will be disgusted with such a man. The marriage will fall through. Meantime, troops and supplies will reach Marie of Guise. The whole bottom will drop out of this fine plot; the affair is finished."

Guillaumont bowed and departed. Diane regarded Campbell reflectively.

"You see, monsieur, how simple it is to let rascals defeat themselves! We are relieved of a traitor, the intrigue that threatens war is turned into a jest, the Regent of Scotland is reinforced, the English are checkmated. And all because of a message delivered."

Campbell looked at Thorn, who yawned vastly.

"All because of a dog, madame."

"Oh! Tell me about it, and about that wound you bear!"

Campbell complied. He was aware that the group of ladies had drawn closer, at a sign from Diane; he glanced at them as he spoke, telling what had happened and how Thorn had been found.

"So you would not recognize this Lady Anne again?" inquired Diane.

"Unfortunately not, madame; it was dark outside, and I could see little of her."

"Then let me present you. Ladies, this is M. de Glenlyon. Come, Lady Anne, your quick wit has served us well this night! Your cheek, child, your cheek!"

Campbell found himself bowing to a young woman all red and white, whose laughing eyes dwelt upon him amusedly. He touched her cheek with his lips, as the custom was, then swung around as Diane addressed him.

"Monsieur, what is your desire? You speak French too well not to be of great service here, if you desire to remain in France."

"Why, madame, I scarcely know," said Campbell. "I must let my friend Angus know that all is well with me—"

"See that word is sent to the man Angus, Lady Anne," said Diane quickly. "Where is he, monsieur?"

Campbell gave the location of the house in town, and Lady Anne left the room. Then Diane continued:

"You have plans, ambitions, hopes. What are they?"

"Only to serve my queen, madame."

"And your queen is the Dauphine of France. Very good, monsieur! Then you shall remain here, for the present…. Ah! What is it?"

A chamberlain had entered. He came forward, bowing, with word that the King desired to know if Madame de Valentinois would receive him. There was an instant flurry among the ladies, but Diane assented calmly:

"By all means. We shall be greatly honored, and I desire to present this gentleman to His Majesty. Remain, monsieur."

To Campbell it was unreal, fantastic, incredible. This tall, stalwart man with the fringe of black beard, the regal bearing, the magnificent garments and jewels—the King of France! Diane curtsied low. The King raised her, kissed her hands, laughed, and turned to Campbell, who went to one knee and kissed the extended hand. For an instant he met the profound, bold black eyes, noted the peculiar contraction of the left eyebrow, heard the voice of Diane as from far away, and realized that Henri was speaking to him.

"Indeed, monsieur! It gives me great pleasure to welcome you. Any gentleman of Scotland is an honor to our surroundings. What's that, Diane? Of course, of course; there's the very spot for him! Equerry to our little Marie; when she arrives, he'll greet her in her own tongue as a pleasant surprise, eh? It will carry only five thousand crowns a year, but we may arrange better in time. Here, monsieur; do me the honor of accepting this token of our favor as a pledge against the future. And, Diane, let one of your ladies take him at once to St. André, who will arrange for lodgings and all else, including an advance upon his salary. My felicitations, M. de Glenlyon!"

IT WAS all a dream, beyond credence.

He had slunk into this room a hunted man, his life at stake, his future all awry. He walked out with Anne Haworth holding his hand and laughing at his confused air, the King's diamond on his finger, Thorn stalking grandly between them.

Equerry to the Dauphine, a post at court, the royal favor assured, all danger swept away in an instant—why, it was a regular sunburst of glory!

Then, outside in the antechamber where a number of the King's gentlemen chattered and stared at them, Anne Haworth halted and looked hard at him.

"Glenlyon, eh?" she said. "Not as good a name as Campbell, but more fortunate. And there's one thing to settle. Do you still lay claim to Thorn?"

Campbell met her half-laughing eyes. Fine brave eyes, ablaze with an eager light; dark eyes, a merry open countenance but one filled with character.

"Did you send word to Angus?" he asked.

"I did. And Thorn belongs to me, do you understand?" The dark eyes were no longer laughing. They were intent and passionate. "To me!"

"Not a bit of it," said Campbell. "Is he a crawling serf to be the mere property of any person? Rather, a friend. Let him choose. Go to the door, yonder, and call him."

Impetuously, she obeyed, crossing to the doorway and swinging around with a swish of skirts. She extended her hand and called the dog.

"Down, Thorn!" said Campbell quietly.

Thorn looked at her, his curved tail moving. He looked up at Campbell, looked again at the girl who called him, then sank down, head on paws, at Campbell's feet.

"You see? He has decided for himself."

A touch of anger lifted in her cheeks.

"Why, I wonder, did the Regent pick you for such a mission?"

"Because your father, who is the Regent's steward, recommended me," said Campbell. "And because an unknown gentleman might get through, where some great lord could not."

"And now you'd steal my dog! That's what one might expect of a Campbell of Argyll. They're all cattle rievers in the west country."

"No," he said, lightly amused. "A Campbell of Glenlyon. That's title enough, my lass, if it's a title you're looking for."

"*My lass*, indeed! You presume on short acquaintance. Lady Anne to you, Campbell lout! Mind your manners, now you're at court."

"Aye, your father said you had a harsh tongue," he rejoined easily. " 'A harsh tongue like her mother, and like her a heart of gold and the ambition of an angel! And a tidy hand with the broom or the cookstove.' I doubt if you'd handle the cookpot well, however; you seem a fine lady indeed, though I owe you great thanks for serving me so well this night."

"Not you, but our queen!" she said stubbornly, as though fighting to keep up her hot impetuous temper. "You're harsh enough of tongue your own self, it seems; the touch of the King's hand has set you up mightily. The man who asked help in the cold night sang a different tune."

"Did he, indeed? God forbid!" said Campbell. "I'm sorry for that, Anne Haworth. You have the bloom of Scots mists in your cheeks, and your father's pride in your eye; a bonny lass, and no harm in the word either. Not cut to a standard pattern, like these French ladies who are all alike; but hot porridge one minute, cold porridge the next.... Why, you're a woman in a thousand! Hasty word, and quick smile afterward, like sunlight and shadow on heather."

He smiled at her, but his words died and his smile failed. Weakness, a sudden let-down from crisis, sent everything swimming before him. He saw her as through a mist.

"What is it?" Her face changed. "Why, you're pale!"

"Nothing, nothing, mere weariness," he said. His head

cleared. "Come along, let's get the job over with and a lodging found. Who's this St. André we're seeking?"

"The Master of the Household, and a great noble," she rejoined, then came to him and put out her hand to his arm. "Please, Malcolm Campbell! It's true I've a quick tongue, and spoke you harsh; but the thought of you keeping my dog was a cruel one and goaded me. You'll not take Thorn from me? I brought him from Scotland three years ago. My father raised him." She was all friendly now, her dark eyes alight with pleading. The soft warmth and beauty of her went to Campbell's heart.

"You'll not take him? He's known you but a little while, and me all his days!"

"No, I will not," said Campbell gravely, striving to overcome the weakness that gnawed at him. "I'll not lift a hand to take him from you." He paused an instant, then went on: "But there's more to the story than you know. We've been stung and whipped by the same lash, and that's a strong bond. Also, he owes me his life and knows it. So if he follows me, I'll not say him nay. To you he's but a dog, as I'm only a Campbell lout. To me he's a friend and comrade whom I need sorely. So like that or like it not, as you please."

He stooped to touch the dog's head, felt the quick tongue lick his hand, and scarcely remembered what followed; nothing mattered. He had won his race with death, and was aware only of the consuming weariness upon him.

CHAPTER IV

THE FLIGHT of the Earl of Arran was only a two days' wonder at court, though it was destined to be far more than this in the annals of Europe. If the chief of the Hamiltons were gone, however, others of the name remained. More than once, Campbell caught a flash of the scarlet-and-blue Hamilton tartan among the stalwart figures of the Guards, like an evil omen.

Those three days before Mary Stuart and the Dauphin arrived set Campbell firmly on his feet again. His wound had healed as by magic, good food and rest worked wonders. Thorn stuck by him like a shadow, but of Anne Haworth he had seen no more except at a distance.

On the third morning, when word of Arran's sudden flight was no longer a secret, Campbell was watching the grooms exercise certain horses belonging to Mary Stuart, as part of his new duties, when he saw Black Angus and two other resplendent figures in Highland dress approaching. He himself, as befitted his position, had acquired a quietly rich court dress of blue Genoa velvet, but the Guards retained all the panoply of the Scots regime.

Campbell was getting fairly well shaken down. Most of the French nobles and officials treated him with indifference; a few with hostility; still other few with fawning subservience, since the King had twice stopped and spoken briefly with him.

"Come away, Malcolm," sang out Angus, drawing near. "Here's two of the lads off duty to have a word with you, so call their names and prove if ye be a Scot or no."

Campbell glanced at the kilts and bonnets, and held out his hand, smiling.

"By the badge of broom and the blue-green kilt, you're both Forbes of Craigievar," he said, meeting warm grips. "My father's often spoken of a Long John Forbes who raided the border with him in the old days."

"Myself, at your service," said one of the two, a towering, lanky man with reddish-gray beard. "And this is my cousin Alec, the best man in the company with crossbow or long bow; and it's heart's pleasure to meet with your father's son. Come for a walk up the glen, man, and we'll have a bit talk before noon meat."

On guard duty, the Scots Archers carried no bows or targets;

the kilt and plaid were one, in that period, to be used as a cloak by day and a blanket by night, while the dirk and belted claymore were weapons enough. A glance at the serious face of Angus told Campbell that something was afoot; dismissing the grooms, he joined the three and walked with them among the trees behind the stables and outbuildings, while Thorn nosed about the undergrowth.

"So you're a fine gentleman of the court, Malcolm of Glenlyon," spoke up Alec Forbes, who was red as his long cousin, but beardless.

"Aye, he is," said Angus. "And looks better than of late, with his beard shaved clean and his braw new clothes and bit of a sword."

"He'll do, if he can use a sword," observed Long John critically. "Though he lacks in years. Twenty-four, at a guess. At that age. I had grown a beard that'd turn a sword-cut."

Campbell laughed. "And still would, by its looks," he said, eying that flaming though somewhat grizzled beard. "Twenty-six, to be exact. I don't suppose you're taking me here among the trees to discuss the weather?"

"Small chance," grunted Angus, and glanced around. "Here's a good spot. Alec, keep an eye out while we talk!"

"Better, let Thorn do it," intervened Campbell. Evidently there was some need of privacy. "Thorn! On guard, comrade! Guard!"

Thorn wagged assent and stole off among the trees.

"Losh! He's all but human!" said Long John admiringly. "Well, well, let's to it. Angus, broach the matter and don't be long-winded."

"My wind's my own," said Black Angus composedly. "Malcolm, it's well said that red tartans aye keep company in the devil's train! In the company are Ramsays and Erskines and Scotts, such Lowland gentry as you'd expect to be consorting with Hamiltons—"

"Lowland yourself," broke in Alec Forbes. "Since when did

"Oh!" said Campbell, comprehending.
"A warning, eh?... I thank you."

the Douglases ride north of the Clyde? But it's red tartans and no mistake. Go on with it."

"The point being," pursued Angus, pawing his beard, "that Mounseer Glenlyon had best watch himself of nights and turn a soft word to any evil wind that blows; for if he gets into a quarrel, he's ended. There's Silken James Hamilton, a fine gentleman of the court, and cousin of Arran. Silken James is a braw lad himself and has French steel at his beck, and Scots dirks to help."

"Oh!" said Campbell, comprehending. "A warning, eh?"

"Just that, aye." Long John nodded. "Many a Scot has become more French than the French, comrade; but not us. A plague on all Frenchmen, say I!"

"Silken James, eh? So that's your name for him," said Campbell reflectively. "I thank you for the warning—"

"Oh, it's not ended; it's just begun," intervened Angus. "Long John was on guard last night, and speaks French poorly but kens it well, and bends his ear to the keyhole when the chance comes—"

"You lie, you black heathen!" said Long John placidly. "They were in liquor and talking loud, that's the truth."

"Who?" demanded Campbell.

"Hamilton, and Montmorency, brother of the Constable, and Baron de Castelnau, and the Prince de Conde, nephew of the Constable, and Charles de Gondi, Master of the Queen's Wardrobe."

"That damned Italian?" exclaimed Alec Forbes. "Why, it was a conspiracy, no less!"

Long John nodded. "Exactly, cousin. A conspiracy. Backed by the Queen's friends. Does this Mounseer Glenlyon know anything about our Italian lady of the beautiful leg and fine hand and devil's heart?"

"Get on with your yarn," snapped Alec Forbes, keeping a sharp lookout upon the trees around. "He doesn't need to know. We serve Mary Stuart, and to hell with the Italians and Frenchmen to boot! That's all any honest Scot needs to know."

"You're long in the wind as Macleod's piper yourself," grumbled Long John. "Well, here's the way of it. Mary Stuart and the Dauphin reach here tomorrow. Malcolm Campbell, or Mounseer Glenlyon, is to be drawn into a duel and stabbed in the back, at the first chance. Silken James got that as his price for saying aye to the others, joining the Queen's party and lending his aid."

"In what?" demanded Angus impatiently. "What's the point of it all?"

"Well, I don't know." Long John fingered his red beard. "I didn't get it clearly. It's something about the King's helmet, and an astrologer's prediction. You know, the Italian woman believes in these cursed astrologers and has one herself. Oh, yes! There was one thing more—"

The other two broke into imprecations.

"The saints preserve us from thick wits!" growled Black Angus. "The King's helmet, you say; an astrologer's prediction, quoth'a, his wits all run to length! Where's the sense in this fools' talk?"

"Wait," exclaimed Alec Forbes, clapping his cousin violently on the back as though to dislodge a choked thought. "Out with it, John! Notch shaft and let fly! What's the one thing more?"

Long John, with knotted brows, tugged at his beard.

"Blessed angels, help me!" said Black Angus, rolling his eyes to heaven. He leaned forward, caught Long John by the shoulders, and shook him violently. "Man! Wake up! You know well that the Italian woman hates the Guises. You know that Le Balafré, the Duc de Guise, is the support and stay of Mary Stuart and of her Scots inheritance; you know that Mary of Guise is Regent of Scotland and sister of Le Balafré! Speak, for the love of God! Think! Remember! What devil's work are these French and Italians brewing?"

"Let go. I have it, I remember now!" exclaimed Long John. "It was about killing Le Balafré."

A GASP shook Alec Forbes. Black Angus, jaw fallen, stared from widening eyes.

"And you remember, all of a sudden!" he cried in gusty anger. "I suppose if they talked of murdering the King, you'd forget that, too! Well, let's have it."

"It wasn't much, really," Long John said apologetically. "The court moves to St. Germain and Paris in June, to celebrate the double marriage of the King's sister to the Duke of Savoy and of his daughter to Philip of Spain—"

"We know that, dolt," interrupted Angus. "Everyone knows that. And this is the first week in May. And the sun is shining.

Speak, or by the nails of God I'll choke it out of you! What about Guise?"

"Oh! He's going to Paris in a few days, and to Lorraine. Something about his estates and a sick man, his steward. It's not clear to me at all," rumbled Long John, desperately scowling. "Anyhow, Hamilton goes with him and few or none of his own suite, and an escort of the Scots Guards is given him…. Yes, that's right. A special honor. Given him by Mary Stuart, that's it. Hamilton said he would arrange it. And when they get to Orléans, Le Balafré is dead!" Long John raised his head and gazed around triumphantly. "That's it, upon my word! That's exactly it! Everybody was very happy about it, and Hamilton is to be made a marquis or duke or something."

Campbell listened with more of curiosity than any other emotion. The assassination of a French nobleman, however great, was nothing to stir his heart. Such matters were the order of the day; in Scotland they were of common occurrence, and by no means rare here. Henri of France had come to the throne because his elder brother was poisoned. But, when he saw the effect upon Angus and Alec Forbes, when he saw how they were white and shaken to the depths, he comprehended that there was something more here than he knew.

"WHAT IS it?" he asked. "What does it mean? Do we care if these depraved and degenerate French nobles murder one another?"

Alec Forbes choked at this, but Black Angus turned patiently to him and started to speak, then broke off.

"No," he said sharply. "We've done enough talking here, comrades. Scatter! Take Thorn and walk on, Malcolm, and circle back. We must show up for mess or they'll suspect. Meet me tonight after the change of guard, in the gardens on the north side, by the new tower. And leave Thorn at home. For the love of God, don't fail to come!" he added urgently. "You don't know what—"

He broke off, at a sign of caution and alarm from Alec, who

pointed. All turned. Thorn had come into sight, head erect, ears pricked up; he uttered a low growling whine, then burst into a leap and was gone.

" 'Ware!" exclaimed Angus, putting hand to sword. "Whoever it is, no friend!"

"No friend?" exclaimed a ringing, laughing voice. "After the change of guard tonight, you say? So, Black Angus of Kilspindie! And Long John and Alec Forbes—oh! And our fine new equerry, Monsieur de Glenlyon, with the King's baubee glittering on his finger!"

She rose up and stood looking merrily upon them, Thorn gamboling about her knees.

"What's it all about?" Anne Haworth looked from one to the other. "A fine lot of conspirators you are! So you trusted Thorn to keep watch, eh? You sorry rogues! What's the secret? Speak up, Long John Forbes! You know me well; speak up!"

"Why, Lady Anne, about—about Le Balafré," gulped Long John, before Angus hit him in the midriff with heavy hand and doubled him up.

Rising, Angus glowered at the girl.

"Naught for your ears, Anne Haworth," he said gravely.

Her laughter died. "That may be, Angus; but you know me, and I know you," she said steadily. Her gaze touched on Campbell, lightly. "You're true men, you and Alec and Long John, and I'd not see three good men make fools of themselves before Frenchmen. I don't know what it's about, but you should know that Anne Haworth is as good a Scot as any of you—"

"It's no secret for you, mistress," began Alec stubbornly, but Campbell laughed softly and took the word from him.

"Why not, comrades? This lass is one of us. She knows the court and its ways better than all of us put together. There's good sense to what she says. Her wits may well save us from somehow making fools of ourselves. If she can keep the rendezvous with us tonight, Angus, I say let her do it!"

"Thanks, Glenlyon," said the girl quietly.

Black Angus exchanged a look with Alec, and after a moment lost his frown and nodded grudgingly.

"All right; ye say well there's sense to it, Malcolm. But mind, no word to her now!"

"Done with you," assented Campbell. "And best split up here, as you said. Lady Anne, may I escort you back to the chateau?"

"I'll be glad," she replied, and gave Black Angus a long, steady look. "All Scots together, Angus, those of us that are true folk! You can depend on that."

"Aye, we ken it well," spoke out Alec Forbes. "But there's sore work ahead for all honest men."

His words, with their Highland burr, echoed in Campbell's mind as he walked away with Anne Haworth. "Sair wark, sair wark ahead!" That meant the whirr of goose-feathered yards and the ring of steel, stout hearts girt in by treachery and the ominous pooling of crimson blood in the sunlight…. The thought passed, as Anne Haworth spoke.

"Well, Glenlyon? I suppose there's no use asking you now?"

A smile twisted his wide, strong lips as he silently shook his head. The wound disfigured those shaven features, but it was a strong face, high-boned, the gray eyes set wide and holding a curious feel of inner power and assurance. Her gaze dwelt upon him as they walked back among the trees, with Thorn padding at heel.

"There's something about you," she said, "that reminds me faintly of two people. Of Lady Diane, and of a man I met. Not that you look like them. Just something about you that gives the same impression of quiet and depth and strength."

"Indeed?" His eyes warmed upon her. "Who was the man?"

"A physician, a famous astrologer by all accounts, whom the King summoned here. They say he comes from a family of converted Jews, in the south. His name is Nostradamus, or Notredame in French."

"Oh!" Campbell stopped short. "Why, that was the man I told you about! The physician who came to the tavern! He's here in Blois, or his assistant is. I didn't see him, for my eyes were bandaged. Angus says he was a fey man, with second sight, a man of wonder."

"He's the greatest physician in France today," said Anne, "but he has many bitter enemies. He doesn't hesitate to speak his mind about quacks and impostors; his profession is filled with them. I've heard it said that he'll be burned at the stake for sorcery one of these days. Well, here we are back again! And— look, look!" Her voice leaped swiftly. "She's coming back from her ride—the Queen!"

"The world's full of queens, it seems," said Campbell lightly, as he watched the file of superb horses clattering into the court-yard ahead of them. "Which one?"

"There's only one Queen of France, stupid! The Italian woman."

She went on speaking softly, eagerly, her voice interpreting the scene to his eyes, as grooms sallied forth to take the horses and guards formed up and saluted.

The central figure was that of Catherine, riding the side-saddle which had been invented to display her one attribute of beauty, a superb leg and ankle. Somber despite her show of jewels and gold, a dumpy and inelegant woman, her features held a darkly severe force of character that was singularly un-pleasant but impressive.

There were not many in her suite; a number of Italians who had come with her from Florence, the Gondi brethren, Strozzi, officials of her household, guards, equerries, half a dozen of her ladies. She was, as she had been these many years, a nonentity, a person of no importance in France; merely the mother of the King's children, despised as the daughter of merchants and unloved by any. All her life she had been totally eclipsed by Diane de Poitiers.

Unloved, powerless, despised—and yet the Queen of France.... The hand of Anne Haworth tightened on Campbell's arm.

"Heaven help France if she should ever get power!" said the girl under her breath. "She's astute, crafty, vengeful. The pride and arrogance of the Guises have held her crushed; she has fed on hatred for years. She hates them with all her heart. She hates Diane, yet fears her terribly, as some evil thing fears and hates the sunlight! She hates our Mary Stuart, as the unloved thing hates that which all men love. But she has ability, she has.... Look—do you see that tall man with the gray beard, in the black robe? That's her astrologer, Ruggieri. He's her physician and star-gazer; they say he knows all the future. She moves in the dark places, like an otter under water."

"Faith, you seem to detest and fear her!" said Campbell.

He felt a shiver in her hand.

"Who doesn't? The Dauphin is a boy of sixteen; Mary Stuart is only seventeen. Mere children! But while the King stands between, Lady Diane is safe from her. While the Guises keep their vast power, Mary Stuart is safe from her."

"Why, you speak as though she were actually to be feared by them!" said Campbell in astonishment. The girl looked into his face, her eyes wide and set.

"And why not? It was a Florentine who poisoned the Dauphin and made Henri heir to the throne! They had never expected Catherine to be a queen."

Campbell frowned slightly. He remembered those broken phrases Long John Forbes had uttered—"something about the King's helmet, and an astrologer's prediction." The words made no sense for him, yet he, too, felt a slight shiver creep through him, as though it came to him from the girl on his arm. Then she spoke, with abrupt change of subject.

"Tell me, Glenlyon; what's back of you, what's ahead? What has your life been?"

"Oh, schooling and war," he responded. "I've ridden the Border, raided and harried, learned my letters and a bit of Latin, learned sword and bow and lance."

"But the future? Where are you heading? What's your ambition?" she persisted. They had come to the courtyard and were halted there.

"To do my best," he said quietly. "Your father once said to me that in these days of blood and fire a Scots gentleman should aim at only three things in life: unsullied honor, courage in the darkest hour, and sword kept at razor-edge. Damned few men I know are able to claim all three, at least in Scotland!"

Her hand squeezed his arm and then fell away.

"Fewer still, I think, in France," she said. "I've changed my mind about you, Glenlyon. I think that I may like you after all. I'll see you tonight at the tower in the north gardens. And—you may keep Thorn, since he seems to want you, with my blessing!"

She was gone, with her gay laugh. But Campbell comprehended that those words had not come easily to her lips, and his heart warmed to her.

CHAPTER V

CAMPBELL COULD well understand that if Black Angus had secrets to discuss, it would be the height of folly to discuss them within the walls of the royal chateau; they could be only for the open air, where the stars alone might overhear.

An hour after darkness, when the guard had been changed for the night, he left Thorn in his room and made his way to the south gardens. There was no longer any overt danger for him; the search for Malcolm Campbell had ended with the flight of Arran. Although many of the Scots Guards eyed him with surly glances, he was safe from them... thus far. Not for long, to judge by Long John's warning.

He was thinking of this as he paced out along the paths toward the new tower, which with scattered piles of stones marked the unfinished building operations of the late King François. Yes, the vengeance of the Hamiltons would seek hard to find him out, and soon. There were Scots to help, also.

Many of the Guard had never seen Scotland, but had come from families settled in France since the day of Louis XI or earlier. Others had come across ten years ago with the child queen, Mary Stuart—men like Long John or Angus. These stuck together tightly, distrusting and damning Frenchified Scots and Italians and French alike, and serving their queen alone.

"Too bad there aren't more like them," reflected Campbell. "Too many Scots give allegiance to their clan or its head, and none to their queen! A traitor like Arran is still chief of the Hamiltons and well served by them. And this Silken James, this Hamilton who's at court here, may well command the dirks and bows of many an archer of the guard and many a Frenchman besides. Murder's their game, a dozen swords against one and no quarter given!"

He had seen nobody in the darkness; but now came a stir, and a brawny shape uprose in the starlight, almost beside him. It was Angus, who had been waiting with his tartan wrapped about his shoulders, and who now spread the thick wool over a block of stone.

"Sit ye, Malcolm of the scarred brow! I've put an order in with the Guards' outfitter for a six-yard tartan of the Campbell greens and yellow. It'll come from the Paris stocks in a few days, and may serve at need. I had news of our physician this night."

"Who? Notredame?"

"The same. He's gone to Orléans to attend some great folk there.... Ah! Here's the lass."

From the pleasure-walk that overlooked the dark Loire, Anne Haworth came tripping nimbly, wrapped from head to heels in a dark mantle. She welcomed a seat on the big plaid tartan, and chuckled softly.

"Pleasant news for you, Angus Dhu! They say that Silken James, although he's a Hamilton, is to have temporary command of the Guards, until some Scots noble of sufficient rank is given the post."

Angus smothered an oath, then broke forth.

"There's the proof, Malcolm, d'ye mind? Captain of the Guard! And he's the one to go with Le Balafré! Be sure, he'll take along only those of his own choosing."

"Guise, again? What about the good Duke François, the best soldier in France?" demanded Anne quickly. "What's this secret?"

Black Angus plumped it out, just as Long John Forbes had recounted it, names and all. To it, he added the warning given Campbell, and wound up all out of breath, while Anne sat, chin in hand, and said no word.

"Well, what do you think of it?" asked Campbell.

She turned to him.

"That you're a doomed man unless you can restrain your temper."

"That's to be seen. I mean the other thing, about Guise? He's Mary Stuart's uncle, of course, but I don't see why Angus and Alec Forbes should be so worked up about it."

"Then it's high time you did," growled Black Angus. "First, this scarred Guise is the best man and the greatest prince in France, second only to the King. Also, he has a claim to the throne himself, and a good one. He's the idol of the army and the people love him for a blunt, brave fellow. In fact, he's one of the few Frenchmen I'd take off my bonnet to with a good grace."

"True, he has the eyes of a soldier," said Campbell.

"A man's man. Well, he's to be murdered! Why? Because the Italian wench hates and fears him. Because he stands in the way of all the rascals. Because he supports Lady Diane, and our Mary Stuart. Because he's a grand man who won't sully his honor or stain his hands with filth. And who's to murder him?"

"Silken James, apparently," Campbell replied. "And capable of the job, to judge by the little I've seen of him."

"You miss the point!" fumed Black Angus. "These rascals wangle it to have Mary Stuart give him an escort of her archers under Silken James himself, to Orléans. Guise gets there a dead man. What then? The fury of the army, of the Guise faction, of all the French people, is turned on Mary Stuart. They'll say she murdered him, her own uncle! That's the end of her and of the Scots Guards as well, d'ye mind? Perhaps of Lady Diane too; they'll drag her into the mess somehow. You never saw such a country for lies and liars, Malcolm!"

"Scotland doesn't do so badly at that, herself, these days," said Campbell. "But I see your point, yes. And behind it all, behind these men who plot—"

"The Italian woman, of course."

"Say you so, Lady Anne?" Campbell turned to the girl. "Now you've heard all. What think you of it?"

"Oh, there's nothing extraordinary about it, except that this time they fly at high game," she said reflectively. "Assassinations aren't unusual. And if the power of the Guises were broken, Catherine would profit vastly; at the same time, it'd be a shrewd stroke at little Mary Stuart. Poor child! Because she has brains, and pride, and will some day be Queen of France as well as of Scotland, Catherine hates her like a viper."

"Then you think Long John heard aright?"

"Of course he did. But are we to make fools of ourselves? Careful, Black Angus! What's in your mind to do about it?"

"Warn Mary Stuart. Also Le Balafré."

"Pish! His life is threatened always; he'd pay no heed to warnings, nor credit them. And she, after all, is only a girl, with little power. What could she do?"

"All right, then," said Angus sullenly. "Carry the word to Lady Diane."

ANNE REFLECTED on this. "No," she said at length. "That would save Guise; but those others would slide out un-injured. Better to shatter the sword in Catherine's hand, than merely to ward off the blow. This is a matter for Scots to handle for their queen. At least, that's my rede. Those rascally Scots who serve Hamilton could well be spared."

"Well said," approved Campbell. "Let Scot kill Scot, eh? All hands suited. They're doing that in Scotland every day."

"None of your sarcasm, thanks," she riposted. "By the way, I might advise you that Thorn has been trained to protect his master's back. If you have need, give him the word: 'Back to back, Thorn!' He'll not fail you."

"Anyone in France has need of such protection," chimed in Angus gruffly. "Well, lass, what's your mind about this matter?"

"Let the matter come to a head," she said. "If you see it coming, if this journey of Le Balafré's really takes place, with a Scots escort, then you'll know what to expect and can act accordingly. I'd say, give the only warning with a yard-long shaft and the edge of your sword! It's taking a big risk, of course, but it's a game for Scots archers, not for highway police of the marshal."

"There, by God's hand, speaks a woman after my own heart!" swore Black Angus admiringly.

Campbell laughed softly. "Amen to that! Count me in if the time comes, Angus. Meanwhile, a dozen things may turn up to spoil the plot. Well, is that all? I'll see you safe back, Lady Anne."

"What about your own safety, Glenlyon?" she demanded.

"Oh, I'll take care of that, never fear! I can turn the other cheek like any monk."

Black Angus grunted skeptically under his breath. The girl rose.

"Very well, then. Don't forget, Angus, that Ian Cameron of Lochiel will return tomorrow with the queen, our queen. He'll be a good man to take into your confidence in this matter of Le Balafré."

"Aye," said Angus. "And good night to the two of you!"

CHAPTER VI

C AMPBELL WALKED along beside the girl, circling about the upper end of the buildings to reach the
postern gate on the opposite side.

"You must be very careful," she said softly. "You've no idea
how clever they are about murder, here; it's not even regarded
as a crime, unless the victim is of the blood royal. Don't let
yourself be tricked into any action."

"Thanks, my lass," he said gratefully, patting her arm.

"Don't call me that!" she exclaimed. "I'm not your lass, nor
anyone's. It's like using the French word *mademoiselle* to any
girl of noble blood; nothing less than an insult! And I don't
care for intimacies. There's enough loose talk and action everywhere, without my taking part in it."

"Heigh-ho!" said Campbell, astonished. "Are you some great
lady, far above the ignoble ways of mortals?"

"I do hope to be," came her voice in grave assent. "If you
knew of the unspeakable vices, the depravity, the degenerate
customs that have spread like poison through all the upper
classes in France until they're flaunted openly—why, you'd be
sickened! There's not a breath of clean air at court, except in
the apartments of Diane de Poitiers."

"Who is the King's mistress," said Campbell slyly.

Anne made indignant response.

"Not in the way you mean! She loves him; he loves her; it's
real love. There's never been a hint of indecorum or scandal.
And there are other women, too. Don't you realize that all the
power here is wielded by women? But it is. That's my ambition—to reach some such eminence."

Campbell was more and more astonished, as she went on
speaking with an earnest revelation of herself; but he was not
astonished at her, only at the conditions she laid bare. Though,

as she pointed out to him, England was ruled by a queen, as was Scotland.

Somehow he had always thought of France and Italy as lands where gallant knights and lordly princes ruled with despotic power. So they did, indeed; but they were mere puppets. From Italy had spread feminism; in the salons of great ladies, the centers of culture, were pulled the strings of power and rule. The finger of Diane de Poitiers could reach over the whole of France, and so could the fingers of other women, less noble.

Mary Stuart absolutely ruled the boy Dauphin, in their mutual love. In Orléans, in Paris, in Lyon, the nimble brains of women determined the course of history, as in Italy and elsewhere. These women could dispute with philosophers in Latin, like Mary Stuart herself; they wrote books, scribbled poetry, ordered affairs of finance and law.

The great nobles, who could at most scrawl their own names with effort, bore resplendent titles, swaggered under jewels and orders, and did as nimbler wits desired them to do. Never was the power of women greater, because it was universal and not publicized. Marguerite de Navarre was shaping the course of the new religious ideas. The Duchess d'Etampes managed the shameful treaty that laid France prostrate before Spain.

Nor did these women who swayed destiny need to make use of feminine arts. No court circle had ever been so chaste, so intellectual, so influential as that of Anne de Beaujeu, daughter of Louis XI of France; and Diane, who had been a lady of honor in that circle, imitated its austere brilliance in her own.

"I WOULD do the same, if I could," said Anne Haworth simply, gazing up at the dark pinnacles of the chateau under the stars. Campbell, who had been fascinated by her words, by her open thoughts and ambitions, wakened abruptly to reality.

"If you could! But you can't. You never can," he said. "Too many such great ladies have poured into these channels all the frustration of their lives; we're humbler folk, and happier, thank

"You're a doomed man unless you can
restrain your temper," said Anne.

heaven! There's the whole answer to your dreams, Anne Haworth!"

"Shame!" she exclaimed vibrantly. "You just can't comprehend such things—"

"Can't I, though?" he broke in. "Why, as a boy I used to dream of dedicating myself to search for the Grail, to wearing shining armor like another Bayard, to ride like another Bruce over the English hosts and the Border towns! And what does it simmer down to? As I grew used to the weight of armor, to the swing of sword, to the smash of steel on helm and shield, these things changed. Now I do what I can, and do it well, that's all."

"Content with small things?" she said scornfully.

"Perhaps. If I smash the helm of a man-at-arms, it might be

the helm of an English baron; does me as much good, anyhow. You might whisper wise words into the ear of a prince. Instead, you give your rede to a Campbell lout and a bearded archer, and they love you from their hearts for it; and that's more than the prince would do."

"I should not have called you a Campbell lout; I'm sorry for those words," she said softly. "Forget them and forgive. Good night."

They entered at the postern gate, passed the guards and separated.

NEXT DAY came Mary Stuart and the Dauphin, glittering figures surrounded by a throng of nobles and guards and court ladies, advancing with a wild skirl of pipers to meet the King, who received them. A pallid, puny boy, this Dauphin; his wife

a blonde mischief, a girl impetuous, ardent, brimming with the
life and vitality he so sadly lacked; yet they were much in love
and showed it unashamedly, with the confidence of children.

Campbell, in the forefront of the throng, stared wide-eyed
as the young couple dismounted and Henri embraced them.
Catherine was here too, waiting until the King's greeting was
done. The carriages, from which the travelers had changed to
horses in order to make a more impressive arrival, rolled clouds
of dust from the roads. The pibroch of *Bratagh Bhan* or the
White Banner, the gusty pipe music of the royal Stuarts, skirled
and screamed lustily from the strutting pipers and filled the air,
until the French nobles grimaced and put hands to ears, and
even the King laughed and waited until his greetings could be
heard.

Scotland's queen! It was Campbell's first sight of her, and he
yelled frenziedly with the other Scots, swept by an emotion
born of old tradition and distant heather and a personal enthusiasm. For this girl with the long face and straight nose, the
slender, exquisitely molded features, the narrow eyes and russet
masses of hair, was not exactly beautiful; but her smile was
captivating, and she exerted an instant fascination upon all
around her. All, that is, except perhaps one.

The Queen of France stood looking on unmoved, a thin,
mechanical smile lifting the corners of her full lips, no spark in
her dull and lifeless eyes.

The bagpipes droned into silence, voices arose in a hum and
a buzz, laughter broke forth, everything was suddenly in motion.
Campbell became aware of a man beside him, speaking, tugging
at his arm; an usher in the King's livery of white and black, the
colors of Diane.

"M. de Glenlyon! His Majesty has commanded your pre-
sentation at once!"

The rest was almost a blank to Campbell. He found himself
kneeling, touching his lips to the singularly beautiful hand of
Mary Stuart; he was so absorbed in her and in her words that

he was aware of nothing else, until he heard the King laughing heartily.

"Faith, Marie, you've bewitched him! He doesn't even know that I exist!"

"Pardon—your pardon, sire," exclaimed Campbell in abrupt confusion, summoning up desperate hasty phrases of courtiers' parlance. "It's true that I was dazzled... the blaze of sun and the clear whiteness of the moon for once are met and blended in an ecstasy of beauty!"

Not another man there would have dared utter such a speech in front of Catherine de Medici; for the symbol of Diane de Poitiers was the crescent moon, as all knew. Yet the words of Campbell were quite innocently spoken.

He was disconcerted at the sound like a gasp from all around. Henri, delighted and beaming, presented him to the Dauphin, then to the Queen. Those eyes sent a chill through Campbell; he divined a quiver of fury in them.

"Come to my apartment in an hour, M. de Glenlyon," said Mary Stuart, her lips twitching slightly. "I'm anxious to hear the latest news from Scotland and from my good mother, and it seems to me you have a very pleasant and honest turn of speech."

That was all. As the group broke up, Campbell sighted the scarred, bearded face of Guise, saw the duke was laughing heartily, and caught sight of a beckoning hand. He made his way to the tall, soldierly figure. The nobles around made place for him, and Le Balafré took him by the arm and spoke softly at his ear, chuckling the while.

"Monsieur, I could love you for that speech! But if ever I saw rage in a woman, it was in the face of the Italian wench. If you can use a sword as you do your tongue, well and good; but have a care. Should a pinch come, call on the Cross of Lorraine for help, and you'll get it."

Disconcerted and perplexed, Campbell went his way, aware that glances and whispers went up wherever he appeared. He had no explanation until he joined a group of Scots around Black Angus; then he had explanation enough, and stood utterly aghast.

"If you were a Frenchman," said Angus, "you'd be headed for a cell or worse, this minute! Aye, though the King liked it fine. Now you're a marked man and no mistake. Innocently said? Maybe, maybe, but who'd believe that excuse? Nay, make the best of it now, take credit for a bold tongue, and be damned to the lot of them!"

It was another story when he was ushered into the presence of Mary Stuart, with the Dauphin lolling beside her and eyeing him with listless gaze. He bent over her fingers and found her laughing openly at him, while the ladies around eyed him and passed comments among themselves. He was glad that Anne Haworth was not here.

"Malcolm Campbell of Glenlyon, is it?" said the young Queen in English. "Well, my good Malcolm, have you discovered what you said downstairs?"

"I have, madame," said Campbell. "And God knows I meant nothing by it!"

"Too late now, Glenlyon," said she. "Aye, give the devil his due! But I'm sorry for your sake, my friend; really sorry," she went on more soberly. "It's a cruel jest of circumstance. Carry it off bravely and fear not. I'm glad to have you as my equerry."

"Madame, permit me to leave here and go back to Scotland," he said "I'm a booby, a fool, in these surroundings."

"Afraid, Glenlyon?"

His head jerked up He met her clear brown eyes, and reddened.

"No, madame. But the servant owes prudence, lest the mistress be blamed."

"Prettily said. I'm able to take my own part, however. What's done is done; stand by it, then, and I'll stand by you! Now for your duties; I'll go riding each morning and shall demand your attendance."

In another half-hour, Campbell of Glenlyon was a full-fledged member of the court, falling into the groove of his scanty duties; a man picked out among all the rest for vengeance, a man marked down for punishment; a man glittering with the honors granted him, but with death at his elbow and hatred dogging his steps and envy watching him with furtive waiting.

For this was the lot of every man worth his salt, at the court of the Valois. From the princely Guise to the lowliest cup-bearer at table, there was no standing still; one walked in peril, and the higher one rose, the greater was the abyss below.

CHAPTER VII

THE DAYS flitted past. In the four massive sections of the chateau, each with its barrack-like accommodations for the royal followers, the artificial life of the court went its way, with riding, hunting, diversions, intrigues.

Campbell kept much to himself. Of the Scots Guards, he saw a good deal, and fell into friendship with Ian Cameron of Lochiel, an attendant of Mary Stuart; a deft, silent giant equally at home with pen or sword, who had been educated for the Church and had gone into the Army by preference

Anne Haworth he saw now and again, but seldom in private. The scab over his eyes disappeared, leaving a slight scar that worried him not at all. With each day he fell into greater friendship with Thorn; the two were together constantly, and Campbell could never sufficiently admire the intelligence, the sedate dignity, the absolute devotion, of this great Irish hound.

For the moment, all matters of crisis seemed pushed over the horizon. There was nothing to justify the warnings of Hamilton vengeance. Indeed, he several times encountered Silken James, finding him smoothly courteous and amiable. Nor was there any indication that Guise meant to leave Blois. He and his most unchurchly brother, the Cardinal de Lorraine, occupied the Hotel de Guise in town, with their immense suite which rivaled that of the King.

Still, Campbell had indication enough that his tremendous *faux pas* was not forgotten nor himself approved. He met with scant friendliness from the French nobles in general and from many of the Scots in particular. Others eyed him askance because he kept Thorn ever with him, instead of quartering the hound in the royal kennels; whispers of sorcery reached him, and some said openly that Satan served him in guise of a dog. And this was perilous. No man was safe from suspicions of such a kind.

It was Guise who gave him warning of this, one morning as they coursed afar. The King had brought down his stag, Guise had lost another, and the hunt had scattered. Guise joined Mary Stuart with a brace of huntsmen and Campbell kept with them, Thorn sweeping along with his tireless, effortless lope.

"You sit a horse well, monsieur," said Guise, turning suddenly to Campbell, as they slowed pace. "But I hear some very odd things that might unseat you, if they be not looked after. There's talk that your dog has the intelligence of Satan himself."

Campbell smiled. "I fear that would be flattering Lucifer, Your Grace."

"Well, do something about it, I advise you. Hang a holy medal about the dog's neck, or let him be seen sitting outside the church door," said Guise carelessly. "Anything to stop idle tongues and vulgar chatter. Ignorance and superstition!"

"Strange words from you, my uncle!" exclaimed Mary Stuart, laughing. "Haven't I heard something about an astrologer in Lorraine, and certain warnings he gave you?"

Le Balafré fingered the scar left by an English lance at the siege of Calais, and grunted.

"Ah! That's different. One can believe this sort of prediction, because no one can make head or tail of it."

"Tell me about it!" she begged eagerly. "What astrologer made it? Ruggieri?"

"Upon my word! The
angels of Louis XI!"
said Le Balafré.

"That Italian mountebank? *Dieu,* no!" snapped the duke. "It was Notredame, when he was in Lorraine last year. You know the man; he published a book of rhymed prophecies that not a soul can understand. He's a marvelous physician. The King summoned him here to Blois, only lately, though I understand he's gone to fight an outbreak of the plague at Orléans—"

"But his prediction to you!" she broke in. "Was it really a warning?"

The duke nodded, his strong, dark, powerful features tinged with amusement.

"So he affirmed; but I'm no Italian shopkeeper, to let some rascally astrologer rule my course for me!" said he, with contemptuous reference to Catherine de Medici.

"But the prediction? Please, good uncle!" she begged prettily. "I'm curious, really. Lady Diane thinks most highly of this man, and the King holds him in great regard."

"That's more than I do. The man's well enough, but his talk is twaddle," said Guise. "He drew up my horoscope, and said that peril would come to me with summer of this year. My life, said he, would be in great danger from a branch of the oak, very shortly after I came face to face with the angels of Louis XI. Did you ever hear more fantastic nonsense? 'Beware, beware of the oak-tree, and the angels of King Louis!' Be damned to such folly!"

Mary Stuart gazed at him, her almond eyes opening wide.

"But what does it mean, uncle?"

"Faith, if you could read that riddle you'd have more brains than I!" A burst of laughter escaped Guise. "I'm not likely to come face to face with any sort of angels, particularly those of a king who's been dead these seventy-odd years! And the only angels I ever heard of in connection with King Louis were his hangman and his barber-surgeon!" Guise gathered up his reins. "There's the rest of the hunt, so come along and a truce to silly words."

Campbell, not having clapped eyes on Notredame, had scant memory of the man, but Black Angus had spoken of him with unmixed awe and wonder. Now the name wakened his fancies. An astrologer as well as a leech, and famed for his predictions, eh? It was obvious enough that stout Guise gave no credence to such warnings.

But that night, as he turned into bed with Thorn outstretched beside him, Campbell suddenly started wide awake. A branch of the oak-tree—devil take it! Why, the Hamilton crest was an oak-tree partly sawn asunder; the badge worn in the Hamilton bonnet was a sprig of oak!

"Strange!" he thought with startled wonder. "Perhaps that man Notredame does have the second sight, as Angus claims! More likely, however, it's just a coincidence. Louis XI and his angels, indeed! No, it is just as the duke said: all a lot of fantastic blather."

He went to sleep and thought no more about it.

WITH THE following morning—it was a Saturday—Ian Cameron of Lochiel came to him with more immediate matters. The huge Scot found Campbell at the stables and beckoned him to one side. Lochiel had made for himself an assured place at court; he was steady, deep-eyed, slow to commit himself in any way, and had the general trust and confidence of all who knew him, as a man of great honor and good counsel. He wore a pointed fringe of black beard, in imitation of the King, and had a habit of fingering it as he talked; in place of a rapier, he wore a basket-hilted claymore—it went well with his bulk.

"Angus of Kilspindie has told me about the thing Long John overheard," said he.

"Aye, the plot." Campbell nodded. "What d'ye think about it?"

"It seems like the devil's own work, to my motion," said Lochiel in his somber way. "Late last night, I hear, a courier brought in evil word for the Duc de Guise. A fire has gutted his Paris residence. He's lost incalculable sums in books and rare works of art, and they say his son there was hurt. It looks as though he'd be leaving for Paris in a day or so. In that case—eh?"

Campbell was startled. "It begins to look as though Long John had the right of it."

"That's possible," admitted the other cautiously. "I'd not be sure yet."

"But if Guise does leave, and if he's given an escort of the Guards—"

"Then we'll know it's a plot, as Long John and Angus think, sure enough. He'll not act in haste, though we must; he'll need the King's permission to leave court. And now what's to be done about it?"

"The obvious thing is to warn him, tell him everything!"

Lochiel shook his head.

"I'm not so sure. It's not like dropping a hint in the ear of a comrade. La Balafré is a great lord, hedged in by courtiers and conventions and no end of formality; whatever he says or is said to him, leaks out. He has no privacy here. If one of us goes to him, it'll be all over the place in no time, just as I know what news that courier brought him last night. I'm sore afraid we'd all be brought into public and called on the carpet. Prove it, they'll say. Prove what? How? Against forsworn liars who will make us laughingstocks in the sight of all France? Sheer folly, says Anne, and she's right."

"No doubt," Campbell assented dourly. "Has she anything better to suggest?"

"She has. It'll take some shrewd work from the inside, which she and I can do neatly. Will ye trust to us and ask no questions? Angus has agreed, for the others. The smaller the pot, the fewer the leaks, and this is ticklish business."

The massive, powerful features bespoke confidence. Campbell knew he was sharing in a parlous game, and would have preferred to see a bit of the field ahead. However, this man Lochiel was one to trust implicitly; also, Anne Haworth had a shrewd head.

Campbell nodded. "Aye, I'm content."

"Good. Now, we must have siller to salve itching palms; court officials come high."

"Money?" Malcolm Campbell looked blank. "Why, I've a hundred crowns or so left of my expense-money from Scotland—"

"Not a drop in the bucket; we need slathers." Lochiel cocked an eye at Campbell's hand. "That Valois diamond on your finger is worth five thousand hard crowns at the very least. We'll sell the stone and replace it with a bit of paste, or mayhap pawn it and buy it back with our gains; for there should be loot in this business. The murder of a Guise is something to require high pay. What d'ye say?"

The King's ring? Campbell hesitated.

"I must not only take your scheme on trust, but finance it to boot? You ask a lot."

"All Scots together, Glenlyon."

"Right." Not without a twinge, Campbell twisted the ring from his finger and dropped it in the huge palm. Lochiel nodded and stowed it out of sight.

"Good man! Now, whatever orders you may get, carry them out to the letter and no objections. This may need some fast work. We dare not act until we're sure about Le Balafré leaving and Hamilton going with him. Then we must take swift action; however, we've planned each detail and know it can be arranged. Until later… and God keep you!"

Ian Cameron departed, wearing a pleasant air of mystery and urgent business. Itching palms? Court officials? True, he and Anne Haworth should know their way around the French court. And if Black Angus had agreed, this augured well.

LATER, ON this same day, Campbell came upon Thorn, gaunt and sick and vomiting. In sharp dismay, he sent hastily for the keeper of the royal kennels, a shrewd Norman with whom he had scraped an acquaintance. The keeper came on the run, examined the dog, examined the ground, and nodded sagely.

"See the bits of meat he's thrown up, monsieur? Poisoned, no doubt of it; but he's a wise beast. He got rid of it in time. A bit sick, but no sign of convulsions. He'll be well as ever, this time tomorrow."

"Poisoned?" Campbell went white with anger. "Who'd do such a thing?"

The Norman looked him in the eye. "Between you and me, monsieur, this fine dog has acquired a bad name. Like men, like dogs; the nobler the creature, the more bitter is the envy around him. I've heard nonsense about the devil being in dog's shape. Somebody has given him a touch of the white Italian powder. What cures men will cure dogs," he added significantly.

Campbell cursed the court and all in it, and ended up by depositing Thorn in the kennels for the night and himself seeing to his treatment and care, with the kindly Norman's help. For an English groat, he told himself, he would turn his back on everything here and go home to Scotland.

The groat was not offered, however, and morning found Thorn sound and well again. His collar with the golden plate had been made anew, this time a very heavy, wide collar of thick leather studded with metal bosses. Campbell buckled it about the glossy slim neck and with Thorn proudly beside him took

*Campbell tripped the man, sent him staggering
off balance. He caromed into the staring friar.*

the road down the slope to town. It was a Sunday and he was
free of duties, for the court seldom stirred abroad of a Sunday.

IT WAS a warm, fresh day, and Blois was packed with
country folk, soldiers, merchants who followed the court,
hangers-on of a hundred and one kinds. The streets had all the
appearance of a carnival, and Campbell made his way toward
the bridge with the idea of a stroll along the south bank of the
Loire. He was struggling with his own impulses; more and
more firmly, he was inclined to chuck up everything here and
return to Scotland. He was not made for this life, and he recoiled
from every angle of it. What held him irresolute was the thought
of two women: Mary Stuart, whom he served; and Anne
Haworth, whose good opinion he had come to value keenly.

This affair of Thorn's poisoning, however, with the warning
from Guise, had brought things to the point of crisis. What to
do, he did not know; escape from it all was most tempting.

France was a pleasant land and he was on the highway of fortune at court, yet under the surface was a wave of cruelty and treachery that revolted him. Better, he thought, the crude and simple ways of Scotland. Luxury was dearly bought here.

Thus reflecting, he found himself on the promenade along the quays, crowded with merry throngs, and continued his way to the bridge. This was a massive structure defended by two towers, and was lined by shops and houses. The bridgeway was thick with people; midway, of its length, a throng was massed about a resonant figure, one of the preaching friars who wandered the country eloquently calling for repentance and predicting the warmth to come in no uncertain terms.

Indeed, no prophetic eye was needed to see the gathering furies of bloody civil war, gaining force to burst everywhere in France. It was to avert these furies that Henri was bending all his efforts, with a shrewd wisdom that seemed well assured of success.

Campbell sauntered on and came to the edge of the throng, pausing curiously to listen to the friar. He found himself listening, instead, to a voice at his elbow, the voice of a pert-eyed lackey evidently directed at him.

"So the foreign sorcerer and his master the Devil dare to cast the evil eye upon a holy man, eh?"

A mutter arose from those around, eyes going to Campbell and Thorn. Turning to the lackey, Campbell glanced at him scornfully.

"You need a stick over your shoulders, fellow, and are like to get it."

"What's that?" Another voice leaped up. It came from a gentleman who wore the blue and silver colors of Nemours, and who swung around to glare at Campbell. "No foreigner can threaten an honest Frenchman within my hearing! Who are you, monsieur?"

"Why, who do you think he is?" A laugh broke in. Another man, very handsomely attired, who spoke with a strong English accent, had moved up behind Campbell. He stood tossing a dagger into the air and catching it by the hilt as it fell. A merry fellow he seemed, with white teeth showing as he laughed, but with eyes intent and alert.

"Aye, who do you think?" he went on gayly, jerking a thumb at Campbell. "Not hard to guess. Doesn't he bear Satan's mark above his eyes? The touch of the foul fiend leaves a scar, as everyone knows, and this stout Scotsman has the scar to prove it!"

"Say you so, monsieur?" said Campbell grimly. "My faith, you should know, being an Englishman by your tongue! For it's common knowledge that all Englishmen carry another and less pleasant mark of Satan's devising. Or is that a foul libel, monsieur? Put it to the test, show us!"

A gale of laughter arose, together with curses and sudden howls that quite drowned out the preaching friar. The Englishman went white as death, and stood trembling with sheer rage and passion.

There was a reason for this. The name *taillard* was applied to the English who, said an old superstition, were popularly supposed to be born with tails. It was, indeed, one of the stock insults that passed between Scots and English, and a most bitter one. A later allusion to it by Mary Stuart in Holyrood Palace in the presence of the Duke of Bedford and his suite was destined to give mortal affront to the English ambassador and indirectly cause bloody deeds on stricken fields.

Campbell stepped away. Long John's warning flashed across his mind; he was suddenly conscious of peril. He heard the quick slither of steel leaving scabbard, he caught a storm of imprecations from the raging Englishman, he was aware of a surge in the crowding figures around. Thorn sensed it also; a low, rippling growl came from him, and his hair bristled ominously.

"Sorcerer!" went up a howl. "The sorcerer and his familiar spirit!"

"Careful, messieurs," Campbell said coolly. "If you have Satan to deal with, you're running great risks. If not, you're making a sad mistake!"

Here where the friar stood was a break among the shops and houses, and also in the bridge parapet; an open stairs went down to the water at this point.

As he spoke, Campbell strode straight at the thickest of the throng before him, hand on Thorn's collar. His assured air, the bared fangs of the dog, gained place; the men moved aside, the women uttered little cries and scattered hastily, the ragged friar stood all astare, not comprehending what was happening among his auditors.

Suddenly, from the corner of his eye, the wary Scot saw a glint of steel and a lithe moving shape. A swarthy Italian was in the very act of leaping at him from one side and behind, a long poniard thrusting in for the kill.

Campbell caught the outstretched arm and jerked it, tripped the man, and sent him staggering across the stones, dear off balance with his own force of movement. A yell of rage and dismay escaped the Italian He began to fall, threw out his arms, and caromed into the staring friar, who was in turn knocked off his footing.

Italian and friar together went tumbling through the opening in the parapet, across the landing, and off the bridge entirely. A chorus of shouts and screams arose from the crowd; some went streaming and clattering down the stairs to rescue the friar, others rushed to get at Campbell. Staves whistled in air, steel flashed, a howl of hatred rose:

"He assailed the friar! The foul fiend whisked him into the water with one flirt of his tail—kill, *kill!* He has drowned the holy man! Death to the sorcerer!"

A stick crashed against Campbell's skull, knocking off his hat. He glimpsed the Nemours partisan, rapier out; an Italian voice was bawling curses, with steel to back them; the Englishman, sword in hand, was leaping forward.

No help for it now; he was in the trap! He had done his best to evade and to spare bloodshed; now it was fight or be mobbed to death....

"Back, Thorn! Back to back, Thorn!"

WITH THE shout Campbell moved forward, not back—forward, where they least expected him. His sword flickered out. Trained in many a Border affray, he became a figure of wild ferocity. Behind him, Thorn whirled around, huge, springy-legged, poised with murderous snarl and fangs bared.

Small wonder that burghers and country folk scattered wildly; but there were others here—the Nemours gentleman, shrill-tongued lackeys, dark Italian laces, halt a dozen soldiers with steel out. The Englishman leaped forward, raging, his sword awhirl, and Campbell met him as he came.

Armor was still used in this day; a rapier was more for cutting than for thrusting; the art of fence was quite unknown. Dirk in his left hand, Campbell warded that driving English blade, and slashed with his own. His sword-tip slithered from the Englishman's chest and slit the surcoat asunder, to reveal a glitter beneath. A shirt of steel links.

"Assassin! *Taillard!*" Campbell's voice pealed. "A Guise, a Guise! A Scotland!"

Small hope of any aid, with the chateau clear on the other side of town. The Englishman was cutting and slashing like a madman, a lackey was slipping in from one side; behind, the savage menace of Thorn held the ring of weapons at bay. Campbell bided his time; no use wasting sword-edge on that steel coat.

THEN, SUDDEN as a falling bolt, he leaned forward; his blade whistled; then he sprang erect again, and his grim laugh sounded. A frightful cry broke from the Englishman; his sword fell to the stones, the pommel still gripped by the hand. That hand had been shorn clean off at the wrist. He went staggering backward and was swallowed up by the crowd, where men tried to stop the flow of blood and yelled for hot pitch in which to dip the stump. A smith ran with red-hot iron from his forge and they used that instead.

Soldiers and lackeys rushed headlong at Campbell. The clash and batter of steel lifted upon the tumult, as swords struck fiery points. He wounded one, then another. The Nemours gallant pressed forward, and Campbell's blade engaged him, checked him for a moment, then slashed him across the face and sent him reeling out of the fight.

There was a moment of respite. The bridge by this time was massing thick with people, a frantic tumultuous upcry was rising high. Campbell's eyes flickered desperately around; no hope of evasion, no escape, no help. The cry of "sorcery!" was spreading afar.

Cruel faces of hate ringed him in. No accident, all this; he saw men speak one with another, saw nods of comprehension passed, saw weapons firmed and readied as the circle closed in. He was done for now; he had been warned against this very thing; there was no mercy in those faces, only a cruel and fierce exultancy.

Someone gave the word. A yell arose, and they came rushing in from front and sides and rear. Campbell met the rush with cut and slash, putting forth every effort to save himself from the thirsty steel; in the midst, the pressure lessened. The men before him fell away. A frenzied horror swept them and was echoed in their voices.

Something terrible had happened, behind Campbell.

Among those attacking from the rear was an Italian, leaping in with sword and poniard. He thrust with his stiletto at Thorn, while his sword swept at Campbell's back, but did not reach it. The great hound, evading the stiletto, leaped straight at the Italian's throat, bore him backward with his weight, stretched him on the stones with his gullet ripped open, and stood over him red-fanged to menace the others. They fell back pell-mell with cries of mad terror.

"Satan himself!" Yell upon yell chimed up. "Bring spears!

Arrows, somebody! They've killed the holy man! A silver bullet for the sorcerer! Arrows!"

"Here we are, comrades!" A gay voice arose, an Italian voice. The men in front of Campbell hastily made room. A swarthy, laughing man stood there, cranking his crossbow—a Genoese mercenary. He set quarrel in place and lifted the weapon.

Something flitted across the sunlight with a whir and a dull, deadly *"slap!"* A howl of agony escaped the man; his hand was pinned to the butt of his crossbow by a long gray shaft. Above the faces of the crowd, Campbell glimpsed a figure standing on the bridge parapet, an inordinately long, lanky figure, bow in hand: Long John Forbes.

"A Scotland! All Scots together, and be damned to all others!" yelled Long John, and came bursting through the crowd, flailing out with his bow. He went down, lost the bow, came up sword in hand, and rushed to Campbell's side.

"Alec's on the way, and Angus," he panted. "Did ye mind the shot? A good shot it was."

"Too late," said Campbell, seeing the surge in the crowd. "They're coming. Back to back, Thorn!"

A surge, indeed, but not as he thought. A wild, frantic voice shrilled fury; men were dashed aside; through the serried ranks broke the dripping figure of the ragged friar. He beat at the naked steel around with his bare arms, and dominated them all.

"Peace! Peace!" he shouted. "This is murder; stop it, in God's name! Down with your weapons, you fools! No one's done me any hurt. This is a man, not a sorcerer. Here, look and see if Satan's here!"

As he cried out, he flung himself at Thorn. The hound whipped around as though to meet attack, then checked himself and stiffened. The friar swiftly made the sign of the cross over him; Thorn put out head, nuzzled the gaunt hand, wagged his long brush, and then faced about to meet danger elsewhere; but there was none.

Weapons were lowered. Wondering exclamations burst forth; the harangue of the friar drove home the effect. In vain three or four men urged killing, and lifted hot insistent voices—that ragged barefoot friar had stifled the passion of the crowd.

"Guise!" rose a yell. "Guise and Scotland!"

There was movement, a flash of tartans and badges; Long John Forbes relaxed and wiped the sweat from his forehead.

"That'll be Angus," said he, "and high time, too! But it was a good shot, Glenlyon; aye, a comforting shot. Alec himself couldn't have made a better."

His bleak, dour eyes rested on the crossbowman opposite, who was shrieking in new agony as those around tried to free his hand, pinned by the feathered shaft to the butt of his crossbow. "I never did think much of those mechanical wonders," he added thoughtfully. "You can have all your Genoese crossbows and powder-guns to boot; give me a yard shaft and a Scots arm, and I'll make a lummox out of them all! Well, well, here's Silken James the Captain himself, and a pack of fine gentlemen from the court; now there'll be hell to pay, no doubt."

And there was.

CHAPTER VIII

HAMILTON, ACTING Captain of the Scots Guard, and court officials, and town officials, and Italian officers demanding vengeance—and against them all, a ragged barefoot friar, whose name Campbell never learned, but whose vehement force brought their rage to nothing.

Hatred there was in plenty. Though Hamilton dissimulated his own, others did not; the outcry against Campbell was heavy and hot, and against the dog who had slain a man. It grew fierce and bitter, indeed, but the honest friar stood against it like a rock, and cried down the lies that were shouted, and shamed other witnesses into telling the truth. Then the Italian who had started the brawl and had been picked up senseless out of the water below, was brought forward, and someone recognized him as a servant of Catherine de Medici. That was enough. A Guise adherent let out a yell and new fury arose, this time against all Italians.

There the matter came to nothing and was dismissed, and Campbell went back to the chateau with Thorn stalking proudly beside him, and Black Angus swearing in his beard because he had missed the fray.

"However, all's well that ends well," he said.

"And I'm ended," declared Campbell quietly. "I've had enough of this cursed life. I'm off and away for Scotland as soon as it can be decently done."

"What'll Anne Haworth say to that?" queried Angus shrewdly.

"She can like it or not. If she prefers the Valois court, let her have it."

In this resolve Campbell was obdurate. During the rest of the day, however, he saw nothing of Anne, which was just as well.

That night Ian Cameron of Lochiel stopped him hurriedly, as he was passing through the corridors after supper.

"Glenlyon! I'm in the devil's haste; a bare word with you! It's happened!"

"What's happened?"

"What we heard would happen." Lochiel glanced around hastily. "Le Balafré's off in the morning, after the King's *lever;* Hamilton and half a dozen of the Guards go with him. I'm taking the order now," and he showed a paper in his hand. "This means fast work for us all. Luckily, he'll take the journey slowly, as he'll be in no haste."

So saying, he bustled off before Campbell could respond.

MAY WAS out, June was in; that evening the chateau was in a stir of talk and rumors, to which Campbell paid no attention. He took Thorn for a walk late, and turned in, conscious only too bitterly of his own position.

This latest affair had finished him, he felt, whether he so wanted or not. He was aware of jests flying about at his expense; he had heard one himself, regarding the Scot who jousted against a barefoot friar, using an Italian as a lance. He had an idea that he would find things unpleasant for him in the morning, when he attended the ceremonial of the *lever* or rising of the King and the Dauphin.

His forebodings were well founded.

With morning, he broke his fast early, left Thorn in safety, and joined those who were flocking to this function of the day's beginning; a function which might be said to be the great daily act of devotion of the entire court. Here gossip was exchanged, here plans for the day were formed, here friend and enemy alike met on a common footing; here princes of church and state mingled with the mere nobles and officials to give homage to the greatest personages of the blood royal.

In the enormous guard-room of the chateau, with its magnificence of hangings and mosaics, with splendor on every side, log fires smoldered in the two gigantic hooded fireplaces. Pages and guards abounded in this huge room; here were the Queen's maids of honor and those of the Dauphine, here were nobles crowding in, and courtiers, all packed in throngs and all in their own places, for each move here was ruled by rigid convention, which none but the greatest nobles might transgress. Cardinals, chancellors, secretaries of state, presidents of law courts—all the highest in the world were here, waiting for admission to the royal chambers adjoining, or for the King's forthcoming.

Campbell had only to listen to hear things about himself, for malicious tongues were on every side, and malicious eyes watched to see what impression words might make upon him. They made none, except to deepen his resolve not to linger in these surroundings.

He picked up plenty of information about others, as well.

*"Could this be it, monsieur? Can you explain how
it came into possession of a jeweler of the town?"*

The King and Diane de Poitiers were leaving soon for Chenonceaux, that splendid chateau of the royal mistress, where
fêtes were to be held in celebration of the double marriage
ahead, welding France to Savoy and Spain.

Then to Paris, before the end of the month, for more celebration and some jousting, a sport of which the King was fond
and in which he was very skilled. Also, a new Captain of the
Scots Guard—here Campbell pricked up his ears—had been
appointed. The Count de Montgomery, of Scots-French family,
was to receive the honor; he was a courtier of the King's own
circle and a soldier of renown and promise, also skilled in jousting.

So, everything was movement, change, a perpetual stir;
France had no capital except its royal chateaux, and the court
demanded something new every week or month. The King

cared not, for he was always busy, always hard at work or hard at play; but this heavy-hanging splendid thing called the court was always avid of something different, always bored with life. Scarcely settled at Blois, now it was turning back to Chenonceaux and Paris.

Paris? The prospect of this turbulent city did not attract Campbell; he was out of humor with everything French. Suddenly he caught a glimpse of Anne Haworth. She was with the maids of honor of Mary Stuart, and any communication with these young women was strictly interdicted by custom, at the moment. However, he caught her eye. She smiled and flung him a gesture he could not interpret. She seemed flushed, excited, eager.

Guise appeared, walking with his brother the Cardinal de Lorraine. Then, abruptly, the ushers threw open the doors and the crowd pressed forward to witness the King of France getting out of bed.

Campbell felt a touch on the arm.

"M. de Glenlyon?" A gentleman of the bedchamber was bowing to him. "Her Highness the Dauphine, Queen of Scotland and of England, requests your attendance in the private apartment of the Dauphin, on a matter of urgency. Will you have the kindness to follow me?"

Campbell assented and followed his guide from the huge armory and around to a private door of the royal apartments. Two musketeers of the French guards stood at this door; they saluted and permitted the two men to pass. Campbell was ushered through into a small room known as a closet, adjoining the bedrooms of royalty.

He advanced, bowing—then his heart contracted. He found himself in the presence of the Queen, Catherine de Medici. She sat in a chair with a high back, while two of her Italian women arranged her hair.

"Be at ease, monsieur," she said in her expressionless way. "My daughter-in-law, who summoned you, will return in a moment. Meantime, I should like to ask you a question or two. Am I mistaken in thinking that upon your first arrival at court, the King my husband was gracious enough to present you with a token of his favor?"

"That is true, madame," replied Campbell. He had a desperate feeling of having been trapped. "It was a favor which I did not deserve."

"Where is it now?"

Campbell swallowed hard, yet dared not hesitate.

"I—I cannot say, madame. To my everlasting regret—"

She smiled slightly, as though relishing his discomfiture, then opened her hand to display the King's diamond lying in her palm.

"Could this be it, monsieur? If so, can you explain how it came into possession of a jeweler of the town?"

Campbell flushed. He had to lie, and hated it; inwardly, he cursed Ian Cameron of Lochiel. He rallied, and bowed.

"That is it, madame. I regret to say that one of my comrades was in the most desperate straits for money; having none myself, I allowed him the loan of this ring as a pledge, to be redeemed later."

Catherine extended the ring. "Take it, monsieur."

Still flushing, Campbell obeyed. She went on coldly:

"You are a foreigner, monsieur, and unused to the ways of court—as, indeed, you have made quite plain. I have heard many things said about you which I should be sorry to credit, but in this instance you need instruction. A gift from the King is above price and should be cherished as a royal favor. I cannot permit the dignity of my husband to be cheapened and demeaned to the level of a woman's token. Take and wear the ring, monsieur—and bear in mind that it is now doubly a gift from royalty. When next your comrade finds himself in such dire straits, send him to our treasurer; it ill befits that gentlemen of the court should have recourse to meaner purses. That is all."

Chagrined, astonished, puzzled, Campbell bowed and voiced

Campbell caught a glimpse of the
hooded face. "You!" he exclaimed.

his gratitude. As though not hearing him, Catherine signed to
her women, rose, and departed. He was still standing in frowning wonder when, by the same door, Mary Stuart came into
the room. She was waving a paper on which the ink was fresh
and had just been sanded; she thrust the paper at him, smiling.

"So here you are, Glenlyon! Take it quickly! Was she in here?"

"Yes, madame." On one knee, Campbell took the paper.

"Then I can't stop. That's an order for a horse and equipment.
I want you to do a most important errand for me. A passport
good on all the roads has been made out. Lady Anne will give
it to you. She's in the gardens now. Hurry! And, monsieur, good
fortune!"

She extended her hand for him to kiss, then turned and
hurried away, picking up her skirts like a hasty girl.

ANNE, IN the gardens! Campbell made his way out of the
chateau reflectively; he did not know what to think of all this,

by a good deal. That unexpected interview with Catherine had left a chill in his heart; why, he could not say. The order in his hand permitted him to take a horse, saddle and such other equipment as he desired, from the royal stables, on the service of the Dauphine. Why, and for what? No doubt, for the mysterious plans which Ian Cameron was arranging.

"Damn it, why the mystery?" grumbled Campbell. "And why did Catherine give me back this ring? She must have dropped onto the whole affair, somehow; if she has spies everywhere, as they say, then we're all like to find ourselves in hot water! Ah, there's Anne; she may know more than I."

He saw her strolling through the gardens ahead, and hastened to join her. At his call, she turned, with eager greeting.

"So it's done! Good morning, Malcolm—you've seen her?"

"I've seen one too many," he rejoined grimly. "But never mind; first to your affair. Yes, our mistress has given me an order on the stables, and said you would explain some errand she wants done."

Excitedly, Anne Haworth handed him a pass signed by the Chancellor, giving him the freedom of all roads and towns in the kingdom; an essential paper, for hasty travelers.

"You're to go now, as soon as you can get off," she exclaimed. "The errand is to see the steward of the Duchy of Orléans, M. de Villeroy, at Orléans, and obtain from him a statement of accounts which the Dauphine's treasurer must have at once. Do it or not... it's just an excuse. The real errand is to follow the post road to Orléans as far as Nouant. When you get there, go to the Cheval Blanc inn and wait. If Lochiel and Angus and the others don't show up by tomorrow morning, then you are to go on with our lady's errand."

CAMPBELL LOOKED blank. "I don't understand this at all," he said, and frowned. "From here to Orléans is only thirty-odd miles, isn't it? I should be given some idea of what's going on."

Agitation filled her face.

"Please, please! We don't know yet whether Lochiel will succeed; I've done my part, but he had the hardest task. If he can manage it, all will be open; he'll tell you everything. We learned only last evening that Le Balafré was going, that everything had come true as Long John predicted, that Hamilton and certain of the Guards are going too…. Don't you see? It was all true, it means they're going to murder him!"

"All right, my lass; I'll remain in the dark, since you ask it," assented Campbell grudgingly. "I suppose you don't trust me—"

"Don't be silly," she broke in with asperity. "I promised Lochiel; he's afraid that one word, one look, may ruin everything! And after what happened yesterday, you're certainly going to have enough eyes on you."

"You mean, after what Catherine said to me just now!" he rejoined, and at her look of astonished inquiry, laughed grimly and extended his hand. "You see this ring? Here, take it, keep it for me; I don't know what the devil to do with it on a journey and dare take no chances."

He dropped the ring in her hand, and described his amazing interview with Catherine. She listened, alarm creeping into her eyes.

"You don't seem to like it," he concluded. "Well, how do you explain her action?"

"She really takes a deep pride in the King's dignity," she said slowly. "That much of it was genuine. Her spies must have learned that Cameron of Lochiel pawned the ring; you told a lucky lie that fits in with what she knows. Of course, she won't suspect anything of the real purpose, until later. Then she'll put two and two together—then she'll guess at everything!"

"Never mind tomorrow," broke in Campbell. "What about now? Why did she give me back the ring?"

"I've told you why." Anne Haworth was more confident now. "Partly because of the King's dignity, but perhaps still more to put you to shame. She likes to do that. Everyone here calls her the daughter of shopkeepers and leeches; the royal ladies despise her; life is terribly hard for her. When she gets the chance to make herself appear noble and grand, and to shame someone of the court, she loves to do it."

"Oh! You may be right," said Campbell. "Then I'll breathe more easily. I was fancying all sorts of things; a bad conscience is easily touched, eh? I suppose you know all about what happened yesterday."

Anne looked at him, and her eyes danced.

"Well, I've heard stories! Truly, you came off very lucky, and I'm glad. If it hadn't been for that preaching friar, things would have been worse. By the way, have you heard that Montgomery is the new Captain of the Guard? And Silken James, I understand, will get an appointment about the King's person."

"All one to me." Campbell shrugged indifferently. "As soon as we finish with this mysterious affair of ours and Guise is safe, I'm off for Scotland again."

"But you can't!" she cried, hand to mouth, staring at him.

"But I can and shall. This is no life for me, bowing and scraping and fending off steel in the back—well, well, time enough for that when the time comes." He dismissed the subject with a shrug, and his face cleared. "Anne, lass, I'd best get off before something turns up to stop me. So say good-by for the present, and I'll trust you'll have no cause to jeer at me in future."

She put her hand in his. "I wasn't jeering, Malcolm," she said quietly. "If there was a jest in what happened on the bridge, there was death and horror in it too; one picks the laugh to avoid the tears. Danger, yes, and there's danger ahead. A man always faces danger, these days; and I do pray for you to come back safe. Are you taking Thorn?"

"I am, unless you'd rather not," he replied, and she sighed a little.

"Yes, take him; you may have need of him."

Those words, more than any others, showed Campbell that what lay ahead did indeed hold peril of the keenest.

"Good-by," she said, and held up her face. He kissed her cheek; this was their parting.

Campbell went on to the stables, presented his authority to the head groom, selected a horse and equipment, and asked to have it made ready at once. While they talked, a fanfare of trumpets sounded from the chateau.

"That'll be Le Balafré setting out," said the groom. "He and M. Hamilton and eight of the Scots Guards and a brace of lackeys. Think of M. le Duc going on a journey without a suite, like any ordinary man! He's a soldier, that one. And the King permitted him to use the inner courtyard, too; the first time any but the royal family has used it, to my certain knowledge. Well, changing times, changing rules! We'll have your horse ready and waiting in the outer court in ten minutes, monsieur."

So Guise had gone. He himself was going. Wait for Lochiel at Nouant, twenty miles eastward. An odd business all around!

As he made his preparations, Campbell's mind drifted over Long John's report, and on to the leech who had treated his wound in the crossroads tavern. Something about the King's helmet, and the prophecy of an astrologer; no explanation of this. And Brion had given him that singular message, about meeting Notredame again when least expected! Then, the prediction Notredame had made to Guise, a queer lot of words that had no sense whatever; for this very reason, no doubt, Guise had remembered it. Face to face with the angels of Louis XI, and danger coming to him shortly afterward! That made no sense—

"Ah! Yet there was sense in it!" thought Campbell, with a start. "Danger from the oak branch! And now he's gone off with Hamilton, whose badge is an oak tree, and with men who've been specially picked to murder him! That mention of the angels, though; that's but a lot of nonsense."

He whistled Thorn, belted his cloak, and was on his way. Nothing further had been heard about the tartan Black Angus had ordered for him; it might have been useful on this trip, for there was a feel of rain in the air and cloud was mounting the sky. On his way through the chateau, he passed a group of nobles, excitedly discussing the departure of Guise.

To use the inner courtyard, an unexampled honor! And this escort of the Guards… why, the Dauphine herself had arranged it! To be sure, the duke was her uncle, but it looked a bit queer that so many honors were being heaped upon him, Guise or no Guise!

Campbell went on to his waiting horse. So tongues were busy with it already, eh? A good preparation for what somebody most assuredly expected to happen. When word came that Le Balafré had been murdered by his own escort, France would be in convulsions. A plot formed by the King and the Dauphine, jealous of this man who was almost a king himself! Death to all Scots, and the devil take Mary Stuart, Queen of Scots! Yes, it was quite clear now. Lies, trickery, dark and involved intrigue, to work the ruin of some and the death of others, and Silken James the man to turn the card!

"A plague on the lot of you!" Campbell, spurring away with Thorn bounding ahead, took a look back at the royal chateau. "Except for Anne Haworth and a few honest Scots, I'd like fine to cast no eye on any of you again, ever!"

A wish in the morning may come true without warning, as the old saw has it.

CHAPTER IX

THE POST-ROAD from Blois to Orléans and Paris, one of two roads that ran along the bright Loire, went by way of small hamlets—St. Dié, Nouant, the Three Chimneys, and Clery. This last was a tiny place but famous. At the church of Notre Dame de Clery many miracles took place, pilgrims came there in abundance, and King Louis XI was buried in the midst of its nave.

Hard riding could cover the thirty-odd miles to Orléans in

a full day, but it was late in the morning when Campbell rode out of Blois, and he was in no haste. For Thorn it was a glorious freedom; he coursed the roadsides in splendor or trotted beside the horse, disdaining interest in the savage farm-dogs who gave him wary berth or bayed insults after him from safe distance, and the passing peasants who hastily crossed themselves at sight of him seemed to cause him vast amusement.

Campbell got a good noon meal at the inn of St. Dié, and learned by inquiry that some great lord with an escort of kilted Scots had passed this way an hour or so ahead of him. They had aimed to pass the night at the Three Chimneys, said his informant, where there was a huge tavern of ancient fame, with the best wines in all the Loire valley. After seeing Thorn well fed, Campbell mounted and rode on.

The trees were reddening with sunset when he sighted the few scattered houses of Nouant and the post tavern beyond them. There had been many people on the roads all this day, for the valley was well farmed hereabouts, and the post diligence from Orléans was in the tavern courtyard when he dismounted and gave his horse to the grooms. Whistling Thorn to heel, he passed into the tavern and obtained quarters for the night.

He bathed, shaved, and rested for a space. Later, when the diligence had rumbled out of the courtyard and on its way to Blois, he descended to the big ordinary room of the inn, where fowl and roasts were turning on spits before the fireplace. The place was empty of clients, except for a friar of the Cordeliers who sat in one corner, head shrouded in brown hood, before a bottle of wine.

Campbell ordered dinner and made himself comfortable at a table under a wall lantern. The Cordelier rose and crossed to his table, bearing bottle and pewter cup.

"*Pax vobiscum,* my son!" he said in Latin. "Shall we dine in company?"

"Gladly." Campbell summoned up his rusty Latin. "Sit down, Father. You've just arrived?"

"A few minutes after you," was the response. The friar got long legs under the table and relaxed. "In fact," he said in a changed voice, "I had hopes of catching up with you, but failed."

Campbell caught a glimpse of the hooded face in the lamplight, and his jaw fell. It was the face of Ian Cameron of Lochiel.

"You!" he exclaimed.

"Careful, now; no French, Glenlyon! Speak Latin only, then we can be free of our words. Not even English is safe hereabouts."

Lochiel smiled, eased his huge bulk, and sighed happily.

"It went off without a hitch," he continued. "Mind you, gentlemen of the Guards can't go gallivanting over the country like masterless men! I had to arrange for Angus and the two Forbes; they'll be along in half an hour or so. Also, for myself. Just as I arranged the errand for you. We're supposed to be collecting some rent-moneys waiting at Orléans for the King's treasurer. But it had to be delicately done, and in secret."

Campbell began to see light.

"So that's it!" he said. "Well, if you want to catch up with Le Balafré's party, we must push on to the Three Chimneys—"

"Easy, now. I want nothing of the kind."

"But our man may be murdered at any minute!"

Lochiel shook his head, and said no more until the meal had been laid before them and the wine poured, and they were alone once more.

"I've taken counsel with Angus and others, and I know this road very well," he said. "When a great man is to be put out of the way, he can't be killed in any ditch like a common peasant. Mind you, Silken James must come clear out of this; he'll have some fine likely lie made up. He may even be wounded and left for dead, in defense of the duke. But the others must scatter. There'll be a hue and cry through the whole of France. They'll not be safe anywhere in the kingdom!"

"You know who they are?"

"Certainly. Picked men, as Angus had figured. Two Erskines,

*A friar in the robe of a Cordelier, but with
a most unmonklike face, sat reading.*

a Hamilton, two Ramsay brethren, and three others I don't
know. All of them rascals, men for the job."

"And you think there's no danger now, tonight?" asked
Campbell. "The party will be stopping at the Three Chimneys,
ahead."

"Silken James is a canny man, Glenlyon, and these others
have their necks to think about. They'll want a good start on
any pursuit, too. Therefore the job should be done before reaching Orléans tomorrow evening, giving them a clear night's start
or better. The ideal place for it is on the other side of Clery. The
road goes through a forest there. The wood of St. Mesmin, it's
called. That's the spot I'd pick; safe, little traveled, and no one
about to tell tales."

"Very well. But you're taking a long chance."

"Agreed." Lochiel drained his cup and wiped his lips. "The rain's blown out of the sky but it'll be back tomorrow. That's bad; may spoil all our plans. Wet bowstrings notch no shafts. As soon as I get a bite, I'm riding on to the Three Chimneys. That's why I have this friar's garb. I'll steal a word with the duke's lackeys; they'll not recognize me, of course. Just to make certain that all's going as we think."

"I still believe he should have been warned!"

"He was. I sent him a note in a disguised hand; he read it, laughed, and threw it into the fire. Luckily, no one else saw it."

CAMPBELL HELD his peace. He began to see, at last, the scope of what Lochiel had been forced to do, and what he had done.

It was no simple thing to get Mary Stuart's equerry sent on a mission. It was far more difficult to get himself sent on an errand, with three of the Guards for escorts, and to do it with the necessary secrecy. It must have required the utmost finesse, bribery and daring. One word amiss, and the fat would have been in the fire.

"Just what do you propose doing, tomorrow?" asked Campbell. Lochiel frowned and drummed on the table with his fingers.

"That depends. They brought bows along, but they'll probably stick to cold steel for the job, cut down the lackeys and the duke, and put a few arrows into them by way of Scots signature, as it were. Five of us against eight of them, and Hamilton himself, makes nine. If the weather holds fine, it's a good gamble; we have the best shots in the company. If it rains, then we stick to steel. Count Le Balafré with us, and it evens matters."

Campbell drew down astonished brows. "What the devil do you propose?"

"To kill every man jack of them except one, whom we'll make talk later on. What did you expect?"

"I hardly knew," Campbell confessed. "To rescue the duke, perhaps—"

"Fiddlesticks!" Lochiel's face set in hard, massive lines. "Who plays with fire, gets burned. This is worse than fire; it's murder and treason, a damned plot against Mary Stuart herself! You're no boy just out of school, to belch at a killing or two."

"Oh, I'm not objecting! I'll do my share." Campbell shrugged. "But you must have some plan. You can't go it blind. After all, they can dirk him in two minutes, once they begin, and we dare not let them know we're on hand."

"Black Angus has a plan for that," said Lochiel. "So have I. Let's wait till the others come up and have eaten. Meantime, I'll go on the eight miles to the Three Chimneys, and back. You'll wait here. No telling what information I may pick up from the duke's lackeys, about their plans. Agreed?"

Campbell nodded assent. Lochiel rose, stalked out, and called for his horse.

Over his meal, Campbell pondered the matter frowningly. He realized that every detail had to be precisely and nicely arranged; and there were difficulties. If Silken James found other Scots on the road, if he suspected anything amiss, it would spoil the whole affair. Lochiel might be deemed overcautious, but it was better to be cautious than to be broken on the wheel.

As for killing Silken James and his eight recreant Scots, Campbell dismissed this with no second thought as a necessary item. Who played with fire, got burned!

H A L F A N hour later came a great clatter of hoofs from the courtyard, and bawling voices and lusty oaths. In strode Black Angus, followed by Long John and Alec Forbes, clapping Campbell heartily on the back and roaring for wine—not that they lacked, for Long John staggered and Alec hiccuped French and Scots together.

Campbell regarded them, amazed. The huge black beard of Angus was gone, revealing a white shaven jowl and pallid chin like a jutting rock. The grizzled red beard of Long John was also gone.

The others roared with laughter at his looks, but Angus sobered and shook his head, with a dour grimace, and pointed at Alec.

"It was him that did it, Malcolm. Him, the beardless creature, taunting us! And I'll not deny that we'd been quaffing wine a bit. However, it's just as well. We don't want to be recognized too soon, especially by those rascals with Silken James. But ye've said no word about our new outfits! We've one for you aboard the pack-horse, too!"

He swung about complacently. Gone were sporran, tartan and bonnet. The three wore steel caps and mail-shirts over leather jerkins; the archers had become men-at-arms, straight swords replacing the claymores.

"Also for less recognition," hiccuped Alec Forbes. "Landlord! Drawer! Where's the wine you promised an hour ago?"

His fist pounded the table. Long John emitted a thunderous bellow. The landlord came running; the joints and fowl were stripped from the spit, a mountain of bread was brought forth; the evening had begun.

"A' Scots together, wi' siller i' the pocket!" cried Long John. "French siller and broad Harry groats, and no bad coin i' the lot!"

Before the bones were picked, Alec was snoring and Long John was staring glassy-eyed on the room. Angus winked at Campbell, and thrust a knuckle-bone at Thorn.

"Leave 'em be, Malcolm! My head's clear enough, and no more's needed. Where's Lochiel?"

Ian Cameron made answer for himself, stalking in from the courtyard like a brown wraith. He took Angus by the shoulder, lifted him out of his seat, and walked him outside to the pump.

He came back presently, sluiced and streaming with water, laughing uproariously. He wiped face and head on the brown robe of Lochiel; then Campbell beckoned them both to a table in the far corner.

"Let's to business," he said brusquely.

"Right," assented Lochiel. "I made the trip, talked with a lackey, and came back. It's as I thought. Le Balafré's at work with the other lackey, who's also a secretary. Silken James and the red tartans have their heads together. They plan to make Orléans tomorrow night, with a wee bit of a stop at Clery. That proves the job will be done on past Clery, in the wood of St. Mesmin."

"How does it prove anything?" demanded Campbell.

"Because the duke is minded to stop for a bit of a prayer at the Clery church, Notre Dame de Clery. It's a spot famed for sanctity and miracles. They'll let him do it; then, once in the forest, they'll finish him. They can ride on to Orléans and Paris, then scatter—there won't be any pursuit till next day at least."

"How d'ye know they'll do this?" asked Angus.

Hamilton slashed at the hurtling shape;
but for the heavy collar, Thorn would
have been beheaded by the stroke.

"It's common sense. If I were Silken James, with such a job on my hands, that's the course I'd follow.

"Right! I agree!" cried Black Angus.

Campbell nodded slowly. "I suppose you're right. I still think it'll be taking a long chance, however. Where shall we be, mean-time?"

"We'll be up ahead!" spoke out Angus. "Mind! We must see the job begun, yet we must not let our man be hurt; it's a deli-cate matter. And they must not see us. One glimpse of a steel cap, and they'll abandon the job."

Cameron leaned forward with brisk speech.

"See how this plan suits you, comrades: We leave here at daybreak and ride on fast. We'll pass the Three Chimneys before the other party's on the move. So we'll get ahead of them, and stay ahead."

"With our necks at stake," said Lochiel. "Then what?"

"At Clery, you stop behind in your friar's robe. Sit your horse

in the shade and tell your beads, or read a holy book; it'll do you no great harm," said Campbell, smiling. "The rest of us will ride on and wait in the first likely patch of forest. We'll tether the horses and wait afoot, for the better use of our bows."

"Oh!" said Lochiel. "And I?"

"When they leave Clery, you follow, but not too closely; just to make sure they don't try any killing there. We'll follow, through the wood or by road, joining you and trailing closely. We can go afoot faster than they'll ride. At the first shout or clash of steel, we'll be on hand."

Lochiel considered, and nodded assent.

"It sounds fairly safe; I had something of the same sort in mind myself. But there's no telling how circumstances will befall. One of us must be in command."

"Well, suppose you toss for it!" cried Black Angus. "Here's an English groat. Call the turn, Malcolm! Winner takes command!" He spun the silver coin.

"Harry!" said Campbell. The groat clattered on the floor and Angus stooped to it.

"Royal Harry it is, and that settles everything," said he, and made a mock grimace. "To think I'll have to take orders from a Campbell! Well, I'll make the best of it, but we must have another drink to wash it down. Landlord!"

IN HASTE the landlord came—bottles in his arms. But just then Long John stood up, towering over his table, his eyes glassy, and swept out his hand toward the three in the corner. His voice lifted dolefully:

"Sair wark, sair wark! Yon's bonny red bluid! The Forbes tartan's a' splotched with it, and the Cameron sporran's adrip with it, mair's the pity! And I hear the mournful keening of the pibroch of sorrow in the glens—"

He shook with a hiccup and sank down again.

"The man's daft," said Lochiel, and bubbled wine into a cup.

Campbell looked at Black Angus, and saw a pallor creeping across his new-shaven face.

"More like, the man's fey," said Angus under his breath, but Lochiel did not hear the words or heed them.

ONE REASON for the amazing popularity of the Duc de Guise was his lack of affectation. Among princes, no prince could be more haughty; among soldiers, he was a soldier and still the Prince, with a frank, blunt, straightforward bearing that won all hearts. His brother the Cardinal de Lorraine was the diplomat of the family; Guise possessed personal charm greater than diplomacy.

Upon leaving the Three Chimneys, he rode with Hamilton, the eight Scots of his escort in the van, his two lackeys following. He wore a riding-suit of buff velvet, with a voluminous black cloak and a hat of black. None but his personal lackey knew that, beneath the velvet, was a shirt of the most exquisite Milan steel links which would turn the point of any poniard. His sword was a plain weapon with black cross-hilt.

Silken James was at his best this morning. If he cherished a natural chagrin at not being retained in command of the guards, it did not appear. His nickname was well deserved. There was nothing obsequious in his manner. His firm, square-hewn features held strength and decision, he had a shrewd grasp of affairs, but he never forced himself or his opinions into the forefront.

In his steel cap and light breastplate, golden chain and sword-hilt, he presented a strong contrast to the dark bearded figure beside him. One would have said that he was the great man here, handsome, soldierly, assured. Certainly he had a grand air, a personality, a force that marked him out. He bestrode a magnificent Spanish jennet given him by the King, from the stud in Anjou where Henry gave free vent to his hobby for breeding thoroughbred horses.

The summer's day was fresh, as so often happens along the Loire, with a high wind shepherding clouds up the sky; but the threat of rain had held off. The eight Scots Guards in the van were armed like Hamilton with steel caps and breastplates, and with quivers and longbows slung at their backs.

"We made a late start, monsieur," said Guise, glancing at the sky, when Hamilton asked about plans for the day. "Clery is only a few miles ahead. I'll make only a brief stop there; I promised Madame la Duchesse to make a prayer on her behalf. Suppose we push on from there without pause for refreshment, and reach Orléans early."

"As you wish, M. le Duc," assented Hamilton. "With your permission, I'll so inform my men."

He touched the jennet with his spurs and caught up with the eight guards. Their gaze questioned him silently. Deprived of their picturesque costumes, they looked the hard, unscrupulous soldiers that they were.

"His Highness desires to push straight on after the halt at Clery," said Hamilton. "No time for drinking—until later."

The eight exchanged a significant look. Hamilton glanced at one of the two Ramsays, and touched the long pistols holstered at his saddle-bow.

"Is all understood?" he asked curtly.

"Aye," rejoined Ramsay, in English. "You flush the stag; we'll do the rest."

Hamilton reined his horse back to the side of the duke, who regarded him smilingly.

"You look excited, monsieur!"

"A harsh word was necessary. Rough fellows, these Scots; they had expected a stoup of wine at Clery."

"Pshaw! Then they shall have it," said Guise. "Rough fellows, perhaps, but honest. If my niece had not insisted upon your escort, I'd have made a quick trip to Paris and back without bothering you. Yes, a soldier deserves his cup; let them have their wine, and you shall accompany me into the church for the good of your soul. Madame my wife tells me that it is a place of miracles. Who knows? You may come out a changed man!"

The duke laughed heartily at his own joke. Hamilton joined in the mirth, as became a good courtier, but there was something dark and ominous in his laughter.

THE MILES ran their length, and presently the spire of Notre Dame de Clery came into sight above the trees. The road led into the hamlet and they approached the church. Just beyond, showed the post tavern. At the entrance of the spacious churchyard was a tethered horse. A friar in the robe of a Cordelier, but with a most unmonk-like face, sat in the shade near the horse, reading.

"Why, here's luck!" said the duke gayly. "We've met two white horses on the road, and now a monk meets us! Here, good brother!" He tossed a coin to the hooded friar, who caught it nimbly. "A trifle of alms, and may it quench your thirst to good purpose."

Before the steps and wide front platform of the church, he dismounted with Hamilton, and beckoned the two lackeys.

"Hold the horses, messieurs, till we come out. And you gentlemen," he said to the guards, with a wave of his gloved hand toward the tavern, "have a hearty draught of wine at my charge. Pay for it, Michel," he said to one of the lackeys, as he turned toward the church entrance.

He strode into the church, with Hamilton at his heels. The change from the sunlight outside to the dim interior left them both momentarily blinded; however, Guise led the way toward the choir and the altar, and dropped on his knees before the sanctuary.

Hamilton followed his example in silence.

After a few moments, the duke rose, crossed himself and glanced around, curiously. Hamilton also came to his feet. Guise took him by the arm, as they turned toward the entrance again, and halted.

"Look, monsieur! Upon my word, it gave me a start; I failed to notice it when we came in. Whose tomb can this be, in the midst of the nave?"

Before them was an imposing tomb, topped by the kneeling effigy of a man, carved in beautiful white marble. About the effigy rose the marble figures of angels.

Hamilton leaned forward to read the inscription.

"Why, it's the tomb of King Louis XI!" he exclaimed.

"Ah, yes, of course; I remember now that he was buried here," began Guise. "They say that he endowed this—this—this edifice—"

His words trailed off and died; he stood in blank astonishment and wonder, staring at the marble figures.

"Monseigneur!" exclaimed Hamilton. "What's wrong? Is anything the matter?"

"No, nothing." Guise replied. "Nothing at all. I merely happened to remember something. Upon my word! The angels of Louis XI! Well, well, suppose we get out of here and on our way."

He strode out of the church and swung up into the saddle again. His features had lost their customary expression of affability; they were set and hard and alert. The eight guards were straggling back from the tavern. Hamilton came to the duke, anxiously.

"If anything has occurred to startle Your Highness—"

"No; merely a thought that occurred to me, an uneasy memory," broke in Guise hastily. He had no intention of confiding the truth to anyone. "If you please, monsieur, I should like to change the order of march. Let my two lackeys take the van and ride well in advance, with two of our men. Four of your men to follow them, preceding us. Your other two guards to bring up the rear."

Hamilton gave the orders swiftly, almost savagely, in an agony of uncertainty and alarm. Something, somehow, had occurred to put Guise on the alert.

"Keep your eyes open, men!" rang his voice. "You two in the lead, uncase bows, notch your strings, loosen shafts! Ramsay, you and your brother do the same in the rear; keep a dozen paces behind us."

The two Ramsay brethren, dour and hard-bitten men, stripped the leathern cases from their bows, bent them to the string, and mounted. The two lackeys with their pair of guards set off, well in the lead. Four of the guards followed; after these, at a little distance, rode Hamilton and the duke. The Ramsay brethren brought up the rear, and as they set their horses in motion, exchanged a glance that spoke volumes; nothing could have suited their plans better than this arrangement, which the duke himself had suggested.

As the two last riders disappeared along the road leading to the near-by forest of St. Mesmin, and through it, the Cordelier by the churchyard gate came to his feet. He put his book away, loosened the reins of his horse, and leaped into the saddle with an ease and agility which was most astonishing in a brown-robed friar.

Those riding ahead, naturally, did not observe his action.

PIERCED BY the filtering shafts of sunlight, the road was picturesque and strangely beautiful. The trees grew massive and wild; this was a royal preserve belonging to the Orléans duchy and no peasant hand dared touch the green trees, no hut or hovel dared show itself within these limits.

Ahead, well away from the hamlet and lost within the forest depths, a clearing showed at one side. Here the road twisted and turned obliquely, as in days beyond memory it had swerved to avoid a cottage or farmstead that had once stood here. Now all signs of a building had vanished; there was only the green-sward of the clearing, with saplings encroaching upon it.

Approaching this spot, Silken James eyed it keenly, a flash of satisfaction in his eyes. On ahead, the lackeys and their two companions were disappearing around the far turn of the road, the four guards behind them were almost at the turn. Hamilton's hand went to one of the pistols at his saddle-bow and waited.

Guise drew a little ahead. He lifted his hand and fingered

the scar on his cheek, his dark eyes searching the clearing and the trees. Silken James was tense, his features set in harsh resolution, his gaze fastened upon the duke. His hand came clear of the holster, bringing the pistol with it.

"It is strange," said Guise, as though to himself, "very strange, this sense of danger! That's what comes of listening to—"

Hamilton sighted along the pistol-barrel, straight at those broad shoulders ahead. Smoke gushed from the pistol; to the sudden explosion, the horses jumped. Amid the rolling smoke, the figure of Guise fell forward, then was thrown from the saddle as his horse leaped and bolted.

CHAPTER X

WHEN THAT pistol-shot rolled through the wood of St. Mesmin, however, a strange thing happened. "It's done!" Hamilton cried out fiercely, peering through the smoke at his victim.

But it was not done. Guise was not dead; he was not even hurt, except for a bruise. What with poor powder and little velocity, the pistol-ball could nowhere near pierce that hidden shirt of Milanese steel. The impact bowed the duke forward, and the leap of his horse tumbled him onto the dust of the road.

He rolled over and came nimbly to his feet, and his sword flashed out. A startled oath burst from Hamilton.

"Finish it, finish it!" he shouted furiously to the two Ramsays.

Their bows were already bent, their arrows notched. At this instant sounded a deadly *whir-r-r* on the air. The vibrant twang of a bowstring, then of another, rang out. One Ramsay flung wide his arms, convulsively; a yard-long shaft transfixed his head from side to side. The other Ramsay screamed suddenly and shrilly, and toppled forward with a feathered butt protruding from his back. The frightened horses went plunging away, one of the brothers dragging, the other lying dead in the road.

"A Guise! A Guise!"

Campbell was breaking out of the green covert, bow in hand. Long John was at the side of the road, grinning grimly, and Alec Forbes with him, notching fresh shafts. Lochiel, his friar's robe gone and his steel cap aglitter, was coming on horseback.

Plunging to a halt, Campbell lifted bow and loosed. It was a hasty shot; the arrow flashed to Hamilton's corselet and glanced off. Aghast and confounded, Hamilton had already driven home his spurs. The Spanish jennet leaped like a deer, whirled madly out of the road at the clear space, and went in panic for the trees beyond.

Long John's bowstring twanged again. Hamilton was gone among the trees, and Alec shook his head at the towering archer.

"Wasted shaft," said he.

Up ahead, the four guards had halted and were slipping from their horses. A scream lifted faintly from around the bend; the two lackeys died there, and the two Scots who slew them came riding back to join the other four.

Guise stood in the road, staring at Campbell as the latter halted.

"Well, monsieur?" he said coldly. Sharp recognition leaped in his eyes. "You! Have you become an assassin, then?"

"No," rejoined Campbell. "This plot was discovered, and we came to help you—"

"No time to talk!" cried Lochiel, drawing rein and slipping to the ground. "Here, monseigneur! Into the saddle and ride the back road, swiftly!"

The duke comprehended in a flash.

"Good men, true hearts!" he exclaimed. "But Guise is no coward, to let other men fight for him!"

"Do it, do it! Ride and go!" commanded Lochiel angrily. "We've men enough and to spare; we were commanded to save you. Besides—"

" 'Ware!" came the warning voice of Long John. " 'Ware a flight!"

Lochiel plunged at the duke, seized him, thrust him on the

horse. Campbell lent a hand. Despite himself, Guise was bundled into the saddle, and he seized the reins. His own steed had followed Hamilton's jennet in among the trees. Arrows streaked along the sunlight.

Campbell pricked the horse with his knife-point, and the animal went away with a frenzied leap, followed by a long shaft that streaked its rump and kept it at top speed. Bowstrings twanged. The six guards ahead had scattered out afoot and were approaching down the roadsides, drawing bow as they came.

Black Angus of Kilspindie rose up amid the green and loosed from his ear. Yells of angry recognition broke forth; a shaft smashed against Campbell's corselet and splintered, the force of it almost knocking him from his feet. The long goose yards flittered and whirred across the broken sunlight, fast as fingers could notch and loose—deadly things in trained hands! Voices of agony and of fury welled up in sharp tumult.

At the edge of the trees, a pistol bellowed. Campbell was in the act of loosing a shaft; the ball struck him under the pit of his upraised right arm. Hamilton, he thought, as the impact jerked him around. As he collapsed, an access of horror seized him, but not for himself. He had a glimpse of Lochiel lying in the road, an arrow in his throat and blood jetting terribly. Then things went dark, the voice of Angus reached him dimly, and was lost.

Sore work indeed, murderous work; these were no amateurs to bungle their job. Long John was coughing out his life among the ferns. Two of Hamilton's Scots, their quivers empty, were darting forward at a run, swords out. Alec Forbes stood against a tree, with a reddened shaft through his body. Yet his bowstring twanged.

"One!" said he, and laid another arrow, and the bow sang again. "Two!" he cried, but there was death in his voice, and the bow fell from his hand.

"SORE WORK, sure enough," said the voice of Angus. Campbell's eyes opened to the words, and to the warm tongue of Thorn licking his cheek. He was lying in the road, his shoulders propped against something; it was Lochiel's body. Thorn stood beside him, and Black Angus sat on the other side.

"Hello!" said Campbell. "What happened?"

"You've got a pistol-ball in your wame," said Angus. "I've done the best I could for it, which isn't much." He was leaning over, working at something as he spoke. "You're well bandaged, anyhow."

Campbell looked around. No one else was in sight, except the dead Ramsay.

"But where are the others?" he demanded.

"Alec just died," said Angus. "I couldn't get to him, more's the pity. He brought down the last brace with two shafts. Losh! It was good shooting, all of it! If that blasted Hamilton hadn't got clear, I'd have no regrets."

"What are you doing there?" exclaimed Campbell, trying to crush down the thought of his friends, all dead. And himself stricken, as he knew.... He lay bandaged with his shirt flung over him; but the hurt and the heaviness of the ball in his body was terrible.

"Working," replied Angus, with a grimace. "One leg's clear, but the ash is so tough my knife won't cut it."

Campbell got his left arm under him, and pushed himself more erect. Then he saw: Angus had a long arrow through both thighs, above the knees. One thigh was clear and dripping redly; he was sawing with his knife at the arrow to clear the other leg. Campbell set his teeth and pushed himself up until he was sitting. Thorn went off, sniffing. Beside the road, a horse was grazing, a few feet distant; it was the duke's horse.

"Guise got away," said Campbell. "There's his horse. He'll send back help from Clery."

"Maybe," said Angus. "Well, I've done my best; I'm done. Too much blood lost."

"Be damned to you!" said Campbell, forcing down his own

hurt. He inched across to the side of Angus. "Here, let's have a look. Why, there's no great harm!"

"Blood gone, strength gone," muttered Angus, sinking back feebly.

"Nonsense. You're tough. Let's see, now!" Campbell picked up the knife and went to work, forcing himself at it though his head swam. He severed the shaft and drew it clear of the wound, then went at the job of bandaging the ripped flesh of Angus' legs.

"That's done, too," he said. "You can't ride. I can. I'll take the horse, here, and ride back to Clery, and make sure of help."

"Good men gone," Angus said weakly. "Sent those rascals to hell first—"

His eyes closed and he lay breathing heavily. However, the blood was stopped; he was in no danger.

Campbell made an effort to rise, and slumped with a groan. His right arm was almost helpless, his chest hammered with pain. After a moment his brain cleared, and he called Thorn.

The great hound came to him. Campbell got an arm about the arching neck. Thorn understood, and gave noble assistance. Getting to one knee at last, Campbell came to his feet and staggered to the horse at the roadside. He stood clinging to the saddle with his good hand, trying desperately to think, to force back the pain and weakness.

Clery! The thought persisted; it took shape as a driving purpose in his brain....

His shirt had fallen away unnoticed; he was naked to the waist, except for the big awkward bandage about his chest. His legs were sound enough, however. Slowly and by degrees he got a foot in the stirrup. Then, with a supreme effort, he was up and astride the saddle, gripping the pommel and the reins desperately.

He came within an ace of pitching down again; luckily, he found the other stirrup in time, but the whole effort sent such intolerable pain throbbing through him that he could scarcely keep from crying out.

Clery! Clery and aid for Black Angus! The others all dead! Long John had certainly been fey last night; he had foreseen this. Well, Long John was notching a string now with Walter of Holgham and Red Wat o'Tyneside, and many another famed Scots archer of olden days....

The movement of the horse caused fresh agony. Campbell hung on, with swirl upon swirl of pain sweeping him and dulling his brain; it wore down presently to a dim monstrous hurt that seemed to envelop him like a mantle. The horse moved on, Thorn ranging along at the roadside. They passed other horses, the steeds of Hamilton's men scattered and cropping the grass, but Campbell did not see them. He did not see anything; his whole will was centered on sticking in the saddle.

TIME PASSED. Fever had mounted to his brain. He was no longer conscious of the pain; he rode with head sunk on his chest, eyes half open, a prey to flitting fancies that made no sense. Even when Thorn voiced a low and deadly warning, it did not reach him. He was quite unaware that instead of riding toward Clery, his mount had been headed in the opposite direction; he was going on through the dark wood, toward Orléans.

Eyes peered forth from among the trees, following that half-naked, drooping rider. Then a horseman urged his steed out of the cover and into the road; Thorn halted and faced about with white fangs bared and a savage growl in his throat, and stood barring the way.

Hamilton's horse halted, with a snort of fear.

An angry curse came from Silken James. His pistols were still empty, for reloading was no simple task. He hurled one of the heavy pistols at Thorn, who deftly evaded the throw and gave another menacing growl.

With a furious oath, Hamilton whipped out his sword and drove in spurs; his horse plunged forward. Thorn, far from giving ground, crouched and hurled himself upward in a leap, directly at the rider. The horse, in panic, reared wildly. Hamilton slashed at the hurtling shape; but for the heavy collar, Thorn would have been beheaded by the stroke. The sword sheared half through the leather and slashed the dog across the shoulder.

What the man could not do, the horse did: The frantic animal was lashing out wildly; a hoof caught the hound midway of his slim length, crunched him to earth.

Hamilton got his mount under control. Thorn tried to rise and could not. He came to his forelegs, snarling defiance, but stopped there. Putting in spurs. Silken James rode on, sword in hand, after the vanishing figure of Campbell.

Presently he caught up, drew alongside and addressed Campbell. The latter looked at him blankly with fever-ridden eyes and babbled nonsense. Hamilton stared at him; then slowly sheathed his sword. Even with bitter desire for vengeance, only the veriest dastard could have driven steel into this half-naked, raving, wounded man; and Silken James was no coward. Besides, it was clear that his pistol-ball had gone to its mark; and in nine cases out of ten in that day, such a wound was certain death.

The two rode on together. Behind them, there lifted faintly, a long, doleful howl; but Campbell did not hear and Silken James only laughed softly. Those hard, resolute features of his settled into ominous lines, however; his task had failed, thanks to Campbell, and now he would be a hunted man far and wide, his very name accursed....

A flash lit his eye, a laugh came to his lips, and he looked at Campbell again.

"Live or die, you damned Scot," he said cheerfully, "at least you shall save my neck for me and make good some of the damage you've done—so ride on!"

The afternoon was late when Hamilton descried a group of riders in the road ahead; Orléans was only a mile farther on. Campbell, half-conscious, was mumbling deliriously as he hung drooping in the saddle. Silken James eyed the group, then caught up the reins of Campbell's horse and pressed forward with unfeigned alacrity.

The group consisted of an officer and half a dozen men of the *maréchaussée,* a force thus named because under the nominal commands of the Marshals of France, it policed the highways and country roads of the kingdom.

"De par le roi!" Hamilton flung up his hand, authority in his mien. "In the King's name!" he cried. "Messieurs, I take pleasure in confiding this rascal to your care."

"Who are you, who dare use the King's name?" demanded the officer.

Hamilton smiled. "I'm the Sieur de Glenlyon, equerry to Her Highness the Dauphine, monsieur. This rogue is one of a band of assassins who attempted to murder the Duc de Guise this same day, near Clery. His name is Hamilton, an ex-officer of the Scots Guards."

Excitement rose high. An attempt to murder Guise! Here was news of the greatest!

"Le Balafré, thanks to a secret coat of mail, escaped injury," Hamilton said coolly. The explanation of his failure to kill Guise was obvious enough to him now. "He rode back to Blois. I pursued this rascal, shot him, and caught him. Put him in strictest custody, I charge you. I must hasten on to do the errands of my mistress the Dauphine."

"The fellow doesn't look as though he'd need any custody but that of a coffin," said the officer dryly. "Congratulations, monsieur; he shall be safely stowed away, never fear! We'll probably find him dead in his cell in the morning."

"I hope so," said Hamilton fervently, and pressing in his spurs, rode on before any further questions could be asked, or his passport demanded.

The group closed about Campbell. His hands were bound and he was led on to the city, whose forty towers rose above the trees and the river; in their midst, most great and grim of all, the prison-tower of the Chatelet, at the approach to the sixteen-arched bridge of stone that led across the Loire.

CHAPTER XI

CAMPBELL WAKENED to abrupt agony.... He lay on a pallet in a prison cell with open barred window. Two men were holding him; a third, a leech, was probing clumsily at his wound and seeking the ball.

"Ha! I've found it!" cried the leech triumphantly. "It went under the armpit; here it is at the front, between two of the ribs! Now for a cross-incision, and we'll have it out in no time."

"Will the rogue recover?" asked one of the men.

"Of course not," said the leech. "Who ever heard of anyone recovering, after carrying a bullet around with him? Gangrene will set in; it always does. Hold him tightly, now, and I'll go after the ball."

"If anyone in Orléans can do it, you can, master," said one of the men.

Orléans! The word flashed across Campbell's consciousness. Was he in Orléans? How the devil had he come here? Then conscious thought was gone in sharp and horrid pain that endured steadily.

After a time he found himself alone and freshly bandaged. Coarse food and weak wine were beside him. He drank gratefully, sat up, got to his feet and staggered over to the barred window. Clinging to the bars, he looked out.

From this window, he could see the tree-shaded promenade along the stone quays, with a little glimpse of the Loire, where boats came up from Nantes with their freight. People moved about, strolling on the promenade; behind all, houses rose up along the steep bank of the river.

Something moved slightly, opposite. He looked again; it was a dog lying there, head on paws. A dog—why, it was Thorn! Campbell stared in blank astonishment. A cart came along and the dog moved, stood up, lifted head to sniff the air, then lay down again, all his attention fastened on the Chatelet opposite. Another dog came past; Thorn bared white fangs, and the other went hastily on.

Thorn here, watching the place! Campbell knew Thorn must have followed him, somehow; too far away to call or whistle, however. But how—how had he come to Orléans?

The door-lock screeched; the door was flung open, and his answer came. Men flooded into the cell; guards, city officials, a grave scribe with inkhorn and quill and paper. They began to interrogate him. His name was Hamilton and he had made an attempt on the life of the Duc de Guise—

"No such thing!" cried Campbell furiously. He poured out his name and all about himself—and was met with blank derision.

When, presently, he comprehended this to be a fact, and learned how he had come here, he settled down to meet the situation with common sense. He perceived with what cunning Silken James had gained himself time to escape the hue and cry, and tried to make his inquisitors realize it. He described the entire plot, he appealed to Guise himself as a witness, to Black Angus or anyone of the court who knew him. This whole affair was an absurdity, said he, and could be readily disproved.

Unfortunately, his fever had set in afresh and affected his coherency. Worse, his inquisitors had no understanding of Scots names, and were already confused betwixt Hamilton and the Earl of Arran.

"You rogue, do you think the Duc de Guise can be called like a common person to serve as witness?" said the provost's lieutenant, in charge of the affair. "Or anyone of the court? Give us no more lies! You'd be put to the question this moment, had not the leech certified your inability to stand a racking."

Matters went from bad to worse, Campbell lost his temper and his head, and at last they left him amid curses and threats.

By this time his brief lucidity had passed into a torrent of fevered fancies.

Next day coherence returned for a space. He found himself at the window, calling Thorn; the dog was there, settled in the same spot, watching the grim Chatelet with unfaltering gaze, but could not hear his voice. The inquisitors returned, as did the leech, and the same procedure was repeated; it ended in the same futile manner. Torturers were brought and set to work to extract the truth; but Campbell promptly fainted, and the attempt was given up.

Another day came. Clinging to the bars, Campbell gazed afar and saw Thorn still in place, still watching. It was like an hallucination to him now. He raved, laughed, wept, and staggered back to his straw pallet, cursing and shouting until weakness claimed him. Toward evening he reeled to the window once more.

Thorn was still on watch; beside him, this time, was a man, apparently talking to him. Black Angus? No. Campbell strained to see more clearly.... A man in dark robe and the square biretta of a doctor, who put out a hand to the dog's collar and went away, Thorn accompanying him unwillingly but peaceably.

Campbell remembered little more; another day and another, and he tossed on his straw bed, unable to think or speak. His inquisitors did not come back, nor did Thorn. He was abandoned by all, and the realization was horrible.

THE NEXT thing he could realize was Thorn: The cold nose was against him, the eager tongue licking his cheek. He laughed wildly and fondled the dog with weakly failing hand, thinking it a dream; but it was not. Something stung and burned his wound with such agony that it brought him for a moment to clear consciousness.

A man was bending over him, a man in a square biretta, with piercing gray eyes.

"Yes, this is he," said the man. "Here is the scar of the injury I treated before. You know me, M. de Glenlyon?"

"No," muttered Campbell. "Did Thorn bring you here?"

"He did not. I was on my way here with orders from M. de Guise, when I met him. He is safe; he will recover from his hurts." The visitor straightened up and glanced around. "I will vouch for everything," he said to someone else. "Carry him to the house I am occupying, which belongs to the Duchesse de Valentinois."

"Oh," exclaimed a voice. "The house of Diane de Poitiers, in the Rue Neuve?"

"Exactly. And look to his safety, messieurs; the Duc de Guise will be here tomorrow himself, and will inquire most strictly in all you have done regarding this man!"

Campbell's wandering senses fled again, and for a while he had no further conscious moments.

He did not see Guise on the morrow, but his rescuer did. Gray eyes, very red cheeks, a grizzled brown beard, an air of almost majestic calm and restraint, long quiet hands and a gravely composed voice; such was Michel de Notredame, doctor of arts and medicine. Now he stood quietly while the Duc de Guise talked in his fluent, vivacious manner.

"You have done well, M. de Notredame, and I am greatly rejoiced. I am on my way to Paris and shall not wait to see Glenlyon." Le Balafré laid a heavy purse on the table. "Spare no expense, I charge you, for I am greatly in his debt."

Notredame inclined his head. "His condition is serious, but he will recover."

"Under your care, that's assured," said Guise heartily. "As I told you, it was most remarkable how the prediction you made me came to pass. This brings up the other matter I mentioned, the request of my niece the Queen Dauphine. When can you visit the court, which will soon be established in Paris?"

"I have no business at court," Notredame said calmly. "I am busy with this outbreak of the plague here, in the poorer quarter of the city. These folk have need of me."

"Careful, monsieur! These canaille are of no consequence whatever."

"There we differ, monseigneur," replied Notredame, with dignity, though a flash lit his eyes. "The poor and friendless and obscure—the canaille, as you term them—have an equal importance with kings, in the sight of the Creator."

"No doubt, no doubt, but certainly not in my sight," said the duke lightly. "Now, Madame my niece has requested that you visit her, to tell her of the future. From one already twice a queen, such a request is a command."

"That is quite true," replied Notredame. "But the court has physicians who are far better than I: Master Chretien, for example, the foremost physiologist of the age; or the great Ambroise Paré, king of all surgeons, who saved your life at the siege of Calais."

Guise betrayed a certain impatience.

"I am not accustomed to argument or objection," he said coldly. "No other physician has your ability to combat the plague; but this is not a question of physicians. Either from God or Satan, you have knowledge of the future."

"What comes of God works no evil, monseigneur," stated Notredame. "There is no lack of astrologers who would rejoice at such a summons. Ruggieri, for example, who serves Her Majesty the present Queen—"

"Upon my word, monsieur, are you determined to affront me?" exclaimed Guise, pale with anger. "It should be enough when I say that the Dauphine desires your presence at Paris."

"Monseigneur, I have no knowledge of the future," said Notredame. "I can, it is true, obtain such knowledge, which may or may not be exact. I have been of some small service to His Majesty the King, at his command, but already I have been away from my home and family for some time."

Guise regarded him narrowly. "Maître Michel, you have a name for wonders, both at court and among common folk. The peasants plant their crops by your advice. You prate of horoscopes and astrology, but I have heard it rumored that your dealings might be with sorcery rather than with the stars. A crafty man, Notredame! Have you some reason for this evasion?"

Skilled as he was at concealment, Notredame could not entirely hide a flicker of uneasiness. The duke saw this.

"Good! You have a reason. What is it? I order you to tell it!"

"Monseigneur, there are perils which may be averted, as in your own case," Notredame replied with slight agitation, "but there are also happenings which cannot be averted. Of such it does only harm to speak."

"I understand what you mean; all men must die, eh?" Guise nodded. A smile flashed across his scarred face. "Come, I'm a soldier; for once, speak the unveiled truth! Do you predict my death?"

"No, monseigneur. You will live for a year, two years; but you will have witnessed, before you die, four kings on the throne of France."

The duke stiffened suddenly. "Good God, man! Do you know what you say? François, Henri, the Dauphin—" He broke off abruptly. "Why, this is nonsense! The King is in perfect health, although it is true that he has much pain from his teeth. Nonsense!" Yet, with the word, he bent his brows on Notredame intently. His tone changed. "Is this your reason?"

"You have forced me to say what I did not want to say—" began Notredame.

IN UPON him broke the duke, with almost savage insistence that would not be denied.

"Then go and tell my niece, do you hear? She is already Queen of Scotland in fact, and of England by right; it will do her no harm to be told that she is to become Queen of France as well! When shall you be in Paris?"

Notredame sighed. "In ten days, monseigneur, I shall depart with my assistants and M. de Glenlyon. But, I beseech you, say no word to anyone of this conversation."

"I'm no such fool. You have my word," said Guise with a species of wondering contempt. "What nonsense, what arrant nonsense! The King is barely forty; he's good for another twenty years. Why, his death would plunge the world into ruin! Beware of yourself if you spread such reports, monsieur! I shall send my niece word to expect you within two weeks; see to it. Fill her pretty head with any such fancies you like; after all, the wife of the Dauphin may well expect to be Queen some day. But no nonsense! *Adieu,* monsieur."

The duke strode out of the room, called to his waiting attendants, and was gone.

"Plunge the world into ruin, indeed!" Notredame drew a deep breath. "Many a king before Henri has died, and the world moves on regardless! Well, I have hidden the real reason behind one that to him seemed more important; and still I have failed. So I must go to Paris. What is written, cannot be averted."

He sank into a chair and struck a bell on the table. His composure returned; he was impassive and inscrutable as ever, when Brion entered and stood expectantly.

"You rang, Maître?"

"In ten days we must go to Paris, Actæus. Where is that prince of healers, that marvel of the age, our good M. de Fobert?"

"Oh! André has gone to make the rounds of the plague patients, Maître Michel, with the new powder you gave us."

"When he returns, warn him that we shall have to work within a few days, all three of us. How is the son of Scotia and his dog?"

Brion showed his white teeth in a smile. "Both doing excellently, though he's weak."

"I shall visit him in a few moments. Has he done much talking?"

"More listening, Maître. I have told him everything. His only question is why you call me Actæus when my name is Brion."

He laughed again. Notredame smiled slightly.

"Well, there need be no secrets from him, though he may

not understand. Actæus, whom the goddess Diana changed into a tree because he surprised her secrets—a good name for you, my friend and pupil! We have often sat at the feet of Diana, and shall again, though I shrink from the ordeal just now facing us. Yes, we have shared many secrets."

"And the shy goddess has not yet changed me into a tree," said Brion, laughing. Then he sobered, with a look of surprise. "You say there need be no secrets from Glenlyon? That is something new, and most astonishing!"

Notredame nodded. "Yes, Brion, but I have enemies. All those who do good have enemies, and the forces of evil are abroad in the world, increasing hourly in strength. This man Glenlyon, as he is known, does what I cannot do; he sheds blood, in the cause of good. I am not anxious to become a martyr, as you know. Death at the stake, the death of a sorcerer, makes no appeal whatever to me. That is why I profess astrology; for judicial astrology, the alleged science of reading the stars, is protected by Holy Church."

IT WAS quite true that Notredame—or Nostradamus, as he was known in the Latin tongue then so universal—pretended to astrology, a science which in private he dismissed with contempt and disdain. Twice had his books of Centuries been published, under the King's favor. These quatrains, numbering nearly a thousand, predicted the events of history during the coming four hundred years; but they were couched in language so unintelligible and profound that their meaning was entirely lost to the public at large.

Yet, for his son who was still a boy in Provence, Notredame had set down a key to these prophecies of his. He kept this key a dread secret; he had a horror of suffering the fate of a sorcerer, and in all that he wrote, he adopted a symbolism designed to veil his actual meaning from vulgar understanding.

Thus, in conversation with his two chosen pupils and assistants, men of remarkable gifts, he referred to the occult practices which they shared as "sitting at the feet of Diana the goddess." This, in effect, had the simplest of meanings, as Campbell soon was to learn. Notredame himself, behind his assumed airs of mystery, was the simplest of men and the kindest.

To Campbell, lying in a room overlooking the garden, so weak that he could scarce lift hand to caress the head of Thorn who lay beside him, the very aspect of Notredame was magical. This man who sat by the bed looking at him and talking with him, exerted an extraordinary personal force; Campbell, then and later, attained a comprehension of what it was.

"The Duc de Guise was just here," Notredame told him abruptly. "He has confirmed your identity, to the city officials; you have nothing more to fear. The man Hamilton has vanished, although search is being made for him. Therefore you may return to your post at court whenever you so elect. In ten days I am leaving for Paris, and shall take you with me. By that time, you'll be quite able to travel. You must be recovered by then— you must!"

"I owe you thanks beyond measure, Maître Notredame," said Campbell earnestly. "I owe you my life; Brion has told me of all you've done for me."

"I shall confide a secret to you; I have done nothing," said the other gravely. "I am an agent, nothing more. This is a teaching of the greatest importance."

"Whatever it means, whatever you think it means, you're an angel!" Campbell said, smiling. As though he understood the words, Thorn rose at this moment and went to Notredame, put his head on the physician's knee. "Look!" exclaimed Campbell. "He knows it too! Did you ever see a dog speak more plainly of gratitude? He knew what I was saying!"

"He felt it, you mean." Notredame smiled at Thorn and touched his head. "Yes, when I saw him, in the street, I knew you were there; the rest was simple. You will go back to your post at court?"

"Never. I'm not used to such a life. It revolts me."

"So? Then what? One must live."

"Back to Scotland, I suppose. I'm homesick for simplicity and honesty."

"You are, then, wealthy?"

"I have nothing except my father's farm and a few sheep."

"You are mistaken," said Notredame. "The Duc de Guise left a pouch for you. I looked into it and found it filled with gold. It is his way of discharging an obligation. Further, monsieur, you go to Paris with me. The whole world of France will be there to share in the festivities, and of Spain likewise. I think that much awaits you there."

"I'll not return to court, I tell you!"

"You need not. The Dauphine—or as she is more often called, the Queen Dauphine—will discharge you; I shall certify that you are unfit for further service. Simple, eh?"

Campbell eyed the speaker curiously.

"You are a strange man, Maître Notredame. Do you really know all the future?"

"Alas, no!" A certain irritation crossed the physician's face. "Can you not understand what I have said? I know nothing. I only know what is told me by those—" He checked himself abruptly and rose, looking down at Campbell. "I am an agent, nothing more," he repeated slowly. "I give healing and a message of tolerance. Give and take; that is all."

"One of my comrades, who had second sight as the Scots call it," Campbell said, "overheard men talking about this plot against Guise. We acted on what he heard. Also, he heard them speak of some prophecy an astrologer had uttered; perhaps he meant you. And there was something else; something about the King's helmet, which he did not understand. Do you?"

"No," said Notredame. "The King's helmet? No. I am not an astrologer, though I make pretense of being one. Now rest, monsieur. You are safe, you are my guest; my two assistants shall keep watch over you, and I am near if necessary. Your wound is cleansed and well. You have much to do; make yourself ready for it."

He left the room abruptly. Thorn came back to Campbell and curled comfortably at his master's side.

Safe and well, everything cleared away! Strange, what confidence and assurance this man inspired; his power came from a perfect serenity of spirit. Campbell did not worry about what his words might portend; his hand touched gently on the sword-scarred shoulder of Thorn, and he felt the affection of the huge Irish wolf-hound envelop him peacefully, as though bidding him trust in this man whose skill had brought them together again in safety.... He slept, and smiled as he slumbered.

CHAPTER XII

THE MERRY, ever-cheerful Brion, whom the singular humor of Notredame had renamed Actæus, was much with Campbell in the following days. So was the physician's other assistant, André de Fobert, a stoutish pallid man of somber and unsmiling mien, who seemed eternally wrapped up in gloomy contemplation of his own affairs. Yet he talked freely, as did Brion; both had been chosen from among the scholars of Montpellier, the great medical university of the south, by Notredame, who at twenty-nine had been one of the faculty there.

Under their words, the mantle of mystery surrounding Notredame, at least in Campbell's mind, fell away. The man stood forth human, warm, compelling. His first family wiped out by the plague, he had married again. Formerly a man of action enough, he had now withdrawn from the world in great measure; he held it better, said Brion, to heal starveling peasants in a hut than some lord in a castle.

"But," added the dancing-eyed Brion, "don't make the mistake others have done. Don't hold him as powerless and of little worth! Our good Maître Michel has a hand that reaches far, and does nothing without a purpose, though it may be hidden for a time."

"Such as healing me?" asked Campbell, smiling. "And this dog Thorn?"

"Aye, like enough," said Brion more seriously. "My master, whose tongue does not spare charlatans and all workers of evil, has made many enemies; he may well have need of a friend or two. So may others, for bloody and terrible days are close upon France. Besides, monsieur, you are one of those persons fated to accomplish definite things in the world."

"What, are you also a prophet, Maître Brion?" asked Campbell, laughing.

"All of this household are prophets alike," replied Brion curtly. This seemed rather absurd at the moment; Campbell little dreamed what matter-of-fact meaning underlay the words.

On the first day he was on his feet and out in the garden, he came upon Notredame playing with colored pebbles by the fountain. Except for a nod, Notredame ignored him; but as Thorn approached the physician, a careless swish of his tail disarranged the little stones. Campbell called back the hound rather sharply, but Notredame lifted a hand.

"Wait, wait!" he said, and began to laugh amiably, gazing upon the pebbles and then looking up at Campbell. "Perhaps the dog is wiser than us all; yes, yes! You've never learned the Arabian game of chess, monsieur? This is my substitute for it. Aye, Thorn has unwittingly done us a good turn here! Facts, like these pebbles, fall together; here's a new alignment. The other day you mentioned the King's helmet. Now, you know the ways of the court. When does the King wear a helmet?"

"When? Never," said Campbell, "unless he is jousting."

"Of course!" Notredame beamed, his gray eyes very sharp. "And who is the greatest or most powerful person in France, after the King?"

"Diane de Poitiers, or perhaps M. de Guise."

"Wrong." Notredame spoke cheerfully, and scattered the pebbles with a gesture. "Yes, I begin to see clearly, thanks to you and Thorn. From Paris, monsieur, you're going to go on an errand—you and Thorn, and perhaps one or two more. It is not yet clear."

Campbell smiled. "An errand for you? Very gladly."

"For me and for others. We'll learn more tonight." Notredame rubbed his hands as though pleased. "It begins to come clear. A dreary business, a dark and ominous business, even a desperate one. I would gladly avoid it, but dare not. And tonight I shall be told the answers and receive my instructions."

These words made no sense whatever to Campbell. Now Notredame turned to him with an intent air.

"The greatest and most powerful person in France is a woman whom everyone despises. Not a good woman, either; just now she is plotting, or acquiescing in, the murder of her husband. And against my desire, I must help her; like me, she is an agent of destiny. Now tell me frankly. What's your ambition?"

"To return to Scotland," said Campbell, brushing aside what he took to be wandering words; though later he remembered them. "And to take with me, perhaps, a young lady now maid of honor to the Queen Dauphine."

"Her name?"

"Lady Anne Haworth."

"If I offered you the chance to go home again honored and secure, what would you say?" Notredame frowned. "Mind, I say *chance,* and a perilous chance!"

"Why, I'd say thanks again, with all my heart!"

"And you'd be a fool," exclaimed the other. "Scotland? A land of blood and bitter war and treachery without equal! The clouds are gathering dark above Scotland."

"Yet it is still Scotland!" said Campbell, smiling.

"I see ahead; you see looking backward. However, I must go look at the plague patients, and tonight we'll speak with those from whom my instructions come." Notredame produced a knife and began to whittle at a quill. "Tolerance, tolerance! Will Scotland, or France or the whole of Europe, ever learn it except by bitterest anguish?"

He departed, scowling upon his quill and muttering. He did much writing; in fact, several times each day messengers brought letters to the house or took others away. It was not difficult to conjecture that Maître de Notredame kept a shrewd finger upon the pulse of events by means of many correspondents. As for the incident of the pebbles, Campbell straightway forgot it or anything it might signify.

Nor did he give any credence to mystery or talk of predictions. He had a firm Scots belief in second sight or the supernatural as a possibility; he wanted nothing to do with it as an actual practice. As for sorcery—well, sorcery was an evil thing, concerned with incantations and massive volumes and magic formulas galore, whereby one dealt with the Devil in person. And there was no least indication of sorcery about this house.

He dined in the evening with Notredame and Brion, while Fobert served them. Campbell bethought himself again of sorcery, and with a laugh turned to the physician.

"After hearing so many wondrous things about you, Maître Michel, and experiencing a few of them myself, one would expect to see books around you, written by all the great alchemists and necromancers!"

Brion's gaze sharpened, and Fobert looked startled; but Notredame nodded calmly.

"Once I had many such volumes, my friend; my home at Salon, in Provence, was filled with such books. Well, I took my fill of them, and then gave them all to the flames, lest they delude others to the practice of magic. The only magic I know comes from within and works for good. To deal with false or evil spirits is damnation."

"You speak as though evil spirits actually exist!"

The brows of Notredame came down in a grave frown.

"They do. There is no religious belief that does not comprise good and evil spirits. Have you yourself no belief in angels and devils, as the Church teaches?"

"Oh, I suppose so," Campbell admitted. "But everyday life is quite another thing."

"Not necessarily," said the other, and remained silent.

Then Fobert entered hastily.

"Maître Michel! A messenger has just arrived; he is entering now."

"Have him fed in the kitchen, and bring me the message."

Fobert departed. Presently he returned, handing Notredame a missive wound with red cord and heavily sealed. Tearing it open, Notredame read it carefully; he glanced up, his lips twisting in a slight smile, at Campbell.

"The pieces are now falling into shape. Your old acquaintance Hamilton is at the chateau of Minard."

"Minard!" exclaimed Brion. "Why, that is only three leagues from Paris!"

"Precisely."

"Then he has been arrested and taken?"

"On the contrary. He is too well protected."

"By whom?" Campbell demanded heatedly.

Notredame merely shrugged. But Brion spoke out:

"That chateau and its lands belong to the Constable, Montmorency."

"It is not important," Notredame said calmly. "The man Hamilton is not alone there. With him are a number of Frenchmen, an Englishman, and a Spaniard. I do not yet know who the Frenchmen are. The Englishman is Sir John Preble, of the suite of Throckmorton, the English ambassador. The Spaniard is the hidalgo Don Almiro de Soto, one of the commissioners from Madrid attending the royal marriages…. Here; this is for you, monsieur."

From his own packet, he took a single sheet ot paper, folded over and sealed. It was addressed to Malcolm Campbell, in his care. Astonished, Campbell tore it open; his face changed, and swift pleasure came into his heart. There were only a few lines of writing, in Latin:

> I am rejoiced that you are well and safe. The ring is safe. Angus is here, recovering. Come soon; she whom we serve has need of you. So have I.
>
>   Anne.

Campbell glanced up, his eyes alight.

"It is from her!" he exclaimed. "Then, your message is from the court, also!"

"In an hour or two," said Notredame, "we shall have a message from a greater court, my friend. Play the part of wisdom, and you may learn greatly."

"Wisdom!" Campbell shrugged. "That's the least of my qualities. Tell me, how does one acquire this thing you call wisdom?"

Notredame rose from the table.

"From a beginning and a conviction, a mastery and a fulfillment, wisdom comes quietly and unknown," he said, and strode out of the room. The door slammed.

Campbell looked again at the message from Anne, and forgot all else. She was well; she knew where he was!

One thing he did understand, however. This was that Notredame held many strings in those long fingers of his. Communication was the secret of knowledge, and he must be in communication with many, in touch with the court and others. His information was explainable. Need of him? That was curious, thought Campbell, but pleasant; he wondered why there should be any need of him. Campbell was something of an enigma to himself, as most men are. He did not realize the peculiar steadiness that marked him, the poised balance of mind and body.

THIS NIGHT, however, he had need of all his steadiness. Brion came and changed his bandages, then took a chair by the table at the window, which looked out upon the garden and the stars. Presently Fobert appeared.

Then Notredame came and sat at the table, where a candle burned. With him he brought quills and inkhorn and paper. It was all quite calm and matter-of-fact, but suddenly Campbell realized what was going on, and a thrill shot through him as he lay watching. The veil of mystery was about to be lifted before his very eyes.

"It is perhaps a pity," the bearded physician said gravely, "that the world is so little advanced in comprehension of things unseen! We are all true believers, yet the accusation of sorcery would be swiftly leveled against us, as indeed it is already, were it known what we do here. I trust in your discretion, M. de Glenlyon; you yourself are comprised within the purposes of destiny."

"You know well that you need have no fear of me," said Campbell, so attracted and drawn by the man's personality that he could ignore what he considered to be an aberration of thought. "So you're about to consult your oracle?"

"You named it well; an oracle indeed," was the reply. "Some consult the stars, as is lawful; we go beyond them, direct to those in the other world. We three have found in one another a certain sympathy and understanding. Yet to few men is it given to use the same means. To one the stars, perhaps, in all truth; to another the ball of crystal, to another the mediation of the spirits, good or bad."

"And to you, perhaps," said Campbell, smiling, "the quality of utter tranquillity, of complete composure, which you so possess!"

Notredame darted at him a penetrating glance.

"Yes. That is the oracle of Diana the goddess; that is the bond among us three. To attain such composure, such mastery, is most difficult. One must be born with the gift."

While speaking, he took the hands of his two pupils; they

likewise joined hands. To the skeptical eye of Campbell this meant nothing.

"If it's so easy," he asked, "then why couldn't anyone foretell the future in this way and guard against it?"

The three men exchanged a smile. Brion replied:

"Easy, my friend? To see clearly is not easy; it demands relaxation. Can you shut off all the workings of the brain and sit composed, without thought? Try it sometime. The brain is an unruly servant. And one should welcome the future, not guard against it."

"And not avert accidents?" queried Campbell.

Brion laughed a little.

"Certain ones may be averted, others not. What folly drives men to seek to learn the future, when they cannot change one jot of it?"

"Wrong; they may profit by the knowledge," said Notredame quietly. "A man who has a knowing mind may correct and change his minor course by will and knowledge. The major orbit is beyond his human power; what he did yesterday has to do with what he does today. That is written, as they say. The event which to him seems unexpected, may have started to occur a century ago."

"When I roll a stone downhill," said Campbell, "it goes downhill!"

Notredame chuckled. "A good illustration! At first the stone could be arrested with ease; then it is more difficult; and finally impossible without an accident to stone or impediment. Your stone seems to bound down erratically; but a careful study of its course will show that it answers the laws of weight, mass, speed and angle of deflection, laws as yet unknown to mankind. So it is with a life. Yet wisdom and purpose may convert a disadvantage into advantage, a biting sorrow to an enduring faith."

"But," argued Campbell stubbornly, "you say that what is written cannot be averted!"

"True. Yet how little you can understand of the truth!" Notre-dame sighed softly. "There is predestined fact, the totality of all that is or was, and there is the balance to this: man's own free will. Again, his will is determined by his own past. A series of dying echoes, the two in time become one, like a twin star. And there is a veriest grain of weight that is a propulsive to the whole, and always the deciding factor; this is the force of the original concept of the ego—"

His voice died. Silence settled upon the room like a living, sentient thing. Campbell frowned and gave up any effort to argue or even to comprehend. He perceived that Notredame was a master of humanist philosophy—the queer and incom-prehensible system of thought which the monks and schoolmen had carried to extremes.

He sat tensed, waiting, expectant. What would come of this sorcery? For to his notion it must be some form of sorcery. The art of clairvoyance was as yet unknown by name; it was sedu-lously hidden behind other names.

Astrology, the conjunction of the stars? The burning of incense? The mutter of spells and incantations? The conjuring up of spirits? None of these things happened as he lay watch-ing. After a time, a quill began to scratch paper. Notredame had freed one hand and was writing; his other hand held those of Fobert and Brion, who sat with eyes closed. There was no ceremony, no formality; merely the silence of relaxation and the pen-scratching.

Notredame laid down the quill and sat again as before, quite immobile. Once more he began to write, frowned and hesi-tated; Brion prompted him with a low mutter of Latin, and he went on. In this way an hour passed.

The three separated. Notredame passed the paper to the others; they read, wrote down comments and additions of their own. It was a common enterprise, then!

Fobert stood up. "This is the last time," he said. "I am going back to Provence."

"Yes, you shall go," said Notredame. "You shall take with you all we do not need. Brion and I go on to Paris. Come, and I'll help you with your packing."

He and Fobert went out of the room. Brion snuffed the candle and sat there. At length he turned to Campbell.

"Well, you have seen, you have heard. The master has received knowledge and instructions. Those in the other world have spoken to us; that is the way it has come, always. The predictions of the future, the Centuries, came that way, and we disguised their meaning. Well, that is the end. It is a very good thing that you don't know what was said…. The matter will not be easy for you," he went on, as though speaking to himself. "Yet you were sent to the work; a gentleman of Scotland from across the sea, a man born to a sword! Only you could do these things."

With a gesture of farewell, he too rose and left; Campbell remained alone with Thorn. What message and instruction had Notredame received? He did not know; evidently it was to be kept secret. Or had he received anything at all?

A level-headed man was Malcolm Campbell. He had been told much, but he himself had seen or experienced nothing. He had been brought up in a Scots belief in the supernatural and made no attempt to deny its possibilities; but just now he retained a somewhat skeptical point of view, while at the same time giving Notredame full credit as a man of exceptional gifts.

There was no doubt that far and wide, from highest to lowest, Notredame was regarded as one who knew the future, an astrologer of wondrous talent, a physician of renown; and, in some quarters, as a downright sorcerer. Now, in plain words, Campbell had been told exactly how this master of the occult worked; and he put precious little credit in the whole affair.

"What's to prove he was in communication with the other world, as he terms it? Nothing," Campbell told himself. "I heard no voices and saw no specters. That, of course, is no conclusive argument. Yet the man's no liar; neither are his disciples. Therefore, the obvious answer is that they're all three victims of self-delusion!"

He blew out the candle and turned in, undecided what to think. Notredame was no charlatan, and might very well suffer from delusions; at the same time, his influence and even power were far-reaching. His knowledge of the future was, to Campbell, questionable. More likely, he reflected, Notredame was so amazingly in touch with happenings all over France that he could not only foresee but actually mold in his own hands the events to come.

Upon this conclusion, Campbell—deeply impressed but by no means credulous—turned over and went to sleep.

WITH MORNING, he was tempted to think it had all been a figment of his own fancy; but there was the note from Anne to prove otherwise. *"She whom we serve has need of you."* Mary Stuart? She who could call upon all Scotland and France as well, had need of one slightly known Scots gentleman? It did not make sense!

He shaved, dressed, broke his fast and went down to the garden with Thorn. He saw only the housekeeper, for Notredame and his assistants had all been summoned to the plague-smitten quarter of town.

Campbell fingered his wound. It was healing; tonight, Brion had said, the bandages would come off. His weakness was passing, too; indeed, he was playing about the garden with Thorn, when the housekeeper came hurrying out to him.

"Monsieur! Monsieur! There is a gentleman here with a letter. He says someone must sign a receipt for it. Can you write?"

"Enough," said Campbell, laughing.

He followed her into the house. She had admitted a booted and spurred cavalier into the salon, where he stood with a heavily sealed missive in his hand. Campbell dipped a quill in ink and signed the paper extended to him, and took the letter.

"So you are of Maître Notredame's household, monsieur?" asked the cavalier in accented, lisping French.

Campbell assented.

"For the moment, yes," he began, and checked himself, for as he met the other's eyes, he recognized the man. It was the Italian he had knocked off the bridge at Blois, the man said to be in the service of Catherine de Medici.

"Oh!" he said. "You!"

The other bowed, and departed to his waiting horse.

When Notredame came back, Campbell gave him the letter, which bore a superscription in Latin. The physician tore it open, glanced at it, and turned to Brion, who had come home with him.

"We must leave a day earlier than I had hoped, for Paris," he said. "Another command, Actæus; this time from the King, yet written by his secretary! That is odd."

"And sent by the Queen! That is still more curious," said Campbell.

The physician regarded him narrowly.

"By the Queen? By Catherine de Medici? What do you mean, monsieur?"

Campbell told him of recognizing the man—and Notredame looked thoughtful.

"Hm! The command is from the King. But the letter was written by his secretary; it was sealed by the Queen and carried by one of her gentlemen. Obviously, therefore, he knows nothing about it, and she desires to make certain of seeing me."

Campbell smiled. "Has a prophet need of deduction?"

"He has, indeed," said Notredame, "when he deals with a Medici. What troubles me, however, is your meeting with this Italian. That may have consequences."

"Well, I'm in good shape to meet them," Campbell replied, laughing. "Look! My arm's in excellent shape, and I'm quite myself again, thanks to your skill."

"You'll need all you have, unless I'm mistaken," said Notredame. "Come, Actæus! We must get those things packed for

Fobert, if he's to get off south today. Above all, the Limousin casket with my most private papers, and its leathern case."

Fobert returned for the noon meal. His horse and a pack-animal were ready; he himself, obviously eager to get away, was ready soon afterward. A strange man, this Fobert; Campbell thought to himself that Notredame had made a very odd choice of helper and confidant. Yet his trust in Fobert was evident. Campbell was in the courtyard saying good-by when Notredame brought out the Limousin case in its covering.

He himself had seen it once or twice; always locked. It was a curious casket, made by the great master of enamels, Limousin, for the late King François, and by him given to Notredame. It was exquisitely made of blue enamel and gold; not large, yet capacious enough for papers.

"I confide my secrets and treasure to you," said Notredame, giving the leather-cased object to Fobert. "Stow it in your own saddle-bags, I charge you, and place it in the hands of my wife when you arrive at Salon."

"Master, it shall be guarded with my life," said Fobert earnestly, and stowed it away with care. *"Au revoir!* May God keep you!"

"And you," returned Notredame. *"Adieu,* my friend and pupil—*adieu!"*

At the moment Campbell thought nothing of it. But afterwards, it occurred to the Scot that Notredame, in thus replying *"Adieu!"* instead of *"Au revoir!"* had uttered a word which, on French lips, was most significant.

CHAPTER XIII

O N T H E day they set forth on the three-day ride to Paris, Campbell looked most unlike the half-naked wretch who had arrived in Orléans.

Thanks to the munificent gift of Guise, in which Notredame had refused any share, he was superbly mounted and accoutered, and was clad in a serviceable suit and cloak of wool mingled with silk, a fabric which Diane de Poitiers had made highly fashionable. What was more to the point, he wore beneath his jerkin something on which Notredame had insisted: to wit, a sleeveless shirt of fine steel links. Further, Thorn's collar had been repaired, and Campbell had brushed the lordly hound until his coat gleamed.

Brion observed the horses and the sumpter mule, and grunted, as they awaited Notredame.

"This won't be much like our entry to Paris four years ago," he grumbled, for he had a love of state and show and pomp. "Then the Constable, Montmorency, came to call upon us and the King received us, and ordered our lodging at the Cardinal of Bourbon's palace. Now we're evidently going to slink into the city like country-folk."

"The safest way!" asserted Campbell.

So they took their road, and Orléans faded behind them into the blue distance.

Why Paris? Campbell asked himself the question more than once during those three days. Why was he going? He was not sure. It was, for him, no return to court. It was not Anne Haworth's appeal. His heart was intent upon Scotland, yet he was going to Paris. He put the question frankly to Notredame, and the physician nodded.

"I go because I must," said he. "It is the same with you. Remember, you have not yet been dismissed by your Queen; you must finish this matter honorably. We shall do it together. Then your work and your way will lie before you."

"I am greatly in your debt," said Campbell. "What you say, that shall I do."

"Good," replied Notredame. "Leave it so and do not vex yourself."

The advice was sound, but Campbell noted that the adviser did not take it to himself. Maître Michel de Notredame was in a frowning mood from the moment Orléans fell behind and

his worry was obvious even if the cause were hidden. He rode wrapped in his cloak despite the warm weather, and his usually cheerful countenance was drawn and set.

Brion partook of his master's mood, being curt and uncommunicative; his usually bright eye was cheerless, his laugh was not in evidence. Thorn was the only joyous member of the party. Once Notredame remarked this, fastening his piercing gray gaze on the hound.

"There goes one who can afford to frisk and play," said he dourly. "His work is done; ours lies ahead."

What he meant by this, however, he did not disclose....

Boisseau and Mondesir fell behind them, Chatres and Longjumeau were passed, and at length they came into Paris of an afternoon, late. Once past the barrier with its customs

*A bellow came from her: "Help, Malcolm,
for God's love! Messire Ronsard! Help!"*

examination, they headed for the inn called Soleil de Provence,
in the St. Germain quarter.

Here Notredame was received with impressive honor; ample
room was made for this distinguished guest and for his companions.

Once arrived, Campbell went to the physician's room, found
Notredame alone, and demanded their program.

Notredame, with some evidence of agitation, complied.

"Brion has gone to take word of our arrival, monsieur. If the
Queen Dauphine receives us this evening, well and good."

"You speak as though our business with her were of scant
importance!" said Campbell.

"Other matters of greater importance await me, or us," Notredame replied. "You have slight confidence in me?"

"I've every confidence in you," Campbell said frankly, "but little in what you term your instructions from the other world. I've the deepest gratitude for all you've done for me, truly, and I'm at your service as you may desire; but you can't expect me to share or be satisfied with a vague occult belief enveloped in mystery."

"No; that is the pity of it. There must be a beginning and a conviction," said the other almost sadly. "Very well, monsieur. Accompany me, hear and understand all that is said, then act as you see fit. You are under no compulsion. I cannot explain to you what you and the world are not ready to comprehend. We await Actæus, we dine, we wait upon your mistress; tomorrow we see the Dame de Valentinois. Do you accept?"

"Gladly," said Campbell. "I hate to be in the dark, that's all."

"We are all in the dark. The future is gathering, gathering; like a cloud mounting the sky, it gathers force and momentum invisibly," said Notredame. "But the way must open to us all, to you and to me…. Ah, here is Brion!"

Brion came in, eyes alight. Mary Stuart would send one of her gentlemen to bring Notredame at nine o'clock.

"Good!" exclaimed the physician. "You must stop here, Actæus; I am expecting a courier at any hour with news of Fobert, and he must not be missed. And now to dinner, messieurs!"

"The future is gathering, like a cloud mounting the sky!" The words lingered with Campbell and expressed aptly what had been dimly growing and impressing itself upon him during these latter days. Perhaps it was a mere delusion of the senses, he told himself, upon which those words neatly fitted; or perhaps it was an idea adroitly implanted within him by Notredame. None the less he had been vaguely conscious of gathering forces afar that were now rushing to culmination, as in the

deathly quiet before a storm one feels the approaching convulsion.

NOTREDAME SUDDENLY was in better spirits, as though this summons had dispersed his deeper worries. He laid out a thick golden chain and a gown trimmed with fur, to wear later; not for warmth, but for display. The sumptuary laws strictly limited the wearing of *vair*, or sable, to the great nobility and the royal family. That these laws had in the case of Notredame been lifted by the King himself, four years previously, was a token of high distinction which the physician dared not omit in presenting himself at court.

All through dinner, in fact, Notredame talked garrulously, almost gayly. He told how Cinderella's slipper of *vair*, denoting her rank, had on the lips of story-tellers become *verre* or glass—meaningless in fact, but far more dear to the hearts of children. He launched into a discussion of Provencal and medical phrases, disclosing a curious and abstruse knowledge of such matters, and closely questioned Campbell upon certain aspects of Highland speech. He was, in short, a different man; and when preparing to depart, he laughed and jested with Thorn, and ordered Campbell to bring the dag along.

"Bring him, bring him! He's known at court; why not? And, I advise you, return him to the lady who first owned him. I have an idea that he too has a part to play in the matters of destiny. He has already shown as much."

Mary Stuart's gentleman arrived; he was one whom Campbell knew slightly. With much bowing and polite phrases he set forth with them through the narrow, twisting streets. Now and again archers of the watch stopped them, instantly passing them upon recognition. Paris was well guarded at night and had sore need of it; the city was filled with adventurers and rascals during these days of celebration.

The turreted palace of the Tournelles, still a royal residence although fated to end its days all too soon as a horse-market, came into view ahead. Here, said their guide, were quartered the royal family and the greatest nobles of France and Spain, just arrived from Chenonceaux with the King. And here, in the Rue St. Antoine, were to be erected the magnificent barriers with which the celebrations were to be closed. The King himself, and Guise and others were to take part in the jousting; the age of chivalry was barely ended, and jousting was still the keenest sport of the great, who held their position by virtue of birth and physical prowess rather than by favor and possessions.

Upon reaching the palace, a lofty mass crowned by numerous towers and pinnacles which gave rise to its name of Tournelles, the visitors were passed by the guards and led straight to the private apartments of the Dauphin and Mary Stuart. In the antechamber waited a number of the household gentlemen and ladies, who greeted Campbell joyfully—and Notredame with great respect, for the Dauphine was impatient to receive him.

Campbell's eye swept the place in vain; Anne Haworth was not here. But, a few moments later, upon entering the private chamber of Mary Stuart, Thorn escaped from him eagerly and the little queen broke into vivacious laughter as the tall wolf-hound greeted Anne.

"Here's a breach of all etiquette, certainly!" exclaimed Mary Stuart merrily. "I'm nothing, dear Anne, and you're everything! Greeting, gentlemen, greeting!"

Amid the formal salutations, which the ready tongue of Notredame handled admirably, Campbell could exchange only a look and a smile with Anne Haworth, who with the other ladies was sent beyond earshot, Thorn accompanying them. He kissed the fingers of Scotland's queen, and Notredame spoke for him, alleging his inability to continue at court.

"However, M. de Glenlyon is acquainted with my secrets," went on the physician, "and is eager to remain in your service, madame."

"Very well, very well," said Mary Stuart impatiently. "It shall be so arranged; if you prefer Scotland to her Queen, monsieur, there'll be no objection. And perhaps I shall avail myself of your services in a day or two. Now, Maître Notredame, I sent for you because I insist upon the privilege of a woman: curiosity!"

Campbell was dismissed. He joined the ladies, touched his lips to Anne's fingers, and stood silent with her, as ceremony demanded.

What was happening between Notredame and Mary Stuart? Impossible to tell at the moment; but, from the suave bearing of the physician, Campbell strongly doubted whether he was uttering grave prophecies, and Notredame later told him as much.

"One does not confide in a child of seventeen, monsieur, the secrets of the other world. Rather, one says only what the ears of seventeen would most love to hear."

Indeed, the countenance of Mary Stuart evinced only wonder, joy, and vivid interest; she clapped her hands gayly and her gaze fastened upon Notredame in delight and marveling as he responded to her questions.

CAMPBELL FELT a slight pressure on his arm, and caught the soft murmur of Anne Haworth at his ear: "Madame Diane wants him to come to her hotel tomorrow, an hour before noon. Come with him. I shall be there."

Campbell nodded and met her eyes for an instant.

"Understood," he murmured almost inaudibly. "Can you keep Thorn now?"

Her face lit up with gladness. She nodded silently. Campbell stooped and touched the dog's neck.

"Stay here; down, Thorn!" he breathed, and met understanding in the dog's eyes.

The voice of Mary Stuart was lifted and reached them.

"You will do it, Maître Notredame? The horoscopes of me and of my dear François?"

"Madame," said Notredame, bowing, "I shall consult the stars this night and send you the results tomorrow. Remember, any fool can watch the stars and calculate their courses; it is the result of these calculations that is important, the deductions drawn from them and what is told therein! This, madame, is the whole secret of astrology."

Mary Stuart was more than delighted; she was transported with joy at what she had heard. She presented Notredame with a jewel from her finger. She called Campbell and spoke of his services in ardent terms.

"You shall hear from me shortly, monsieur," she promised. "Madame my mother sent you to me, and I shall return you to her, eh? Good night, gentlemen!"

They retired, bowing. Thorn remained; Campbell was inwardly rather bitter about this.

In the antechamber, he took Notredame's arm and delivered Anne's message.

"Excellent, excellent!" exclaimed the physician. "Now out of this place, quickly, for haste presses and I fear that destiny is at her work."

A guard and an escort of link-boys saw them back home to the Soleil de Provence in all honor.

There Brion came hurriedly to meet them, excitement evident in his manner.

"News, Maître Michel!" he exclaimed. "A courier with a message from Fobert, just as you predicted! Good news, I trust?"

In his room Notredame took the message Brion handed him, tore it open, and crushed the paper in his hand.

"He was attacked by thieves on the way south," he said. "The Limousin casket, with all my most precious papers, was stolen. Now get me the inkhorn and the quills, and leave me."

He took the evil news, thought Campbell, with surprising calmness. And with morning, he was serenity itself; once more Notredame was impassive, composed, apparently quite untroubled. Campbell questioned Brion about it, and had only a shrug and a guarded word for response.

"I know no more than you, Monsieur de Glenlyon; my master has his own secrets. And his own enemies, let me add. If you're curious in the matter, go down the street to the inn of the Three Pilgrims and you'll hear enough."

Campbell was sufficiently curious to saunter along the street, drop in at the Three Pilgrims, and ask in English for a morning draught. Being taken for a foreigner with small knowledge of French, he was soon listening to the avid chatter around him, most of which concerned Notredame.

A Latin distych was being passed from hand to hand amid howls of laughter; it was clever enough, being entirely a play upon the words "Nostra Damus:"

> Nostra damus cum falsa damus, nam fallere nostrum est,
> Et cum falsa damus, nil nisi Nostradamus.

Campbell read it and smiled. "We give what we have, and what we have is false," he paraphrased it in brief. He was astonished, however, at the bitterness of those who were talking around him. This was a meeting-place, he gathered, for certain poets and writers of the court and the city. They were assuredly attacking Notredame hotly, accusing him of sorcery and magic, with a virulence that could be accounted for only on the score of envy.

"I had it straight from my cousin, who's a groom at the royal stables," said one, "that the Queen herself has taken up the matter and she has sworn to have him burned as a sorcerer! We're likely to see some fun yet, if that be true."

"Aye, but does Catherine stand with the heretical reformers or with the Church?" asked another. This switched the subject into a still more heated discussion, for the topic of religious hatred, soon to burst with full force throughout France, was one which made passions rise swiftly. Campbell paid his score and retraced his steps thoughtfully enough; it was evident that Maître Michel was indeed facing the enmity that was the certain accompaniment of fame.

He was scarcely back when Notredame came seeking him. Campbell donned cloak and sword-belt, and they departed in the direction of the Tournelles. The house of Diane de Poitiers was directly opposite the palace.

"Tell me something, Maître Notredame," said Campbell, as they walked along. "You have made friends and enemies with your oracular utterances, yet you seem to have small thought for money or fame. What, then, is your purpose in life?"

"To do what I must," said Notredame composedly. "And to save myself. Like all men, monsieur, I have been a fool in my time; the consequences are closing in upon me, I fear. I hope to avert them, do what good I may by the way, and retire to Provence to live out my life—a simple purpose.... What, if I may return the question, is yours?"

"Oh!" Campbell smiled, thinking of Anne Haworth. "Someone else once asked me that: It is to do my best."

"You may soon have the chance," said Notredame.

The two came to the residence of Diane de Poitiers. Opposite was the palace, with its guards and pomp; here was a stately calm assurance, as soon as they entered. They were expected, and were taken to an upper room where a number of ladies surrounded Diane, who lay upon a couch dictating letters. She received them very graciously; she had heard of his withdrawal from court, it seemed. She met the composed regard of Notredame with her own quiet, level look, and then gave him her full attention.

"Well, Maître Michel? I understand that you have a question to ask me. Do you desire that this gentleman should retire?"

The ladies had drawn away. Notredame shook his head.

"No, madame; he is in my confidence. A question? Yes. I should like to know whether you have ever considered what might happen, were His Majesty to die."

For an instant Diane eyed him, startled.

"No, I have not; why, the very thought is incredible!"

"Yet death comes to all men, madame. In such case, what would happen?"

"Oh! I see your meaning," she replied thoughtfully. "You

mean, what would happen to me. Yes, that's it. Well, it's not a pleasant thought. Of course, I'd have the support of the Duc de Guise."

"Assuredly," said Notredame, "provided he were here to give you support."

"And there's the Constable, Montmorency."

"Who would betray you in a moment."

"True," she murmured. "The Dauphin would then be King; and Mary Stuart would be Queen."

"Yes, madame." Notredame bowed. "A boy of sixteen would be King; therefore, France must be ruled by a regent, until he becomes eighteen."

"Just what are you aiming at, Maître Michel?" she demanded, sitting up and meeting the calm eye of Notredame. "You have a purpose. What is it?"

He spread out his hands in the Provencal manner.

"Ah, madame! My only purpose is to make you consider the contingencies of mortal existence, to prepare against what might happen unexpectedly, so to rule your affairs that no evil can reach you! Believe me, I hold your abilities in the deepest respect; but the aspect of the stars leads me to think that great calamities are about to befall France—"

She broke in upon him with some asperity:

"You are impertinent, Maître Michel! The stars? I pay no heed to such nonsense, as you well know. Let others play with horoscopes; I prefer facts. If it comes to warnings, then I may be the one to warn you."

Notredame bowed again. "I shall receive your words with due respect—"

"Well you may!" she broke in again. "Let me tell you that accusations of sorcery are being made against you, and only the favor and interest of the King—" She checked herself and turned abruptly to Campbell. "M. de Glenlyon, will you do me the favor of waiting in the other room? What I have to say is only for the ear of Maître Notredame."

Campbell at once withdrew to the anteroom. Here, to his joy, he found Anne awaiting him, and understood that Diane de Poitiers had sent him away with this in view. Together they went to a window overlooking the courtyard, sank on the cushioned seat, and Anne laughed softly.

"What, you don't ask after Thorn? I couldn't bring him here today. But he's well."

"I'm not," said Campbell irresolutely "I have the feeling things are under way.…. What things? I don't know."

"Well, you've obtained your dismissal from court, although I believe that our mistress is sending for you later today," said Anne. "What do you intend? Scotland?"

"I don't know that, either. What about you?"

"Oh, I'm settled where I am!" she responded, then gave him a sidelong glance "That is, unless I go back to Scotland. My father has written; he thinks I should return."

"So do I," exclaimed Campbell quickly. "An admirable idea! Then return; I'll go too—I'll escort you, in fact!"

"No," she said gravely. "I've promised Mary Stuart to remain with her as long as she needs me. If she were to become Queen of France, I'd go home in a minute, for then she would have to surround herself with French women alone. My hopes and dreams have all changed; the reality is not what I thought," she added, a little bitterly. "How right you were, how right! Well, let it pass for the moment; other things are happening. By the way, Angus of Kilspindie is here."

"Black Angus? Good, good! Where is he?"

She shook her head. "I don't know; not with the Guards, for he's left them. He was crippled by his wounds—"

Her words trailed off. Notredame was approaching.

Campbell rose and presented him. Notredame bowed.

"Madame, forgive me for having taken your liege knight; it is not for long," he said to her. "I trust that your mistress the Dauphine is not angry with him?"

"Indeed not, Maître Notredame," she replied. "On the contrary, I believe she intends to ask his service at once, on some matter; she spoke of it briefly this morning."

"We are all at her service," Notredame replied gravely. "She will have dire need of those who serve her, now and later. She is one of those persons crowned with greatness and with ill fortune alike. But now we must be off, for I have finished my work here."

Campbell touched his lips to Anne's hand; there were a thousand things he wanted to say, but what he read in her eyes was for the moment enough. He was forced to depart with Notredame, who hurried off in silence. Only once, on the way back to the inn, did Notredame break this silence, and then it was as though speaking to himself.

"One more interview remains, the last, the most terrible of all!" he murmured.

"You'll see the King?" Campbell asked.

Notredame shook his head.

"No. It was not he who sent for me—but Catherine, in his name. Ah, that little Queen of yours, Mary Stuart! Clever, headstrong— Well, she shall have her little hour of brightness and success, before the forces of evil close in upon her. When she summons you, go by all means."

"Naturally," said Campbell. He had begun to think this this worthy physician talked too much; also, he was inwardly embittered and angry. So Anne had determined to remain as long as Mary Stuart was Dauphine! That might be for years to come!

Back at the inn, they found Brion gone. Notredame turned to Campbell, came to him, took him by the arms and looked into his face for a moment.

"My friend," he said quietly, "we have followed many diverse threads; now they begin to come together, now comes what was written and what not the wisest man could overturn. I have trusted you, with reason; you will not betray my trust, as did Fobert."

"What!" Campbell started. "Betray you? He, your pupil and

co-worker? But the message said that he was set upon by robbers—"

Notredame smiled slightly. "Who knew what to take and where to find it, yes. This is our farewell; we shall meet again, I think, before long, but not alone. You are healed, you are again strong, and your work awaits you."

"But I have none," said Campbell. "That's just the trouble, Maître Michel! I'm at loose ends—"

"So you think; you'll learn differently. Take my blessing, for what it's worth to you. Sooner or later, all roads come together and the troublous winds are hushed, and man reaches understanding. It is better to do what one can, to do one's best, and to be content, than strive to attack the stars. That's your virtue. You are an honest man in a world of deceit and treachery, and I honor you. Farewell."

"Farewell, if it must be," said Campbell, gripping the hand whose touch seemed so alive and invigorating. "But I don't see why you say farewell now."

Feet pounded on the stairs, a fist hammered at the door. To Notredame's word, it opened to show the innkeeper.

"Monsieur!" he cried at Campbell. "Monsieur de Glenlyon! There is a gentleman below who is seeking you, a gentleman from the court."

"Who is he?" demanded Campbell, astonished.

"M. de Ronsard, the famous poet. A great gentleman, monsieur! He asks that you come down to him. He has come, he said, to take you with him."

Campbell glanced at Notredame, who laughed and waved his hand.

"Behold the response to your question! That is why, monsieur. Farewell again!"

And Campbell repeated the word which he had heard Notredame use to the departing Fobert, and whose use he now comprehended—the word *"Adieu!"*

CHAPTER XIV

DESPITE THE deafness that had driven him from diplomacy into poesy, Ronsard was gay, merry, filled with overflowing energy. Born to the court, an adept in its ways, he saluted Campbell most courteously. Although only thirty-five, he was already known as the greatest poet in France.

"I was sent to command your presence, monsieur; the Queen Dauphine desires to see you in private," he said. "There's no haste, however. She's riding at the moment with the Dauphin. And I'm famished. Shall we have a bite and a bottle of wine?"

"I'll not say 'no' to that!" rejoined Campbell gladly.

They settled down in the ordinary of the inn, and over the wine Ronsard waxed voluble. He fairly worshiped Mary Stuart and made no secret of it.

"What a delicious handful! What a lovely child!" he rhapsodized. "And when one thinks her most a child, what a clever woman is suddenly revealed! This Tudor lady of England, this Elizabeth; do you know her? No? Nor I. Three years I spent in England, and never had a glimpse of her. She was not much thought of in those days. But I learned English—'To your health, milord! Goddam! Good day and how are you? To the devil with you, and a pox take you!'"

He laughed heartily at his own knowledge of English, which had not apparently been picked up in court circles. Then he rambled on about Elizabeth.

"A cold one, they tell me, with a most curious and inexplicable pride in her own virgin state. And certainly she works coldly enough, by means of agents and spies and ambassadors; but our Dauphine is a match for her any day in the year."

Campbell listened smilingly. It seemed to him that Ronsard was sizing him up rather keenly and studiously as he rattled on. The Frenchman's enthusiasm ran from Mary Stuart to her maids of honor.

"Lovely creatures, these fair Scots ladies; at least the King found one of them very lovely: Miss Fleming—you do not know her? No, she has not been at court lately. But they are lovely, eh?" He winked knowingly at Campbell. "I seem to remember that you found them so when you were at Blois, monsieur. Or at least one of them—the one that had a dog—the cool and aloof one."

"Lady Anne."

"Yes, yes; a magnificent creature!" Ronsard blew a kiss from his fingers. "It was the same one. Why, you should have seen her; she was magnificent! She stood and said never a word, as though overcome by shame and chagrin, while our little Dauphine berated her. Aye, took her dismissal as though it meant nothing at all to be leaving the most glorious court on earth!"

Campbell set down his mug. His first thought was that the debonair poet was drunk; yet, though Ronsard did not neglect the wine, he was not under its influence.

"Who in the fiend's name are you talking about?" shouted Campbell at the other's ear. "Not Anne Haworth?"

"Why, certainly! It was something about that huge dog of hers. You needn't shout, monsieur; I don't hear well, but just the same I catch more than people imagine." Ronsard nodded sagely.

"Anne, you say? Dismissed?" Campbell stared.

"Aye, and before everybody! But you did not know? A thousand pardons!" The deaf poet ran on with apologies and excuses, to which Campbell scarcely listened.

And to think she had not said a word about it; in fact, had said just the contrary! Yet in their talk Campbell had felt something amiss. "The reality is not what I thought," she had said, almost sadly.

Yet it was only an hour ago that he had parted from her, and she had given no hint! He bethought himself, ordered more wine, plied Ronsard with it eagerly, and got evasive replies, with a few grains of truth. Yes, it had happened this very morning, early. Thorn had somehow displeased Mary Stuart or the Queen, the poet said. Such a monstrous hound had no place in a palace, anyway.

"Lucky fellows, you Scots!" Ronsard was feeling his wine now. "Always around her, always at her service, while people like me must stand afar off and sigh in secret, or else make poems about it!" Chuckling, he emptied his mug, and Campbell refilled it quickly. "Not bad wine, this; I must bear the place in mind. What's the brand, Val de Loire? I didn't know it could be had this side of Orléans! To your health, monsieur!"

Anne dismissed! No wonder she had seemed changed. Where was she now? Campbell asked. Ronsard shrugged to the repeated question. When one was dismissed, he said vaguely, it was like a king dying; no one cared or knew.

"Wrong," said Campbell, glowering over his mug. "I was dismissed myself, only the other day."

Laughter shook the poet. "But you're a man, always of use! A woman is of no value to anyone, except her lover. What are the three most useless things on earth? An unloved woman, a broken soldier, and a masterless dog. There's the subject for a very pretty rondel, my friend!"

"Apparently this Queen Dauphine of ours," Campbell said bitterly, "is quick to dismiss any who displease her!"

"Oh, don't blame her!" came the careless response. "It was not she. It was the Queen, the Florentine, who caused it all. How? I don't know, but Dame Catherine was at the bottom of it, be sure of that."

"Impossible!" exclaimed Campbell. "Why would the Queen want a maid of honor of the Dauphine discharged?"

"And why would the Dauphine oblige her, whom she detests?" Ronsard winked again, with display of vast inward knowledge. "Ha! I told you she was clever, this mistress of ours! But listen! What's happening?"

From the street outside came the sound of advancing tumult—oaths and shouts of men in anger, shrieks of women,

roars of laughter and of fury. Tap-boy and grooms and hostlers
poured forth to see; then they tumbled hastily back, as into the
courtyard of the inn burst a surging crowd.

Ronsard gulped down his wine and hastened out to watch.
Campbell followed him. Across the cobblestones poured the
throng. A huge figure of a woman, hobbling along with a
crooked staff, was besieged by other women who tore at her
and screamed shrill insults and commands. She was fighting
back. Archers of the watch were trying to intervene, flailing
about with their bows. Gamins were shrieking delight and
plucking at everyone within reach.

The huge woman about whom the roar centered began to
strike out with her staff. She beat down an archer, and his
comrades went at her. Crowned askew with a lace nightcap, her
garments ripped and billowing, she burst free and came hobbling straight at Campbell. A wild bellow came from her:

"Malcolm! Help, Malcolm, for God's love! Messire Ronsard!
Help!"

Campbell's jaw fell. Under the nightcap was the shaven jowl
of Black Angus.

A L E A P, and Campbell was in the courtyard, fending off
the archers of the watch. Ronsard joined him, with gleeful
recognition. The archers fell back, the crowd held sullenly aloof.
When Ronsard sent a shower of coins scattering on the stones,
the throng plunged for the money with yells of delight. The
leader of the archers pressed forward to Campbell, and with
him a panting, rotund man in the apron of an innkeeper.

"Monsieur! This man owes us money!" cried the latter, pointing at Angus. "We took his clothes, until he paid the ten crowns
he owes, and another twenty crowns for the damage done last
night. He and his friends were drunk. I am from the Inn of the
Archer, monsieur, in the Rue des Victoires behind the Tournelles."

Hastily, Campbell produced money, paid the man. He turned,
shoved Angus inside the inn, and then began to laugh. Ronsard

was roaring afresh and pressing wine on Angus, who hung between chagrin and fury.

"It's a lie, all of it!" he bellowed. "Whatever they said, it's a lie, Malcolm Campbell! Don't believe a word of it! They stole my clothes, so I took these garments from the washline and came to find you. Everything stolen or robbed…. Ah, more of this excellent wine! To your health, Monsieur Ronsard! I knew your father when he was Master of the Household to the late King François of blessed memory."

Angus not only had been drunk; he was still drunk.

"What's this lameness, and this staff?" demanded Campbell.

"All of a piece with everything," growled Angus. "Wounded in both legs, crippled, out of the Guards! That's the lot of an old soldier, not a friend in the world! But what splendid wine this is, Malcolm! And how splendid you look yourself!"

"Not bad wine, not bad," intervened Ronsard. "Here, soldier, another bottle for you!"

Angus reached for it, but Campbell knocked it aside.

"Not another drop. Come here, Angus! Down with that staff. Off with that woman's nightcap, you ninny! Come along, now. Grooms! Lend a hand!"

BEFORE ANGUS knew what was happening, Campbell had him outside again, and with the laughing grooms to help, got him doused with water from the pump.

"Get back to your own tavern, get your stuff together, and wait for me," ordered Campbell. "These grooms will give you some clothes; here's money. The Inn of the Archer?"

"Aye, that's it," exclaimed Angus, much sobered. "Not far from the palace. Mistress Anne Haworth was to come about noon, for a word with me—"

"Well, get back there as fast as you can," broke in Campbell. "It's past noon now. I must go to the palace; then I'll be along for a word with you and her both."

Angus went his way with the grooms. So Anne had known

all the while where he was, and had denied knowing! Why? Feeling baffled and angry, Campbell rejoined Ronsard, who was still laughing.

"Let's have the truth and cease tormenting me," exclaimed Campbell. "You know something. Why did the Queen want the Lady Anne dismissed? For God's sake speak out, and speak plainly!"

The poet rose, flung down money, took Campbell's arm and walked him out.

"Now, in the open air!" said he. "Monsieur, your appeal moves me; I love you for your love! Yes, the Dauphine wished the Lady Anne dismissed. It was all arranged very cleverly. The Queen was angered and demanded the dismissal of the maid, you understand? So our good Mary Stuart complied. Now do you comprehend everything?"

"I comprehend nothing," said Campbell. "I saw her only an hour or two ago and she said nothing of it."

"She was commanded to silence, that's why." Ronsard's grip tightened. "Be at ease, all is well. Our little mistress is no fool, I tell you! She wanted to send Lady Anne on an errand which she did not wish the Queen to suspect. It was all a secret."

"Is this true?" demanded Campbell.

"Upon my honor."

They walked on. Ronsard steadied after a bit.

"Now see here," he exclaimed suddenly. "For the love of the angels, say nothing about this to a soul, I implore you! I have compassion on all lovers, for I am one myself. I tried to throw you a hint or two in a roundabout manner, but I think the wine must have affected my wits this morning. You forced me to speak openly, so guard the secret."

"Upon my honor," Campbell vowed in his turn.

The palace of the Tournelles appeared before them, with workmen engaged in putting up scaffolding and seats in the Rue St. Antoine, for the jousting.

Campbell found his heart suddenly light.

The deadly spell of inaction was broken. Anne was sent from court, apparently disgraced, but in reality on some secret mission for Mary Stuart! And here was Angus close at hand, awaiting him! He himself summoned upon some service for the Dauphine…. Why, things were turning out well after all! Just as Notredame had said, the threads were being drawn together.

So they were past the guards, on inside the palace, and Campbell was taken to the same room where Mary Stuart had received him and Notredame. She was here now, awaiting him. Campbell went to one knee before her, respectfully. She sent Ronsard away, stationed her maids out of earshot, and said in a voice of excited eagerness:

"Monsieur, I am about to trust you as I would no other, because my mother Mary of Guise held you in her trust. I ask you to do me a service."

Campbell rose and bowed low.

"I am entirely at your service, madame; I hope that I may deserve your confidence."

"Careful, then! Spies are everywhere. Each person around me is watched," she said in a low voice. "Here in Paris, it is the custom for people of rank to employ spies, just as they employ assassins; everyone does it. And when one woman hates another, she neglects nothing at all."

Campbell comprehended that she referred to Catherine de Medici. Now she produced a large, carefully sealed letter, addressed to the Regent of Scotland.

"Take this, monsieur. It is a letter to my mother, who is now at Leith. Take it openly, for I misdoubt lest spies be watching us even now," she said. As Campbell obeyed, somewhat puzzled by her words, she asked: "Did you ever hear of the chateau of Minard?"

That name struck like a knell in his memory.

"Yes, madame. It is not far from Paris," he rejoined. "I understand that the man Hamilton is there, the relative of the Earl of Arran who tried to kill M. de Guise."

"Indeed? That may very well be. I remember the man un-pleasantly," she said in a most indifferent manner. Evidently she knew no details of that attempted assassination. "But another man is at that chateau, which is an old place built by the English when they held Paris besieged. It is small but curious, I understand. Well, this man is an Englishman; he is named Sir John Preble."

"An agent of the English ambassador," said Campbell. "I have heard of him."

"He will betray anyone for the sake of Elizabeth," she said, breathing the words very softly. "I am in communication with him and also with others, at that place. I think they are all cheating me. Well, I want this letter to fall into Sir John Preble's hands."

"This letter?" Astonished, Campbell tapped the missive.

She nodded quickly.

"Yes. He must not suspect that I sent you to him. Pretend to guard the letter with care—but don't risk your life, mind! Defend it, fight for it if necessary; but let him secure it. Do you understand? I want him to have it, to intercept it!"

"I understand, madame."

"And now, here is another." Mary Stuart produced a smaller envelope tied with a ribbon and sealed, but quite blank. "This bears no address; it is the real letter to my mother. The other is false, and designed to give my enemies the wrong information about me and my plans; let them have it. This one, at any cost, must not reach them, even if it must be destroyed! Take your own measures for its security." She paused, slipped the unad-dressed epistle to him. "Can you get rid of the false letter, as I want, and deliver the true to my lady mother at Leith?"

"Assuredly, madame." Campbell's admiration for her took a sudden leap. "It shall be accomplished as you desire; I swear it upon my honor."

"That is the best oath for a Scots gentleman; provided that, like yourself, he has honor upon which to swear! Too many have

not," she said. "Thank you, my friend. Now, if my cousin Elizabeth is served by a rascal who is a knight, it ill beseems my
dignity to be content with less in the case of an honorable
gentleman. Give me your poniard."

CAMPBELL REMOVED his dagger from its sheath
and handed it to her. She struck him lightly across the shoulder
and returned it, smiling.

"Sir Malcolm Campbell of Glenlyon! In the real letter, I
wrote my mother that I had done this, begging her to confirm
your knighthood publicly. And here—" She reached into her
bodice and produced an embroidered purse. "Take this, for the
expenses of your journey. There is also contained a chain and
locket, a gift from my mother. I give it to you, as to a dear friend.
Show it to my mother, that she may the better credit all that's
in the epistle. And at any cost, I beseech you," she added, a break
in her voice, "get the real letter to her; don't let them get hold
of it!"

"It shall be done," said Campbell.

"That is all. Ronsard is waiting in the courtyard with a horse
and passport for you. Go now; go at once—get out of Paris
without delay! And God keep you in His holy care, Sir Malcolm
Campbell!"

What a fiery, beautiful angel! Smart, shrewd, beating these
accursed French at their own game of intrigue, a clever woman
when she most seemed a child, as Ronsard had said! Not until
he was clear outside, did Campbell recall suddenly that she had
knighted him, and that he had not thanked her for the honor.

"Well, deeds are braver thanks than words, as the saying
goes," he reflected, and kept on his way, his head whirling. "She
said truly; get out of Paris and do it fast! I'll stop on the way
and pick up Angus, too."

IN THE courtyard, he found Ronsard and a groom, with a
saddled horse for him—one of the royal breed, as Campbell
saw at a glance. He gripped hands with the poet, swung up to

the saddle, and with a wave of the hand was clattering on his way.

Had Notredame known or guessed this errand, as Anne certainly must have guessed it? The physician's farewell had been eloquent of knowledge. And how suddenly, how swiftly, everything had happened!

Notredame's secret papers betrayed or lost with the Limousin casket; the visit to Diane de Poitiers; Anne's unexpected dismissal, and now this mission confided to him by Mary Stuart.… Everything in a sharply accented succession! Threads drawing together, yes; but he could not understand them, or what they boded.

He had not forgotten that meeting with the Italian gentleman who served the Queen. The warning of Mary Stuart was fresh in his ears; he was glad that he could leave now, at once, without returning to the Soleil de Provence. His money was in the pouch. Under his jerkin he wore the sleeveless shirt of steel links, so soft and pliable that its presence could not be perceived unless the shirt itself were revealed. He had nothing to do except stop and pick up Black Angus; then to find Sir John Preble and somehow manage this peculiar errand of his.

The Inn of the Archer was before him. As he dismounted, he recollected a folded paper that Ronsard had shoved at him. It proved to be a passport, necessary on the roads and at each town or city. He tucked it into his pocket and stepped into the inn, asking for Angus, and came to speech with the same fellow whom he had paid at the scene of the tumult.

"Oh, monsieur!" The man bowed hastily. "The gentleman is not here. He went away, just a little while ago."

"Where did he go, you scoundrel?" demanded Campbell. "Did you drive him away?"

"No, monsieur, no! All the trouble was forgotten. A lady came with a horse for him."

"A lady?" Campbell recollected Anne's engagement with Angus. "A young lady?"

"Yes, monsieur, with a monstrous huge dog. They rode away together."

Was Black Angus, then, implicated in the mysterious errand of Anne? Perhaps.

"When he returns," said Campbell, giving his name, "tell him that I've gone on to Calais and shall await him there, at the White Horse Inn. He'll know the place."

He made inquiries as to the chateau of Minard, mounted again, and took his way out of Paris.

CHAPTER XV

THE CHATEAU de Minard was a small, gloomy old structure built as a fortalice. It was ugly, primitive and without comforts. Around it was a moat—now dry—and an oval wall; against the inside of this wall were the rooms. It was like a solid chunk of honeycomb, into which were cut two segments. That in front was the courtyard, small in size, containing only a well with a stone curb. That in the rear was a garden with three apple trees.

Old and small as it was, the place had an air of solid security, always highly reassuring to persons of rank. Under King François, Minard had for a time been used as a royal prison, a purpose to which it was admirably suited; then it had passed to the family of Montmorency, under whom it remained little more than a hunting-lodge, convenient to the adjacent Bois de Boulogne.

Now it was occupied by the young Coligny, nephew of the Constable de Montmorency, and a few of his friends. With these were Hamilton, Sir John Preble, and Don Almiro de Soto, of the Spanish ambassador's suite.

Upon a warm, clear afternoon toward the close of June, these three last-mentioned, and Coligny, were walking in the garden, engaged in deep conversation. Coligny was young, irresolute, entirely in the confidence of the Bourbon and Huguenot party.

Hamilton was his positive, assured self, and had very much the air of a master here. Don Almiro was a dark restrained man with pointed beard and a silent way of being immersed in his own affairs. Sir John, on the contrary, was bluff, well past forty, and had twinkling eyes whose merriment had steely depths. He had soldiered most of his life, and wore his sword as though it were part of him.

"My dear Hamilton, you're positively a man of genius!" he exclaimed affably. "Who else would have thought of such a thing as bringing us together here? I congratulate you!"

Coligny, who detested any dissimulation, struck in:

"Aim your lance at the right spot, Sir John! Eh, Hamilton?"

"Oh, I deserve little credit," admitted the Scot readily. "Dame Catherine deserves the credit, I assure you! It lay in her mind that we might work together for a common understanding, and we've not done badly. Before she arrives tomorrow, I hope that we shall have reached agreement on some of the moot points at issue."

His eye touched on the tall Spaniard, who nodded.

"Spain is quite agreeable, monsieur," said he. "Her interests are now protected, in case of certain contingencies. It was an admirable idea to pool our resources, as it were, and I have been much gratified by our conversations."

"But," said Coligny gloomily, "there remains the question of Guise."

"True," Hamilton exclaimed. "There I myself failed; but he is marked for destruction, I can assure you. Let your distrust and hatred of Guise be at rest, for a little while."

"More important to me is the question of Mary Stuart," Sir John said. "As you know, there lies the prime point of my own endeavors."

"It shall soon be settled!" said Hamilton confidently. "Come, Don Almiro! We have both received word from Paris within the past hour. This is a time for frankness, I believe."

"You are right," assented the Spaniard. "Very well. The Queen

Dauphine has conferred with her husband; it is no secret that she rules his boyish will entirely. She is sending today, by the hand of one of her maids of honor, to my house in Passy."

"And what is she sending?" prompted Hamilton, with a smile.

"Assurances, on the part of herself and the Dauphin, as to their attitude toward Spain, acceptance of our proposals, and certain proposals of her own," Don Almiro said. "I should add that this is being done with the greatest secrecy."

"Yes," said Hamilton. "Even to the point of dismissing this maid of honor from her service, that Catherine de Medici might suspect nothing!"

Don Almiro regarded him with profound astonishment and uneasiness.

"Indeed! Then—then you are aware of it!"

"Yes," said Hamilton frankly. "Also, I have taken certain measures, to which I trust you will agree. This young woman will arrive at your house; she will find herself taken into custody, and she will be brought here this evening for safekeeping. The Queen desires that she be questioned further. You assent?"

"Oh, of course!" said Don Almiro, plucking nervously at his beard. "Yes, of course."

"Faith, where do I come in?" demanded Sir John Preble affably.

Hamilton turned to him.

"Your interest, also, is protected. Mary Stuart has written a letter to her mother, the Regent of Scotland, and is sending it by a gentleman whom she trusts. That gentleman, whom I know,"—and for a moment, a flash darted from the eyes of Hamilton,—"was to have left Paris early this afternoon. He will be met on the road and persuaded to come here; if he resists, he will be brought."

"Then he must be of value!" said Sir John, laughing. "All I seek is the letter."

"You shall have it," said Hamilton. "Rather, it shall be placed at our common disposal. Once and for all, we shall pierce to the truth; the trickery, deceit and downright treachery of this child who calls herself Queen of Scotland and England, shall be laid bare. As to the man—yes, he is of great value. He is intimately concerned with the project my mistress now has on foot, and which draws her here tomorrow."

"Would it be too curious to inquire as to this project?" asked Coligny.

"Not at all; I was about to impart it to you, monsieur," Hamilton replied. "It is the destruction of the physician and astrologer, Michel de Notredame, who has dared to counter Her Majesty's wishes. I have already obtained his secret and private papers, which will infallibly insure that he goes to the stake. In fact, certain judges and lawyers skilled in the law involving sorcery will be here tomorrow, to witness his arrest."

There was a little silence. Coligny gave Hamilton a keen glance.

"So this is why you desired me to place this chateau at your entire disposal!"

"And that of Her Majesty," said Hamilton, with a nod. "Do you regret it?"

"Of course not," Coligny replied. "Many of the gentlemen whom I represent will be much gratified if this man Notredame goes to the stake. But let me warn you of one thing, monsieur," he added in his gloomy manner. "You speak continually with assurance, and you yourself feel this assurance. It all centers around one point, the point of our entire association: If a certain thing happens, well and good. But so much is left to chance—"

He hesitated. Sir John struck in with a laugh.

"Bah! Let's speak out about it, and be damned to furtive nonsense! You mean, in case the King of France does not survive the week, eh?"

"There is no need of uttering dangerous words," exclaimed Don Almiro uneasily.

"Well, they're uttered!" said Sir John in his bluff way. "Coligny is right, Hamilton. We're leaving so much to chance, that I don't share your assurance."

Hamilton swept them with his eye, and smiled.

"I neither leave anything to chance, nor do I utter any dangerous words," he said significantly. "I burned my fingers once, and learned a lesson. Does that satisfy you?"

OBVIOUSLY, IT did; but at this moment a man approached them. He was one of the men whom Coligny had provided and placed at Hamilton's disposal; these were all men from Gascony or Béarn, who gave their allegiance to the House of Bourbon.

"Monsieur!" he exclaimed, saluting Hamilton. "We've just received word that the gentleman you expected was stopped on the road. He resisted, and killed two men before he was brought down."

"What?" broke out Hamilton angrily. "I gave strict orders—"

"They were obeyed, monsieur," intervened the man. "He was not harmed. Beyond removing his sword and poniard, and binding his arms, he was not even touched. He is being brought carefully, as you commanded."

Hamilton relaxed. "Excellent! Have him placed in the upper room of the west tower, the old prison-chamber. He is to remain securely bound so that he can destroy nothing he carries. Inform me when he's there, and I'll visit him."

The man saluted and departed. Hamilton, with an expression of joy, turned and clapped Sir John on the shoulder.

"You see? My assurance is justified. You shall accompany me; we'll visit him together. The letter shall be yours, though we'll all share its contents. Dame Catherine shall have the man; or rather, the torturers whom she'll be sending."

"But he has killed two of my faithful servants!" exclaimed Coligny. "Is such action to be tolerated?"

"That's for Her Majesty to say. If I have my way, he'll accompany his friend Notredame to the stake," replied Hamilton, and shrugged. "Two men? A mere nothing, monsieur! You play for a stake of kingdoms, and you complain of two men being killed!" A dark and ominous expression crossed his face. "Are you going to complain when the King of France is killed, as will happen before the next three days are out?"

Coligny shuddered slightly. "The threads of destiny are drawing together," he muttered. "Twice it has been predicted that I was to perish from assassination—"

"Then cheer up!" exclaimed Sir John heartily. "Threads form a rope, my friend; and you weren't born to be hung. I'd like to be your age again, *pardieu!* Give me your arm, Hamilton; you're a man after my own heart!"

They stepped away together, laughing; but Don Almiro peered after them, plucking anew at his beard with nervous fingers, and young Coligny was pallid as the dead.

CHAPTER XVI

MALCOLM CAMPBELL, his arms tied, came a prisoner to the Chateau de Minard.... The ambush had caught him by surprise; he had fought desperately, until brought down by ropes and bound. This was on the highway, not a mile from the chateau, whose sinister aspect greeted him with dark forebodings. He had not anticipated that his errand would be accomplished in this fashion.

In the courtyard, he was assisted to dismount. His eye roved the men standing about, the stables under the wall on one side, the stairs on the other, the walls rising above, the curbing of the well by the stairs. Then two guards were shoving him along, while others gathered admiringly about his superb horse, and led it away.

He still had one ray of hope. If they discovered the letter he bore, took it, and let him go again, his errand would be accomplished perfectly; or, if he could escape after it was taken, all would still be well.

He was conducted up the stairs, along a corridor, and into the upper chamber of a squat tower that rose above the encircling wall. His cloak, which had been lost in the struggle, was put about his shoulders again, though the lashings remained on his wrists. He was thrust upon a couch, covered with a tattered, rancid blanket, and his two guards left; a bolt rasped home outside the door.

He looked around. The room held, besides the couch, a table with a candlestick, a stool, a washstand—nothing else. It smelled of damp and mold. A trap in the ceiling evidently led to the roof-platform of the tower. The only egress was by the corridor through which he had entered; but there was a window.

Campbell rose and went to it, and any thought of escape died here. The window was large. It held three bars from top to bottom, three from side to side—stout, massive bars of iron, solid as the stones themselves. Rain and wind could enter, but no prisoner could leave, by this opening. It was above the chateau wall, and on the outside; fifty feet below, Campbell could see the ground and the trees of the surrounding estate.

With a feeling of despair, he returned to the couch and seated himself.

Feet scraped the floor; the bolt rasped, the door swung open. Into the room stepped the bluff, hearty Sir John, with Hamilton behind him, a guard following. At sight of Hamilton's determined, smiling features, Campbell felt himself a lost man. However, he stood up and nodded recognition.

"So you're the chief of the robber band, eh? Isn't that a step backward, Hamilton? Usually a scoundrel begins with robbery and proceeds to assassination, but you reverse the process."

"Hello!" exclaimed Sir John in surprise. "It's an Englishman!"

"No, a Scot," said Hamilton, regarding his prisoner with a slight smile of satisfaction and triumph. "Knighted, I am told, when he was given this commission. Sir Malcolm Campbell, I present Sir John Preble, who has come with me to relieve you of your errand."

Sir John bowed ceremoniously. Campbell did likewise, as well as his bound arms would permit; not from courtesy, but to conceal the dismay he knew must be in his eyes. How much did Hamilton know, who seemed to know everything? However, the next words of Hamilton gave him some reassurance.

"Yes, my worthy Scot, we'll relieve you of what the Queen Dauphine gave you."

"So you've come to take my money, which even your hirelings did not touch!" said Campbell.

"I'm not a thief," Hamilton said with cold disdain, and motioned to his guard. "Search him; take what papers he carries, nothing else."

The man came to Campbell and took hold of him.

"Careful!" said Campbell. "You're a Frenchman, my man; if you dare to touch what I carry, you'll feel the weight of the royal punishment!"

"A Frenchman obeys the Queen of France, not the Queen of Scotland," said Hamilton. "Do as I say."

The guard complied. He tapped Campbell's pockets, and drew forth the passport and the letter addressed to the Regent of Scotland.

"Nothing else? Ha! That's what we want!" Hamilton seized the two papers with delight and glanced at the passport. He gave it to the man. "Here, put it back in his pocket, for the present. Here you are, Sir John!" So saying, he extended the letter to Preble, who took it joyfully. "Now release the prisoner."

The guard obeyed. Campbell stood in silence, rubbing his chafed wrists, trying to hide the feeling of exultation that shook him. Despite all, his errand was accomplished: the letter designed to reach the agent of England had reached him.

"You'll suffer for this, all of you!" he broke out.

Hamilton smiled coldly.

"Indeed? You're not yet able to make anyone suffer, my dear Campbell. You'll remain confined to this room; my men have orders to shoot you instantly if you try to escape."

"By whose orders, assassin?" snapped Campbell.

"Those of Catherine de Medici, Queen of France," replied Hamilton. "Come along, Sir John. Unless you wish to interrogate the prisoner?"

Sir John Preble shook his head. "Not now. Later I may want a word with him."

"He's at your service at any time," said Hamilton carelessly, and departed. Sir John gave a glance at Campbell, and followed. The guard came after them, bolting the door anew.

LEFT ALONE, Campbell extended himself on the couch; and, fearful of hidden watchers, turned his face from the door. Success, success! What he had been unable to accomplish of himself, had been done for him—and done neatly. That he wore a mail shirt was unsuspected; that he carried anything beneath it, unguessed. Their entire attention had been fastened upon that letter....

The afternoon darkened into evening.

Guards came, lighting his candle from a lantern and bringing wine and food. They spoke no word, answered no questions, but went away as they came. The fare was good; Campbell ate and drank heartily, paced the stone floor a while, put out his candle and lay down again. The sough of the wind in the trees outside put him to sleep.

He slept soundly and well—too well, indeed, for he was only wakened when Hamilton and a number of guards appeared. The guards removed his dishes and brought more.

Hamilton stood regarding him with cruelly glinting gaze.

"There's to be a matter taken up today," he said abruptly, "in which you're to assist. Your friend the leech Notredame is concerned."

Campbell stared in unfeigned astonishment.

"Notredame!" he repeated. "What have you to do with him?"

"I? Nothing, except that he intervened after I had put you where you belonged," said Hamilton. "No, I'm not dealing with him, but the Queen is. So are doctors of the law, witnesses, a bishop or two, and others. We also have his private papers, which will back up the accusations against him."

ANOTHER INTERVIEW, and a more terrible one! The words recurred to Campbell's memory. Here, at this place? Yet Notredame had not mentioned it.

"He was summoned in the King's name," Hamilton went on, narrowly watching his prisoner. "I strongly advise you to testify concerning your relations with him."

"So it was you, or your spies, who robbed Fobert!" Campbell exclaimed.

"Aye, and Fobert, his pupil and assistant, will testify against him." Hamilton laughed lightly. "However, it's not my affair; I'm obeying orders. Shall I call in a scribe to take down your testimony?"

"I've none to give," said Campbell curtly.

"Good. Then you'll be tortured to make you talk. And those who serve the chamber of justice in Paris, know how to make stubborn fellows talk glibly."

"Give me a sword, and I'll talk quick enough, to you!" said Campbell.

"Yes, no doubt," Hamilton sneered. "So you refuse?"

Campbell poured wine into the pewter cup, sipped it, then suddenly flung wine and cup together, straight into Hamilton's lace. Instantly, two of the guards were upon him, shoving him back. Hamilton took a step away, wiped the wine from his face, and instead of losing his temper as Campbell had hoped, merely shrugged.

"The choice is yours," he said. "The Queen will know how to deal with you. I'll be back later on, my fine rascal."

He beckoned his man and went out. Left alone, Campbell slumped down on the stool.

Notredame! Why, this was something new, something that threatened him acutely; the surprise of it shook him. If he were indeed stripped and tortured, the secret letter must be found, everything would be lost; he must at all costs avert such a disaster. But how?

There was no way, except by testifying to a pack of lies against Notredame; it was a cruel quandary. Campbell sat hour after hour, tormenting himself with the problem. Noon came and passed; more food was brought; he ate and drank mechanically. Notredame was coming here, or being brought?

It was plain enough now, all of it, and bitterly plain. Catherine de Medici had resolved upon the death of this man, whom she considered as an enemy, and was bringing if about in her own stealthy fashion, by due processes which could not be averted or hindered. She had given Hamilton charge of the affair, and spies had served her well.

"They've got me, too; they little know how they've got me, damn them!" muttered Campbell. "Maître Michel's papers seized, Fobert probably bribed to betray him—and now me! If I don't sign their lies and accusations of sorcery, they'll torture me till I do. And then they'll discover what must be hidden at all costs. My best recourse is to get that little letter out, tear it up, and burn or eat it."

At that moment his door opened and Hamilton, with a number of guards, came in. He looked not only cheerful but even gay; he was wearing a court suit of velvet and fresh linen, and stood laughing at Campbell with an air of the greatest affability.

"I've just discovered something," he observed. "Something curious and interesting and most instructive! Really, my dear fellow, you should have confided in me sooner! However, Her Majesty is here and is awaiting you, so I'll only give you a glimpse and a promise, on the way." He turned to the guards. "Bind his arms behind him; securely, but not too tightly. He's not being tortured yet. Then gag him and bring him along."

Humming a gay air, Hamilton went to the window and looked out, while the guards obeyed his instructions. Campbell made no resistance; he was entirely helpless. If he wanted to destroy Mary Stuart's letter later on, he must keep his head now. His wrists were firmly lashed behind his back. Into his mouth, secured by a lashing around his head, was slipped a pear-shaped instrument of Italian invention. This pear of metal occasioned him small inconvenience unless he tried to talk; then it caused acute pain, and prevented more than a bare croak being heard.

"Very well; ready? Now bring him along," said Hamilton, and nudged Campbell in the ribs. "My friend, you'll have occasion to remember that cup of wine you presented to me this morning! Step out."

Campbell obeyed. Following Hamilton, he passed out into the corridor. Unluckily, he was too occupied with his own predicament, as well he might be, to take careful note of their course; but suddenly he saw Hamilton pause, check the men with uplifted hand, and eye him with infernal glee.

"Something to show you," said he, chuckling. "Yes, it was quite a discovery! I had taken small account of your private feelings, until the matter was disclosed to me this morning. Now look, through this slit in the wall. It was made for archers, so why should it not serve a Scot?"

He pointed to an arrow-slot, shoulder-high, beside him. Campbell was pushed at it, his face was forced against it. He found himself looking through it at a chamber beyond.

He tried to speak; suddenly his face purpled, fury came into his eyes; he almost lost his head in this moment. For he was looking directly into a room where Anne Haworth sat, her chin in her hand; she was staring straight at him, as though conscious of some movement through this arrow-slot.

For an instant, Campbell doubted his own eyes; but there could be no mistake. It was Anne. She wore the same dress in which he had last seen her, of gray and red, with a cloak beside her of like material. It was Anne herself—

At a signal from Hamilton, the guards pushed him on. Hamilton was looking into his face and laughing thinly.

"You recognized her, eh? Then you'd better change your mind about talking, when the Queen questions you. Or else? Torture, later; but first you shall see *her* put to the question, my friend! Stubborn you may be, but that will unlock your lips quick enough. When you see her stripped and laid on the rack, with her pretty body doubled up and tormented, you'll think twice about being stubborn! Bring him along, men. Which one of you has the pistol? Let me have it."

One of the men handed him a long pistol. He examined the priming, nodded, then led the way.

CAMPBELL KNEW little of what was around him; a low, stifled groan escaped him.... Spies, cruelty, torment! Anne, sent on her secret errand, had been caught or suspected; now she was here, in the hands of these men, a helpless thing like himself. And he knew full well with what ruthless determination she would be treated before his very eyes, to break his resolve.

He was only dimly aware of people in a large room, talking and chatting in groups, staring at him as he was led past. Men in flowing robes, in attire of ceremony—what was it Hamilton had said about judges and lawyers? No matter. For here, in the room beyond, something else awaited him.

A severe room with a table and one person seated in a chair before it: a room carpeted and hung with tapestry. And the person at the table, who viewed him with cold dull eyes, was Catherine de Medici herself. The object before her on the table, unopened but removed from its leathern case, was Notredame's Limousin casket, little locks hanging from front edge and corners.

Hamilton bowed. Under the urge of his guards, the prisoner also bowed. Her eyes upon Campbell, she said:

"So, monsieur, we meet again. Apparently, impertinence still becomes you, to judge from your gag. However, you may nod your head if you desire to speak freely in regard to the sorcery practiced by Maître de Notredame."

Campbell shook his head. A frightful despair was upon him. There was no escape; he must talk, he must lie, he must say anything, if it would save Anne! But first, he must destroy that letter under his shirt.

"Very well, monsieur," she said to Hamilton. "Put him in the chair, and stand as I have ordered you. Neglect no precaution; watch this man Notredame carefully. Let him enter, and send away these others. Your faithful presence is enough."

Campbell, mute and helpless, was shoved into a chair behind her, against the tapestry. Hamilton stood beside him, with pistol ready.

Without turning, Catherine spoke again.

"You have discovered no way of opening this casket, Monsieur Hamilton?"

"None, Your Majesty, except by destroying it."

"Then I shall have it opened. It is too beautiful and precious to destroy."

Next moment, Notredame stepped into the room.

CHAPTER XVII

FOR ONE instant he stood, hesitant and astonished, his gray eyes taking in everything before him—the seated woman, Hamilton and his pistol, the helpless Campbell, the table and the casket on it, lit by the warm afternoon sun. Then, without showing his astonishment, he bowed low and respectfully to Catherine de Medici.

So absolutely at ease was he, so perfect was his composure, that Catherine was keenly irritated by it. She relaxed, secure in the knowledge that Hamilton's pistol protected her against any threat from a desperate man.

Etiquette demanded that she be the first to speak. Notredame, apparently ignoring all else, waited in the utmost seren-ity. Catherine's crafty stage-setting had entirely failed of effect, and she bit her lip in annoyance. With a slight gesture toward Hamilton, she broke the silence, her voice harsh and sharp.

"This gentleman is in my confidence, as yonder man in the chair is in your confidence, Maître de Notredame," she said. "Or so, at least, he has told us. He has also given us full infor-mation regarding your practice of sorcery and forbidden magic and alchemy."

Notredame bowed again. "That, madame, is obviously why he has been rendered incapable of further speech."

"You do not appear astonished."

"Not in the least, madame. The stars long ago presaged this meeting."

"Really?" A slight smile of triumph curved the full lips of Catherine and lighted her pallid visage. "Did they also tell you that accusations of sorcery are made against you, that the gentlemen in the adjoining chamber are awaiting your arrest and trial, and that they need only evidence and charges from my lips to conduct you to the stake?"

"Yes, madame," Notredame replied composedly. "But they also informed me that the lips of Your Majesty would acquit me of all charges."

"The stars lied, or your interpretation of them lied," she re-sponded, with something akin to a snarl.

Campbell shifted posture slightly; the chair, pressing against his concealed shirt of steel links, irked him. Then he remained motionless, absorbed, fascinated.

He perceived that he was watching a deadly and merciless struggle, in which the exultant hatred of a crafty and vindictive and powerful woman was pitted against the unaided wits of a man. Or was Notredame unaided? Campbell could not be sure, and he wondered.

"I see you recognize this casket," Catherine said sharply.

"I do indeed." Notredame glanced carelessly at the enameled box on the table.

"I am informed that it contains your secret papers."

"The greatest of all my secrets, madame."

"They shall be given to the world, do you understand?" A trace of furious passion sent color flaming across Catherine's pale cheeks as she spoke. "They shall at once be placed in the hands of those judges and advocates who are waiting in the adjoining room. Nothing can save you now. There are witnesses against you; the forces of Church and State are waiting to seize you. If you dare to appeal to the King himself, he cannot intervene. You have taken too much upon yourself, and now your punishment approaches." Her voice became imperious. "Give me the key of this casket, if you please."

Notredame bowed slightly and reached under his shirt. The pistol of Hamilton lifted and steadied; but Notredame only produced a silver chain upon which depended a small key of gold. He took this from the chain. Quite unruffled, with a poise that infuriated Catherine anew, he laid the key in her outstretched hand.

"Here it is, madame. If you will have the goodness to fit it to the central lock, the others will all open; otherwise they will not."

She put the key into the lock, then paused, looking up at him.

"You have refused to give me your services, Maître de Notredame. You have given help and assistance to those who hate me. You have worked against me in every way possible; now bethink you, was it wise?"

"Alas, madame, I had no choice!" said Notredame quietly.

"Then you have no choice now," she retorted, and turned the key. There was a succession of slight clicks. As with most French locks, the key turned twice, and then the lid of the casket lifted to her hand.

She started slightly, staring down at the velvet lining. There within the casket reposed only a single paper, folded over. She drew it out, opened it, and held it to the light of the windows. The writing was large; it was in Latin, and Campbell, from behind her, could see it clearly.

Hail, Queen of France!
Hail, Queen of France no more!
Hail, greater than Queen, ruler supreme!
Destiny awaits you; take it.
  Farewell.

Catherine stared at the words. She lowered the paper; despite herself, she met the composed regard of Notredame with a troubled uncertainty.

"Queen of France no more!" she murmured. "No papers, no secrets—'greater than Queen, ruler supreme!' What is the meaning of this, Maître Michel?"

"I dare not presume, madame, to interpret what must be entirely clear to you," he said simply. "You yourself are a follower of the stars, fully acquainted with them."

Once again she had become very pale. Her eyes glittered upon him.

"Yes, I am a student of the stars," she said in a low voice. 'Queen of France no more!' That can mean only one thing. Are you acquainted with the prediction of Messer Ruggieri, my astrologer, in connection with the life of my husband the King?"

"Alas, madame, I have scant knowledge of the Florentine school of judicial astrology," Notredame replied.

"Indeed?" she said. "The horoscope of the King predicts that his life will extend only to between forty-one and forty-two years!"

Notredame bowed once more. Campbell caught a peculiar flash in his eye, and knew that his bow was designed to conceal this slight token of exultation from Catherine. Then his voice came slowly and deliberately:

"It should be more accurate, madame. Then it would predict a total of forty-one and one-quarter years, and ten days."

Upon the silence, Catherine suddenly caught her breath.

"You don't know what you say!" she exclaimed in a stifled voice. "The King's birthday was the last day of March. This is the end of June, in the year 1559—"

Still slow, still deliberate, the calm and expressionless words of Notredame went on:

"Therefore, madame, the period is at its end. The predictions of the stars do not vary, they are not to be altered. It is true that the period is almost at its end; due to the errors of chronology covering the ten days, it is positive that the King will not die before the tenth of July."

"You say, you dare to say, that the King will die then!" murmured Catherine in great agitation. "You dare to predict his death as unalterable! Why, this is treason!"

"No, madame; it is only my interpretation of the stars, which are never at fault. The most important thing is the fourth line of that writing beneath your hand."

BY DEGREES, the tremendously impressive manner of Notredame, his unruffled urbanity and quiet force, had achieved its effect. Unthinkingly, Catherine obeyed his voice. She opened the paper and glanced at it again frowningly. Then she lilted her head and darted one keenly sudden and suspicious look at him.

"This was done purposely!" she exclaimed. "This casket did not hold your papers and secrets! It held only this one paper, meant for my eye!"

"True; my greatest secret. Any attempt to deceive the piercing intuition of Your Majesty would be quite fruitless." If the words held hidden irony, Notredame's voice held none. It was bland and smooth. "Yes, I was aware of certain complications. So I venture to repeat those words before you, madame. *'Destiny awaits you; take it!'*"

Upon the room settled a troubled, uneasy, pregnant silence.

Catherine's breathing became more rapid; her bosom rose and fell. When she looked again at Notredame, it was in a certain awe and amazed wonder. She was too clever, too keen-witted, not to abandon all pretense now.

"I understand, Maître de Notredame. You have rebuked me; you have treated me like a child—you who have stood among my enemies, you who have opposed me in every way, you who regard me as a helpless infant—"

"No, madame," he dared to break in upon her, an unpardonable affront. "Like a woman destined to be one of the most powerful characters in history. It is quite true that I have ventured to oppose you in the past; but now the time has come when I oppose no longer. I have been instructed to open your eyes, madame, to reality. I merely tell you that what is predestined cannot be averted. Whether for good or evil, there are certain things which you will do, and I am come to tell you what they are. Remember, I am an agent only, and nothing else."

A slow flush crept into her cheeks. All her life she had been kept in subjection, despised, insulted, without the least influence. These golden words dazzled her, and opened a new concept to her mind.

Almost with a shock, Campbell abruptly realized why they talked so freely in his presence: They were speaking Latin. The blank features of Hamilton showed he did not understand this tongue, and Catherine evidently took for granted that Campbell was also ignorant of it.

"Powerful!" she repeated bitterly. "You forget. Even as Queen of France, I have no power, no friends; deadly foes are all around me. If this frightful prediction is correct, if the King were to die unexpectedly, then I would cease to hold even the title of Queen. And you have the impudence to predict this!"

"I predict an even greater title for you, madame." Notredame spoke with dignity. "Do you wish to hear it? I have not come as a false friend; in fact, between you and me there cannot be friendship, though there may be a mutual respect. If you wish me to show you the inevitable road to greatness, I am ready to make your way clear."

Catherine trembled at these words; she regarded him avidly, credulously—struggling against belief in him, yet yielding to it. She made a slight gesture, and leaned back.

"Speak, then."

"At this time tomorrow, madame, the King will be struck down." Notredame leaned forward, his gray eyes alight. "You will then have ten days in which to act. To such a woman as you, that is more than sufficient. To all others, his death will be unsuspected; you will have a tremendous advantage, therefore."

"But the new Queen of France will be Mary Stuart, who hates me!"

"She does not hate you, madame; she is impetuous, but of a noble character. Be the first to cease hating; give her trust and friendship, and she will give you the same. However, her husband is still beneath the age of majority; therefore, France must be ruled by a regent."

"And that regent would be my bitterest enemy, Guise!"

"Who is also the bitterest enemy of the Huguenots, remember. But the death of Guise is also written. And even before his death, you shall take the power from him."

"I, take his power?" She laughed mirthlessly, yet with fearful fascination in all that Notredame was saying. "What miracles, what angels, would help me do such a thing?"

"Your own will and ability—the help of those who fear Guise—the House of Bourbon, the Prince of Conde, the whole growing might of the Huguenot party!"

She started slightly. "Those heretics!"

"Among them are the greatest nobles in the kingdom, even in your own court. Ally yourself with them. They prefer you to Guise. So would Elizabeth of England, so would Spain; you, as Regent, would be preferred to a powerful warrior."

The eyes of Catherine were alight and sparkling now.

"Ah, what a prospect! But I can make no agreement with heretics."

"A temporary agreement need not be lasting. Think of the Constable, Montmorency! He will join with you gladly. And regard the future!" The eloquent voice went on, powerful and insidious. "François the Dauphin, the King-to-be, is frail and will have no heirs. His brother is a boy of ten. Do you understand, madame? Seize the chance! You will be Regent for years to come! With your ability, you can play with these conflicting forces, subdue them to your will, make each of them serve you!"

CATHERINE'S OUTSTRETCHED hands had clenched. She was transfigured, flushed, excited. This glowing vision lifted before her eyes in all its possibilities.

She was, after all, a Medici; she had every quality of this remarkable family. As she sat here now, a change came into her features. They hardened, they took on new form and shape and resolution. The secret strength and purpose of her character, all the greater because it had been nourished under oppression and subjection, suddenly flashed into sight.

When she looked up again at Notredame, it was with the air of a different person.

"So this paper was your greatest secret! I understand now, monsieur; how childish I was, to regard you as an enemy! But I must warn my husband, do you understand? It is a matter of conscience. Although he loves me not, although he has openly betrayed and despised me, I cannot let him go unwarned."

"Do so, madame. It will be of no avail; I have already warned him!" Notredame spoke with a mournful certainty. "You well know how headstrong he is. This is one of those decrees of fate which no mortal power can avert."

"Nevertheless, I shall warn him. And to you I give my thanks, my gratitude, my promise of protection, even friendship!" She extended her hand to Notredame, who went to his knee and kissed her fingers. He looked up at her with concerned eyes.

"Thank you, madame. As for this friend of mine, this young man behind you—"

"Fear not. Go back to your inn, Maître de Notredame; await there the outcome of your prediction. If it happens as you say, you have nothing to fear and much to hope." She turned and beckoned Hamilton; she was speaking now in French. "Monsieur! Take care of this Scots gentleman for a day or two; treat him with civility, I charge you." She exchanged a swift, significant glance with Hamilton. "If certain matters turn out as I think, he is to be set at liberty instantly."

Hamilton bowed; his dark, powerful, impassive features showed no surprise. Campbell, however, had caught the interchange of glances, the swift and terrible message between these two. He suddenly understood that, if Notredame had won his duel of wits, this woman had none the less played her hand very astutely, with a depth of craft and deceit which no man, whether prince or prophet, could hope to fathom.

She rose, and with Notredame following, left the room. From the adjoining chamber her voice sounded with an astonishing strength and decision.

"Gentlemen, I have found Maître de Notredame to be entirely innocent of any sorcery or dealings in the black arts, and have therefore dismissed and condemned as false any charges against him."

The pistol poked Campbell under the ear. He looked up to meet the darkly flaming gaze of Hamilton.

"Get up! Damme, I don't pretend to understand what's going on; but if you're set at liberty it'll be with a poniard planted under your rib! Treat you with civility, eh? With the civility you deserve, you damned Scot—and the young woman as well. Get up! Move! Back to your kennel, you rogue!"

Perhaps Catherine had not, after all, been astonished at the exactness of the prediction made by Notredame; perhaps she had merely been afraid of his frightful knowledge.

CHAPTER XVIII

THROUGH A sunny afternoon destined to ring down the echoing corridors of time, and indeed to affect most vitally the entire course of the world's history, the Rue St. Antoine blazed with color and rang with voices and trumpets and the clash of arms.

This wide street, which separated the palace of the Tournelles from the house owned and occupied by Diane de Poitiers, had been converted into the conventional lists for jousting. This sport of the great was the last dying knell of the age of chivalry.

Ranged along the scaffolding and boxes were princes and ambassadors and nobles, the highest names in France, the most glittering court on earth. Jewels flashed in the sunlight, gold and silks and rich fabrics were so common as to be everywhere, luxury and sumptuous display were on all sides. The Queens, Diane de Poitiers, all the most beautiful and lordly of women were here; as Queen of France, Catherine de Medici bestowed certain of the prizes, and as Queen of Scotland. Mary Stuart awarded others.

In gilded and splendid armor, four champions defended themselves against all comers; they were Henri of France on his noble steed Compere, the Duke de Nemours, the Duke de Savoy, and François, Duc de Guise. Each in turn ran against any challenger; the lances struck shield or helmet and shattered. To win, the victor must bear himself solid as a rock against repeated shocks, and deliver shocks in his turn; the least yielding or clutching at the saddle-bow would disqualify him. Only the most expert of horsemen and the most powerful of athletes could bear off the prize.

The King, flushed and excited, finished his turn and laid aside his armor. He was clad in magnificent attire of white silk slashed with black, the colors of Diane de Poitiers, decorated in the most superb manner with jewels and gold. He wore silk stock-ings, a custom introduced by Diane, and white shoes fastened with diamond buckles.

From youth he had been accustomed to this sport of joust-ing, which he dearly loved, and it was most likely that he would be today's victor. However, his courses had been run; now he joined Diane and her ladies, watching the succeeding courses with gay laughter and intent appraisal. At his post stood Mont-gomery, Captain of the Scots Guards, in full armor. He was also noted for his skill at jousting, but was taking no part in the day's sport; he was on duty.

MEANTIME, AFAR from the noise and gayety and splendor of Paris, the ominous chateau of Minard lay hidden amid its trees and darkly silent. In the garden under the three apple trees, two men were pacing up and down, talking to-gether. One was Hamilton, the other was Don Almiro de Soto. Somewhere about the chateau was Sir John Preble, but Coligny was gone; as a member of the court he was forced to attend his uncle, the Constable de Montmorency, at the festivities.

"Then you've talked with the young woman?" Hamilton was saying.

Don Almiro assented.

"Yes. She was furious at her detention, naturally. Unluckily, she now knows that the whole stratagem of her dismissal from court fooled nobody; in fact, she seems to know far too much. She pierced through every proposal and suggestion that I made."

"She's in the confidence of Mary Stuart," said Hamilton.

"But she has been dismissed from her service."

"Eh? What do you mean by that?"

"If she disappears, no one will care. She is dangerous, mon-sieur. If set at liberty, she would know far too much about us, for example."

"The devil! I can't keep her here. She's no longer necessary to me, it seems," Hamilton exclaimed sharply. "Besides, this place is only for temporary use. And you can't expect me to kill a woman, Don Almiro."

"Certainly not," said the Spaniard. "We have other ways of handling such matters in Spain. Suppose I were to bring certain of my own men tonight, remove her in a carriage, and take her to Spain. Why not? She would go into a certain place of security and never come out."

"Oh!" said Hamilton. He pondered this suggestion for a moment, and his face cleared. "Yes; a good idea. We must certainly get rid of her. And then you'll have her safe, if you desire to put her to the question at any time. Yes, yes, an excellent plan! Do it at once, tonight."

"Very well," assented the Spaniard. "First we must see if other things fall out as anticipated—But, look!" He broke off sharply, pointing. "Word has come from Paris! There is Sir John!"

Hamilton swung around. Sir John Preble had appeared. He was striding rapidly toward them, but his usually affable countenance was like a thundercloud. Without a word he came up to them, showed a crushed paper in his fist, and extended it. Hamilton took it, opened it, and read the brief message:

"The King has finished his courses. Nothing has happened."

A sharp oath escaped Hamilton. Sir John spoke with chill reproof.

"So you have neglected nothing! So you are very certain, are you—"

"I'm going to Paris myself, now, instantly!" snapped Hamilton furiously. "The fools! I told them what to do and they were afraid to do it. I'll see that it's done. A mere matter of adjusting the helmet."

"But the King has had his turn, according to this report!" said Sir John.

"That, too, can be arranged," retorted Hamilton, in passionate fury. He strode away hastily, lifting his voice in a shout. "My horse, my horse! Do you hear? Saddle my horse at once, you there!"

Behind him, Sir John looked at Don Almiro, who was worried and nervous.

"What is there to do?" he demanded, plucking at his beard.

"For you, nothing; we must wait." The Englishman's eyes flashed. "But I have a bit of business in hand. It may lead to something. I've been thinking over this matter of the Scots prisoner; an idea has occurred to me. A smart woman, this Mary Stuart; she has the devil's own guile!"

"What are you going to do?" demanded Don Almiro in alarm. Sir John laughed and laid his finger along his nose, slyly exultant.

"Wait and see, my friend! Perhaps I'm a match for the devil, eh? Wait and see!"

All this day, Campbell had sat in his room or paced the dusty floor, consumed by a futile fury of expectancy. Freed of his bonds and gag, he was none the less a close prisoner, and his mental condition was not enviable.

Thanks to the scene he had overheard, he was now aware of everything; the King was expected to die this very day. But he, and he alone, could surmise with dreadful certainty that the expectation was in some quarters an assurance. That significant exchange of glances between Hamilton and Catherine de Medici had revealed much to his imagination.

He was not, to be honest about it, particularly concerned regarding the King of France; but he was extremely concerned in regard to himself and his mission. This, despite the promise of Catherine, was vitally threatened. Hamilton's last words to him had indicated as much. He had been a marked man ever since his arrival had caused the precipitate flight of the Earl of Arran. And if Catherine came to power, he could expect no mercy from the vindictive Hamilton, whose influence would be unlimited.

NOON CAME and passed. Campbell was standing at the window of his cell, when a movement below caught his eye.

Something had appeared at the edge of the trees. Then it was gone.

Curious, he looked again. Suddenly his heart leaped. For an instant, a dark shape came into sight, down there; it whisked out from among the trees and back again, but not before Campbell recognized it.

"Thorn!" He cupped his hands and called from the window. "Thorn! D'ye hear me, old fellow? Thorn!"

The hound remained motionless, looking up. Campbell got his arm between the iron bars and waved. Then, beside the dog, another figure came into his sight—the hobbling figure of a man leaning on a knotted staff. The man looked up, doffed his cap, and made a gesture of caution, of warning.

Campbell withdrew his arm. Angus, Black Angus of Kilspindie! Angus and Thorn together! Well, they could do him no help now, except possibly take news of his present plight to Notredame or to Mary Stuart. Yet, if Anne were here in this chateau, why were Angus and Thorn, who had accompanied her on her errand of mystery, at liberty?

"None of it makes sense," reflected Campbell in despair. "Yet the sense must be there, if I could only see it!"

He went back to the window, but both Thorn and Angus had disappeared.

It was afternoon now, to judge by the sun. He was aware that a guard was continually stationed outside his door. Thus, he was not surprised when the lock grated, the door opened and a visitor stepped in. But he was astonished to see Sir John Preble, instead of Hamilton.

Sir John dismissed the guard, closed the door, and came toward Campbell with a sparkling smile of affability.

"AT LAST, my dear Glenlyon, I'm able to speak with you alone!" he exclaimed. "Of Scots extraction myself, I find it deplorable that you're in this situation.

"Your sympathy is a bit late," said Campbell warily.

"No doubt. But I can't help myself. Hamilton's just gone to Paris, and this has been my first opportunity of speech with you. Luckily, these French rascals don't understand a word of English."

"Luckily? Why luckily?"

"Because I want a word or two with you which no one else must overhear."

"On what subject?"

"That of the other letter, the real letter, given you by Mary Stuart."

Campbell felt a sharp pang of apprehension.

"I don't know what you mean, Sir John," he said calmly.

"Come, my dear fellow! You know very well," Preble exclaimed with hearty amiability. "I've been here and there in my time, let me assure you. I've carried messages and I've intercepted them; I've had to use thumb-screw, boot and rack on recalcitrant gentlemen. I know perfectly how these things are done, and after the first glance at this letter you carried, I divined the secret. Where's the other letter?"

"Really, Sir John, you must be out of your mind!" rejoined Campbell.

The Englishman winked.

"Not a bit of it. Now pay attention, my friend. This is between you and me alone! You'll profit by it, I promise you." Sir John spoke swiftly and earnestly. "Hamilton would have you stripped and put to the torture instantly, if he suspected. But why should he suspect?"

Relieved of his first fear lest Sir John had some positive knowledge, Campbell thought fast. The devil had caught up with him; he had to act. But with guards waiting outside, this would be sheer folly.

"Do you expect me to credit a thing you say," he rejoined, "when spies wait at the door, perhaps watch everything in this room? No, no!"

Preble laughed. "So, then, I'm right about another letter! Where is it?"

"Where you'll never find it, unless I reveal the secret," Campbell rejoined.

"Good. Name what you want! Money, rewards, assurances, freedom—"

"First of all, safety from spies," said Campbell. He spoke with a slow hesitation, as though compelled to yield against his will; yet he saw clearly what he must do, and did not shrink from it. "I see no reason to trust you, especially here and now," he went on. "If you wish to discuss this matter, very well; it might be more profitable for me to discuss it with you than with others—"

"It will! I can promise you as much!" exclaimed Sir John eagerly.

"Then I agree; but not now—later," Campbell concluded. "Come back, say, in an hour. Dismiss the guards who are about the door. Let me assure myself against spies."

"Why, gladly!" cried Sir John. "And bring with me an earnest of the promised rewards, eh? I'll do it, of course. And in return, my friend—your silence!"

"Oh, I shall be discretion itself!" Campbell said gravely. "First, where is the young lady who is being detained here?"

"The young lady?" Sir John looked puzzled. "Yes, I remember; I haven't seen her. It's not my affair at all, but that of Don Almiro. He has answered for her silence; I think he is taking certain measures to insure it. How did you know about her?"

"From Hamilton, naturally."

"So?" The Englishman looked thoughtful. "Why do you ask about her?"

"Because I am personally interested in her."

The bluff features of Sir John cleared. "I see; honestly said. I'll inquire about her, then, from Don Almiro. If you serve me, I'll be glad to serve you. In an hour, then!"

He saluted Campbell with a courteous bow, and departed, leaving Campbell to his surging thoughts.

AN HOUR! Destroy the letter, or carry out his purpose, which? Too well did Campbell realize that there was no way to beat the devil about this bush. As he stood in this perplexity, a faintly familiar sound reached his ears. It was the peculiar whistle such as an archer used to warn his companions of something amiss on a night watch.

Campbell darted to the window. There below him, at the edge of the trees, he saw the figure of Black Angus; but now Angus held a bow in his hand. Campbell waved from the opening; then he caught a gestured warning, and saw Angus lift the bow and notch shaft to string.

He jumped back from the window in sharp alarm. What the devil was Angus up to? Then he breathed more freely. If Angus were drawing bow out there in the open, he must be well assured what he was about. And this, after all, was not a castle with guards lining the wall to watch every approach. It was a castle, true, but occupied only by a handful of men who paid no attention—

The faint twang of a bowstring interrupted him. Something fluttered at the window; it passed through, it fell into the room; a long shaft, with a cord fastened to it and trailing.

Campbell was tempted to laugh; instead, he took hold of the cord and drew it in. Was Angus passing him up a rope? This was futile; any escape from this room was impossible. A note? Even more impossible. Angus could not write, and could read only scantily. He came back to the window and looked down. Angus had disappeared; but there was something heavy on the cord. He pulled it in and in. Something clanked against the stones. As he looked down, he saw Angus come into sight again with an imperative gesture. He understood; the cord was to be lowered anew. He waved assent, and Angus vanished.

The cord came in. Another clank from the stones; then he had it—a sheathed rapier, to which the cord was firmly tied. With an exclamation of joy, Campbell seized upon the weapon, freed it, and slid it under his blanket. He tied the end of the cord to the arrow and let this go down again from the window. Angus came out to receive it, then darted back to cover.

Campbell stood at the window, holding the cord's end. No use calling; his voice might carry to other ears, and his words would not reach Angus. What the devil was the archer doing now? As though in reply to the thought, he appeared again and motioned. Campbell drew in on the cord; this time, a rope came with it, a stout hempen rope provided with knots at intervals. Campbell felt his heart sink. Folly! The rope would do him no good whatever, since he was barred from leaving by the window.

However, he drew it in and made the upper end fast to the bars; and over it, to hide it from any chance sight, he flung his own gray cloak. Then he turned from the window. He could not get out, and that ended it; none the less, he was grateful to Angus for the effort. And more, for the sword. The possession of this blade changed everything, made his own desperate resolve settle into cold determination, and gave him a new lease on hope. All things were possible now, even escape!

He drew the rapier from its sheath—a plain weapon, but one of quality, good steel. He left it bared, and threw his blanket over it again. His thought now was with Sir John Preble, and what lay beyond. He had been half determined to destroy the little letter under his shirt, but now all was changed. Escape? It might yet be in his grasp, thanks to that rope! Yet he knew well enough that there could be no escape, letter or no letter, without Anne Haworth. The probability at which Sir John had hinted, terrified him; he knew nothing about Don Almiro de Soto, but—

A sound reached him. He turned his head; he rose and approached the window. To his amazement, something rose beyond the opening. It was the head and torso of Black Angus.

"So ye would not give me a hand!" grunted Angus, gripping the bars.

"Good Lord, man!" Campbell fairly gasped. "I never dreamed

you were coming up! Here, give me your hand! And in broad daylight too, you madman!"

"Losh, it's safe enough; there's not a soul on this side the house," said Angus, panting more than a little. He wedged a foot into the embrasure, clung to Campbell, and rested, peering into the chamber. "Where's Anne Haworth?"

"I don't know. Somewhere in the place."

"I came to find her, and found you instead. That's Thorn's doing. I escorted her on an errand and she did not come back; we followed her here, later. Help me in!"

"You can't get in, nor I out," said Campbell desperately. "It's no use, Angus!"

"Faint words," said Angus, with a grunt. "My legs are bad, but my arms are good and my head better. So I can't get in? If that's wine you've got on the table, I'll get in, spite of Satan himself! Ha! I see a way! Let go, now; let me loose, I say! When I'm past, draw in the rope and leave it, so nobody will see it dangling. We may need it again."

While he spoke, Angus began to exert himself. Over his shoulders were tied his bow and quiver; notwithstanding this handicap, the enormous strength of his arms became evident. Inch by inch, he passed from the sight of Campbell, working his way upward above and past the window, obviously making for the platform or roof of the squat tower.

Campbell dared not breathe or speak; he was tense with dread expectation, lest at any instant the archer lose footing or hand-grip and plunge downward. The stones scraped; nothing happened. Presently the hoarse but cautious voice of Angus reached him:

"In with the rope, man! All's well."

The rope came in and was piled in the window embrasure, and the cloak flung over it. Scarcely was this done when Campbell caught a scurry of sound from overhead, and the trapdoor in the ceiling came partly open.

"Shall I throw it back?" demanded Angus.

"Yes—no, no! Wait!" cried Campbell in sudden acute dismay. A sound of voices came at his room door, and he remembered Sir John. "Down with it, quickly! Someone's here!"

THE TRAPDOOR lowered again; but it did not entirely lower. Angus had inserted something to hold it up a space, that he might hear what happened below.

Campbell swung around and darted to the couch and stood there, as his door was opened. The door was flung wide. Sir John Preble stood laughing; looking past him, Campbell saw the guards disappearing along the corridor.

"Well, the time is up and the afternoon wasting to its close!" exclaimed the Englishman, stepping into the room. "I'm keeping my promise; the men are gone. Come and see for yourself that there are no spies."

"I don't doubt you," Campbell forced himself to say. It had to be done; there was no other way, yet he hated the prospect with all his heart. Sweat gathered on his cheeks.

"Oh, I'm competent to take care of any trouble," said Sir John coolly, clapping hand to sword-hilt, as though sensing the very thoughts of the prisoner. "But unfortunately that rascal Don Almiro suspects something. The accursed Spaniard has been eying me and pulling at his beard. He speaks English, too, so we'd best be about our business."

"So we had," said Campbell, wondering that his own words came so coolly. "Shut the door, then. Did you find where the lady is kept?"

"Damme, I did not!" With an air of surprised recollection, Sir John closed the door and came across to the table. "I forgot all about it. But I didn't forget this." He held up a heavy purse and clinked it. "Gold, ruddy gold, my friend! The promised matter of rewards. Now, was my guess a true one to the mark?"

"Aye, it was," Campbell confessed.

The ruddy features beamed. "Ha! I said well, eh? And you've another letter from Mary Stuart?"

"Yes," said Campbell.

"Then let's have it."

Campbell cast a glance at the closed door. He stooped, and from beneath his blanket slid out the naked sword.

"Too good was your guess, too straight to the mark," he said quietly. "I'm sorry, Sir John Preble; I've no choice now. I've a steel shirt and a steel sword, to be honest with you, and you know too much."

Preble stepped back a pace.

"The devil!" he exclaimed. His face changed; on the instant he became hard, cold, deadly. Campbell was between him and the door. "You fool! Will you force me to kill you?"

"No. You've forced *me* to kill *you*."

Slowly, guardedly, Sir John drew his sword from the scabbard. "This is passing strange, my friend," he said. "Where got you steel shirt and sword, eh? I honor you for the courtesy of warning me, but—"

In the very act of speaking, with no look or motion to put his victim on guard, he leaped and struck like a viper uncoiling to the mark.

CHAPTER XIX

THE LIGHTNING plunge of man and steel caught Campbell unawares. Nothing could avoid that sword-thrust, aimed at his throat.

Sir John had acted well; but as he sprang, his empty sheath caught against the edge of the table. It was the merest trifle and could not spoil his intent; but it did serve to deflect his thrust. Instead of driving into Campbell's throat, the rapier darted full weight against his chest. The steel bent almost double, the impact knocked him backward a pace; but the hidden steel shirt saved his life.

A cry of furious dismay burst from the Englishman. He recovered and thrust again; this time, Campbell's blade flickered.

Steel clashed. Sir John in his turn was caught off guard. The Scot, seemingly so laggard, erupted in a sudden dazzling burst of agility, too swift for eye to follow. Before the combat really began, it was ended.

True, Campbell received an ugly slash across the neck; but his own sword was driven through and through the Englishman, and Campbell wrenched it clear amid a spurt of crimson.

Sir John Preble stood motionless for an instant. Then the sword dropped from his hand and clattered on the boards; he pressed his palm against the reddening gash and stared at Campbell with widening eyes of terror and realization.

"Why, you damned Scot!" he ejaculated, in utter surprise. Campbell stood poised, suspecting some trick, but there was none.

Sir John groped for the table with outstretched hand. Campbell came to him, gripped the agonized fingers, and in two staggering steps Sir John gained the couch. He sank down upon it, still clutching his breast.

"You—you've done it!" he gasped. His face changed, relaxed, smoothed out. The ghost of a smile touched his lips, and he sank back.

Campbell dashed wine into the pewter cup and held it to the Englishman's lips. Sir John gulped at it.

"Thanks, friend," he said. "A true knight, a very worthy gentleman.... What a fool I was! The green fields of Norfolk, the long waters of the Broads glinting in the sunset—"

His voice failed. Campbell leaned over.

"I'm sorry, Sir John Preble," he said quietly. "Truly sorry. It had to be done."

"Faith, I asked for it! So it's come at last!" And with the words, Sir John smiled again weakly. "The sunset's darkening. My ring— Tell her, Agnes Preble—behind the church at Norfolk—the brown house.... Good or bad, I've lived for her. Send her my ring and she'll know."

"It shall be done, upon my honor," said Campbell.

Sir John looked up at him, started to smile, and stopped. His hand fell away from the wound and blood gushed, and he sighed softly as he died.

AFTER A moment Campbell leaned forward, picked up the limp hand, and from its finger twisted the gold circlet. As he slipped it on his own finger, he was aware of a creak and a slam above; the trapdoor fell wide open, and the face of Angus looked down.

"I was ready to finish him at need, but things were too spry for me," said Angus. "He made a good end, considering he was an Englishman; a pity to waste so much wine, though. Here, take it! I'm coming down."

Campbell took the extended bow, and Angus followed it, holding by his hands and dropping to the floor. He stood up grimacing and rubbing his thighs.

"That's bad for these hurt pins," said he. "I'll never get over that wound in St. Mesmin's wood; it tore and ripped my leg-muscles. Ha, the wine! Tell me what you know about Lady Anne. I had to go with her in haste and haven't caught my breath since."

"Where's Thorn?" asked Campbell. Black Angus lowered the bottle to reply.

"Down below among the trees, on guard. I've got three horses waiting there."

Campbell told what he knew of Anne, which was nothing very definite. Black Angus finished the bottle, set it down, wiped his lips on his cuff, and shook his head.

"Our work's cut out for us. If you could drop down the rope and go, that's one thing. But we must find her. Hello, what's this? Money?" He gripped the purse on the table.

"Leave it," said Campbell.

"I will not!" Angus promptly pocketed it. "If you've no use for it, I have. Why were you so set on killing this Englishman?"

Campbell told him, and showed him the little letter on the chain.

"If I go down, take it to the Regent, or destroy it."

"Belike. But if you're down, where'll I be?" Angus deftly strung his bow, tested the string with his thumb, and nodded. "Now what? We've a rope, and it'll reach from the roof above to the ground. Stool on table, and we can get up to the roof. There's the way out; but where's Anne?"

"That's the rub," said Campbell. "We must find her. And there are men about."

Angus, looking unlike himself with the shaggy grizzled beard gone, scratched his head thoughtfully. Sunset, the late sunset of midsummer, had filled the room with glory through the opening above; now it began to fade.

Black Angus lifted his head as though to speak, but suddenly checked himself. He touched the arm of Campbell and pointed to the door. Looking, Campbell saw it move slightly and silently. Someone was outside, listening, trying the door.

With a gesture of caution, Campbell went to it and cocked his ear against the crack. No steps, no voices; merely a sound of heavy breathing. Not the guards, then. Who? More gentle pressure, and the door opened in a jot further, against Campbell.

"Sir John!" said a voice. "Are you there, Sir John?"

Campbell managed a crude imitation of the hearty tones of Sir John Preble.

"Who is it?" he said. "Oh, come in, come in!"

T H E   D O O R was pushed open; into the room came a tall man in a Spanish cape and with a black beard. The cape gave Campbell the clue—the unknown Don Almiro! He pushed the door shut quickly and stepped in front of it.

"Welcome, Don Almiro," he said grimly.

The Spaniard looked at him, looked at the dead man, looked at the burly Angus, and turned deathly pale.

"*Diable!*" he croaked, and swiftly crossed himself.

Angus laughed. "Not a bit of it, my friend! The devil comes from below. I came from above—you see!" He pointed with his bow to the trapdoor.

Don Almiro glanced about and knew himself trapped.

"Well? You wanted Sir John? There he is." With his sword, Campbell pointed to the couch. "What do you want with him?"

Stammering, incoherent words came to the lips of the Spaniard, who was quick enough to recognize the former captive. A drop of blood fell from Campbell's sword-point at his feet, and he shrank back.

"Mercy!" he begged, finding tongue at last. "Mercy! Do not kill me!"

"Where are the guards?" demanded Campbell.

"I—I sent them away. Downstairs."

"Excellent! Well, Don Almiro, I've no intention of killing you," rejoined Campbell, with shrewd judgment of his man. "That is, if you talk freely and speak the truth. You've no sword, I perceive."

"None," said Don Almiro, taking courage. He pushed back his flat Spanish cap and looked Campbell in the eyes.

"Very well. Tell me where the young lady is kept."

"What young lady, monsieur?"

Being almost totally in the dark, Campbell pretended to know everything.

"*Pardieu!* The young lady who brought you a message from the Queen Dauphine, and who is detained here, and whom you expect to spirit away to Spain tonight!" As he spoke, Campbell lifted his sword slightly. With an air of hauteur, Don Almiro whipped his cloak around him, forgetting that a moment previously he had been begging for mercy.

"Do you threaten a hidalgo of Spain, monsieur? I am not your enemy; I bear you no ill will. The young lady of whom you ask is in a room down the corridor and to the right."

"Which room is it?" demanded Campbell, as though knowing the place intimately.

"The one beside the little stairs, monsieur, that descend to the courtyard. Not the large stairs, the small ones," said Don Almiro loftily.

Campbell smiled. "I see. And you have sent the guards downstairs to the courtyard. And Hamilton has not yet returned from Paris. And darkness is rapidly falling."

"There's half an hour or more yet of daylight," exclaimed Angus. "That is, outside!"

"Then make the most of it and prepare your way down," said Campbell. "We'll certainly have to use it; we can't hope to fight our way out with Anne. Meantime, I'll converse with this gentleman."

He smiled again at Don Almiro, who eyed him with uncertainty and began to pluck nervously at his beard. Then he put his hand beneath his cloak.

"If money," he began, "will be of interest to you, monsieur—"

"It will not," said Campbell abruptly. Angus, who had fallen to work, flung a word at him.

"I'll watch the don. You get your slashed neck tied up."

Campbell retreated to the door, put down his sword, and taking out his kerchief began to bandage the slash across his neck. It was in no way serious, but was still bleeding and had begun to hurt abominably. Don Almiro remained motionless, his crafty eyes on Campbell.

"I am not an enemy, monsieur," he repeated.

"So you said before. In a moment you'll precede me out and show me the lady's room."

"With the greatest pleasure," said the Spaniard, accompanying the words with a bow.

Meantime, Black Angus had freed the rope and tossed it up through the open trap to the roof above. Pulling the table beneath the opening, he planted the stool upon it, and stepped up. Seeing that Campbell had bound up his neck and held his sword again, he put out his arms and pulling himself up to the roof, vanished.

"I was a blasted fool!" came his voice after a moment. "Here's a ladder."

He began to lower a ladder of stout timber, got it clear of table and stool, and then descended it. He grimaced again and rubbed his thighs.

"It's hell to be lame, Malcolm!" he said.

"You're better off than Lochiel or Long John Forbes," rejoined Campbell.

"What'll we do with the don, here?"

"Lock him up and leave him unharmed."

"So?" Angus eyed the Spaniard. "Men who pay spies have fat purses."

"Unharmed, I said; and we're not thieves."

Don Almiro bowed. "My honor, gentlemen," he said grandly, "bids me inform you that I speak English."

"I knew it already," said Campbell. "Ready? Then lead the way, and my sword will be close to your ribs. You may stay here if you like, Angus; I'll bring her back."

Black Angus grunted something and picked up his bow. He had unbent it; now he put his knee to it and snapped the bowstring into place again.

Campbell went to the door, opened it, glanced outside and saw no one.

"Come along, Don Almiro. Lead me to her room, and produce the key."

The Spaniard stalked out, wrapped in his cloak and dignity.

"There is no key," he replied. "Only a bar on the outside. You shall see."

Campbell followed him closely. Glancing back, he saw that Angus was coming after them at a limp, but paid him little heed.

AHEAD WAS a fork in the corridor, which went straight ahead. The fork was only a short passage going to the top of a small circular stairway, guarded by a high iron banister with ornamental post. These stairs gained the courtyard by a short cut.

"There is the room." Don Almiro nodded at a door halfway to the stairhead. Here in the interior of the chateau it was growing dark, although an embrasure on the left side, opening above the courtyard, let in light from the east. A heavy bar showed across the door.

"Very well. Have the kindness to lift out the bar," directed Campbell.

Don Almiro complied, lifting the wooden bar from its hasps and leaning it against the wall. Campbell came to the door and knocked. He caught the voice of Anne Haworth from within the room—

The hand of the Spaniard slid from beneath his cloak, holding a long poniard. He sprang upon Campbell, striking with his full weight, driving home the poniard in a deadly blow between the shoulders. The shock, the impact, crushed Campbell forward against the door; but the slender poniard shivered into flinders against the shirt of steel links. One gasp escaped Don Almiro; then he hurled himself at the stairs.

A bowstring twanged sharply. Campbell heard a *"whirr!"* in the air, a crash from the direction of the stairs, and the exultant tones of Black Angus from behind:

"I feared as much; well, *he* wore no shirt of mail, at all events! Hurt, Malcolm?"

Campbell gained his feet, knocked breathless but unhurt. Don Almiro lay huddled at the stairhead, against the iron post, and Angus darted toward him with a grunt.

"Through him as if he were a cornsack, and never a squeak out of him!"

JUST THEN the door opened, and Campbell saw Anne Haworth staring at him, questioning and alarmed; and he clear forgot Angus and all besides, as she cried out in bewildered recognition.

They were holding each other's hands, both of them laughing and talking at once, when Black Angus darted into the doorway.

"Ha, my lady! Well met!" he exclaimed. "No time to lose, Malcolm; look alive! Someone's just arrived with a clutter of hoofs!"

Someone just arrived! Across Campbell's brain flashed the memory of Hamilton. He swung around swiftly.

"Where's the Spaniard?"

"Oh, the don's guarding the stairs," said Angus, and winked jovially as he slapped his girdle. "He's safe."

Campbell thrust Anne toward him.

"Take her, quickly! Off, Anne, off with him, and questions later! Explain as you go, Angus, and get her started down. I'll be along. Quickly!"

Breathless, Anne caught the hand of Black Angus and was whisked into the passage.

Campbell stooped and picked up his sword. Hamilton, eh? Despite the impetuous anger that gripped at him, there was too much at stake to indulge any craving for vengeance now. Let the man go! Killing was gruesome work, needless fighting was folly and madness.

Out in the passage he glanced at the stairhead, startled, then relaxed. Black Angus had recovered his arrow, but Don Almiro must have perished instantly. Now he stood there in a ghastly simulacrum of life, leaning against the iron post,—in fact, tied to it,—the Spanish cloak wrapped around him, his flat Spanish hat pulled low. Angus had taken time to indulge his ghastly fancy.

Campbell turned toward the corridor and the squat tower-room—then halted, not at the medley of voices from the court-yard, but at the sound of feet scraping on the round stairway close at hand. Then at a voice, Hamilton's voice, piercing up at him…. Not at him, either!

"So there you are! They said I'd find you at the tower. Sir John too, eh? News for both of you, great news!" The lusty voice rang with excitement. "I told you the fools had bungled it, and so they had! D'ye hear me, De Soto?"

Hamilton went into a burst of laughter. He was on the stairs—close, ascending! Campbell wanted to turn and run for it, but something rooted him here, listening.

"Does it paralyze you to hear that a king is dead, my dear don? You should have been there. 'One joust more!' he cried out. Insisted on it; forced Montgomery, the captain of his guard, to go into the lists with him; he was mad for it! Someone had told him that Montgomery was the best horseman present. They rode, they struck fair—and the visor of the King's helmet was unfastened. D'ye understand? The lance splintered and went into him, under the visor. And the Queen fainted dead away, the sly puss— Here, De Soto, what's wrong with you?"

Hamilton was but six feet away, pulling at the sagging figure. Campbell saw him, yet could not move. The King dead or dying….

In a flash, Hamilton saw him standing there; then the body of the Spaniard collapsed and went tumbling down the stairs, and Hamilton was dashing upward, sword out and a shout of half-comprehension on his lips. He was indeed far swifter to act than was Campbell.

So Hamilton gained the stairhead, and flung himself like a madman upon Campbell. The King dead, the blow struck, the prophecy sustained! Only at the clash of steel did Campbell waken to life, and then he had all the disadvantage of the defensive. He was beaten back and back, past the room door. With incredible agility Hamilton pressed the attack, sword in one hand, poniard in the other, his features a mask of convulsive fury and hatred.

Campbell was done for, he felt. Instead of one hard-driving

purpose occupying him, his mind was split in different directions: Anne Haworth and the rope, the dead or dying King, Don Almiro tumbling down the stairs. That frightful demoniac face in front of him, blazing at him, blasting oaths at him, seemed to sap nerves and strength. He parried cut and slash and thrust mechanically, yielding and falling back as he fought. Feet were scraping the stairs, voices were rising in hot haste—

He stumbled against the wooden bar that the Spaniard had left leaning on the wall, lost balance and pitched sideways. At the same instant, the men from the stairway came leaping forward, crowding one another to get at him.

The shock of that headlong fall released something in him. Perhaps the blow from that Spanish dagger between his shoulders had jangled his nerve-controls; he never knew. With swords cutting and slashing at him, with Hamilton above him and thrusting down, he was abruptly transformed into a rolling, thrashing madman. Suddenly he was himself again, the trained border fighter, coolest and most capable when death was closest upon him.

A Béarnais screamed to the slash of steel; another caromed blindly into Hamilton; among them upleaped the catlike figure, stabbing and slashing. They broke away. He was clear of them; he was leaping at Hamilton, battering him back, out of the little passage and into the corridor where daylight still lingered.

Now it was Hamilton who yielded and gave desperate ground, who saw the cruel glitter of death striking hard at him. Frantically he fought against its touch; he was wounded, and again; blood sprang on his cheek, on his shoulder. Sobbing for breath as he fought, old dust eddying up from the ancient boards under the hammering feet, Hamilton retreated more rapidly.

From behind, someone stumbled forward with a long lance and the point thrust heavily against Campbell's back. The steel links sent it sliding away. Campbell swung about and his sword caught the man who held the lance, caught him between ear and shoulder in one slashing cut that dropped him above his lance. Then Campbell was hammering again at Hamilton, driving him ever backward.

BEHIND HAMILTON appeared the half-open doorway of the tower room. Campbell could see the room was empty; the ladder leading to the opening above was empty. With the blade of Campbell flickering and cutting at him, Hamilton backed into the doorway, backed into the room. He struck against the table. Not daring to take his eyes from the grim and deadly features of Campbell, he reached out with his left hand and shoved the table from him, hard.

The table was a heavy one. It overturned at this frenzied shove, and fell against the lower end of the couch. Campbell set foot on the empty wine-bottle and it rolled under his weight. He was flung off-balance and came down on one knee; his sword struck the floor and was dashed from his hand.

"Ha!" panted Hamilton exultantly, and darted in with a slash as swift and deadly as a lightning-bolt, designed to finish the helpless, groping man with one stroke.

Then a terrible and unforeseen thing happened.

Movement had been rapid; it was only an instant since Hamilton had pushed the table away. Dislodged by the shock of the table against the couch, the body of Sir John Preble toppled limply forward and tumbled to the floor, the arms outstretched wide, across Hamilton's feet.

The latter caught the motion and leaped aside, in the act of striking. He changed the direction of his blow from Campbell to the thing clutching at him; only as the sword drove home, did he see what this thing was, and whom it was. A wild, choking cry of horror and recognition burst from him.

That instant meant death or life. Without even comprehending what had happened, Campbell's groping fingers found his sword-hilt, and he thrust forward desperately as he came to his feet.... The sword was jerked from his grip, for the blade was through Hamilton's body. Hamilton was gripping at it and staggering away.

Campbell flung himself at the ladder, conscious of men at the door behind him. Whether Hamilton lived or died, he cared not. He hauled himself frantically up the rungs and came to the roof above, and stepped off the ladder; with a heave, he had it up, hauling it away from the clutching hands below. Gasping cool air into his pounding lungs, he gripped the trapdoor and threw it shut.

Now haste was most desperately imperative; they would be up and after him in no time, and his weapon was gone. He saw the rope knotted stoutly to the stones at one side, darted to it, and somehow got himself over the edge. A shout of encouragement came from below.

How he thanked heaven for those blessed knots in the rope! Without them, he would have been lost. Twice they saved him as his hands slipped. He lowered himself as fast as he dared, trying to get his feet about the rope, but trying in vain. Down and down—Ah!

A burst of excited voices reached him. He looked upward and saw figures there against the darkening sky. Desperately he lowered himself, then felt the rope give, and give again. Knives were hacking at it. A frantic hoarse cry burst from him.

Like an echo of his cry, came the angry vibrant twang of a bowstring. Something hovered against the sky and came plunging down, straight at him, brushing past him, a wailing scream on its lips. The scream ended abruptly and terribly…. Then suddenly the rope gave entirely. Campbell felt himself falling; everything ended in a crash that brought darkness.

CAMPBELL WAKENED to eager whines and whimpers, to the touch of a warm tongue on his face, to the dog-smell of Thorn joyously nuzzling and sniffing him. His hand found the dog and he heard the voice of Black Angus:

"Didn't fall too far. Struck on the body of this Frenchman; my arrow's broken, plague take it! Quick with the horses, lass!"

"I'm coming, I'm coming!" That was Anne Haworth's voice; he thrilled to it. Then he felt strong hands under his shoulders.

"Up, Malcolm! Up and away, d'ye hear? Up!"

He came lurching to his feet, coughing and panting and exhausted, while Angus steadied him. Dark shapes came crashing around; horses. Thorn was leaping upon him; Anne Haworth was touching him, pulling at his shoulder.

His senses cleared, his blurred vision came to focus. With the help of Angus, he got astride a saddle and straightened up.

"Where to now?" cried Angus, scrambling into the saddle at his side. "Paris?"

"Paris? No!" Campbell found voice with a burst of words. "Paris be damned! Out and away, away from all this! To Scotland!"

"Aye," said Black Angus. "Scotland it is, then; ride for it, and devil take the hindmost! D'ye hear, lass?"

"Yes!" responded Anne. "I'm with you! Scotland! Scotland!"

And hoofs clattered down the night.

CHAPTER XX

SCOTLAND? WITH Mary Stuart now looking to greater things, as the King of France lay dying? There the account ends, indeed, but there the story could not end except upon a false note; for hardly a rood of Scots ground but fell into a growing welter of blood and tears, in those darkening days.

France, even amid the descending agony of civil war and devastation, had its peaceful happy spots such as Provence, or the court where the Queen-mother Catherine came to power and mastery. But Scotland had none.

Here Scot and Frenchman and Englishman battled one against another; here clan fought savagely against clan, religion against religion, brother against brother, with unending fury, until her very Queen was handed over to the headsman's ax. Nothing in all Scotland remained stable or secure; on every side was black treachery.

Thus the chronicler seeking the record of Malcolm Campbell must wait until by chance—or destiny—certain scraps of information came into his hands.

One of these scraps occurs in the "Book of Heresies," wherein Sieur Florimond de Guisbert battled with his pen all the hosts of evil. He mentions among other things the appearance of Satan himself near Garde in Provence, the fiend there taking the shape of a monstrous black beast like a dog, of no known breed. This creature would have been burned alive by certain peasants, except that he was rescued by the well-known magician Nostradamus, who was thus proven to serve Satan and the black art of sorcery.

This beast, clearly, must have been the Irish wolfhound Thorn. But how came Thorn into Provence? The obvious clue occurs in one of the epistles of Caesar de Notredame, author of the famed "Histoire de Provence," where we find the words:

"I well remember how in the lifetime of my father, Maître Michel of blessed memory, a worthy knight of Scotland came and settled near Garde in our country. He and his lady were intimate friends of my father and I have frequently seen them at our house in Salon. They had many relics of the unhappy lady Mary Stuart, formerly for a brief space Queen of France."

And finally we have a still more direct clue from the very hand of Nostradamus himself. At least it was found among some of the Notredame papers, which came into the possession of his self-styled "intimate friend" Chavigny—that Chavigny who was in reality a mere passing acquaintance, and who published an inaccurate life of the great physician for his own profit.

This fragmentary letter, or rough draft, he did not publish, because its crabbed Latin was obscure and lacked explanation or signature. However, it fits very well as the capstone to this chronicle, whose readers may not find it so obscure or worthless after all. It reads:

"I am glad you are near me again. I am glad Glenlyon finds peace in Provence, this land of sleeping-spells…. Yes, I concealed my meanings with astrology; it was my way, and it paid. There are many who consider my prophecies but the fantastic ideas of a writer; yet much soon will be as I saw through the visions of those years.

"You also have the gift of vision; as one man on earth sees great wealth, another a great city arise, and another may be content to see the fulfillment of what talents God entrusted to him. To each of us his own work….

"I could look ahead; now it is backward they see. But they and I and you alike see three things that are imperishable in this world or the next—fidelity and honor and toleration. Today or yesterday or tomorrow, those who battle against these verities and attempt to dishonor them, shall pass into oblivion as the snows of May melt and run into rivulets and are gone. Three words, in whatever tongue they be written, hold the mystery and truth of existence: Give and Take! *Adieu*."

ABOUT THE AUTHOR

H. BEDFORD-JONES is a Canadian by birth, but not by profession, having removed to the United States at the age of one year. For over twenty years he has been more or less profitably engaged in writing and traveling. As he has seldom resided in one place longer than a year or so and is a person of retiring habits, he is somewhat a man of mystery; more than once he has suffered from unscrupulous gentlemen who impersonated him—one of whom murdered a wife and was subsequently shot by the police, luckily after losing his alias.

The real Bedford-Jones is an elderly man, whose gray hair and precise attire give him rather the appearance of a retired foreign diplomat. His hobby is stamp collecting, and his collection of Japan is said to be one of the finest in existence. At present writing he is en route to Morocco, and when this appears in print he will probably be somewhere on the Mojave Desert in company with Erle Stanley Gardner.

Questioned as to the main facts in his life, he declared there was only one main fact, but it was not for publication; that his life had been uneventful except for numerous financial losses, and that his only adventures lay in evading adventurers. In his younger years he was something of an athlete, but the encroachments of age preclude any active pursuits except that of motoring. He is usually to be found poring over his stamps, working at his typewriter, or laboring in his California rose garden, which is one of the sights of Cathedral Cañon, near Palm Springs.

www.ingramcontent.com/pod-product-compliance
Lightning Source LLC
Chambersburg PA
CBHW061522020726
47502CB00006B/2187